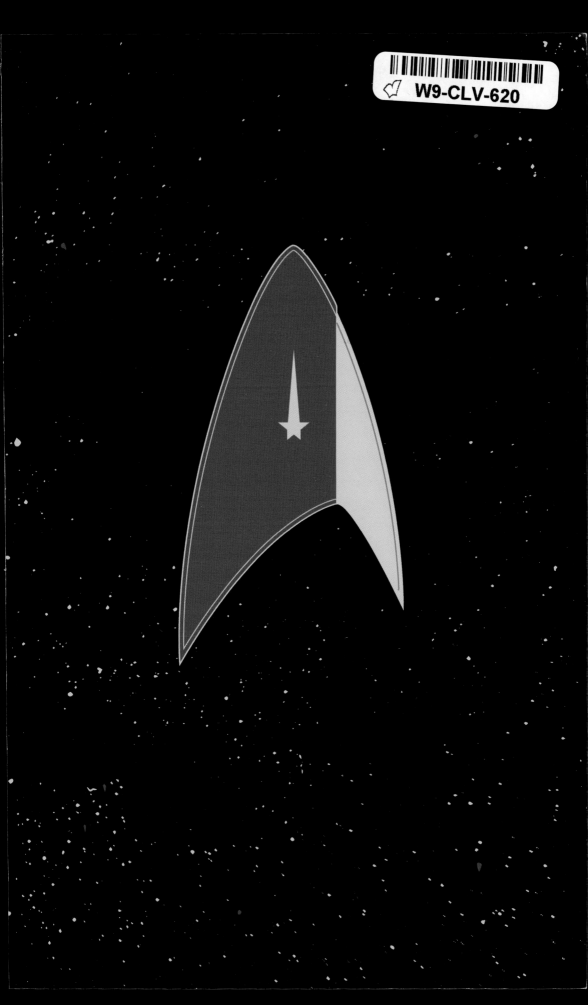

Facebook: facebook.com/idwpublishing
Twitter: @idwpublishing
YouTube: youtube.com/idwpublishing
Tumblr: tumblr.idwpublishing.com
Instagram: instagram.com/idwpublishing

COVER ART BY
GEORGE CALTSOUDAS

COLLECTION EDITS BY
JUSTIN EISINGER
AND ALONZO SIMON

COLLECTION DESIGN BY
JEFF POWELL

PUBLISHER
GREG GOLDSTEIN

ISBN: 978-1-63140-989-9   21 20 19 18   1 2 3 4

Greg Goldstein, President and Publisher
John Barber, Editor-In-Chief
Robbie Robbins, EVP/Sr. Art Director
Cara Morrison, Chief Financial Officer
Matt Ruzicka, Chief Accounting Officer
Anita Frazier, SVP of Sales and Marketing
David Hedgecock, Associate Publisher
Jerry Bennington, VP of New Product Development
Lorelei Bunjes, VP of Digital Services
Justin Eisinger, Editorial Director, Graphic Novels and Collections
Eric Moss, Senior Director, Licensing and Business Development

Ted Adams, Founder & CEO of IDW Media Holdings

Special thanks to Risa Kessler and John Van Citters of CBS
Consumer Products for their invaluable assistance.

STAR TREK

DISCOVERY

THE LIGHT OF KAHLESS

WRITTEN BY **KIRSTEN BEYER** AND **MIKE JOHNSON**

ART BY **TONY SHASTEEN**

COLORS BY **J.D. METTLER**

LETTERS BY **ANDWORLD DESIGN**

SERIES EDITORIAL ASSISTANCE BY **CHASE MAROTZ**

SERIES EDITS BY **SARAH GAYDOS**

STAR TREK CREATED BY GENE RODDENBERRY

ART BY **TONY SHASTEEN**

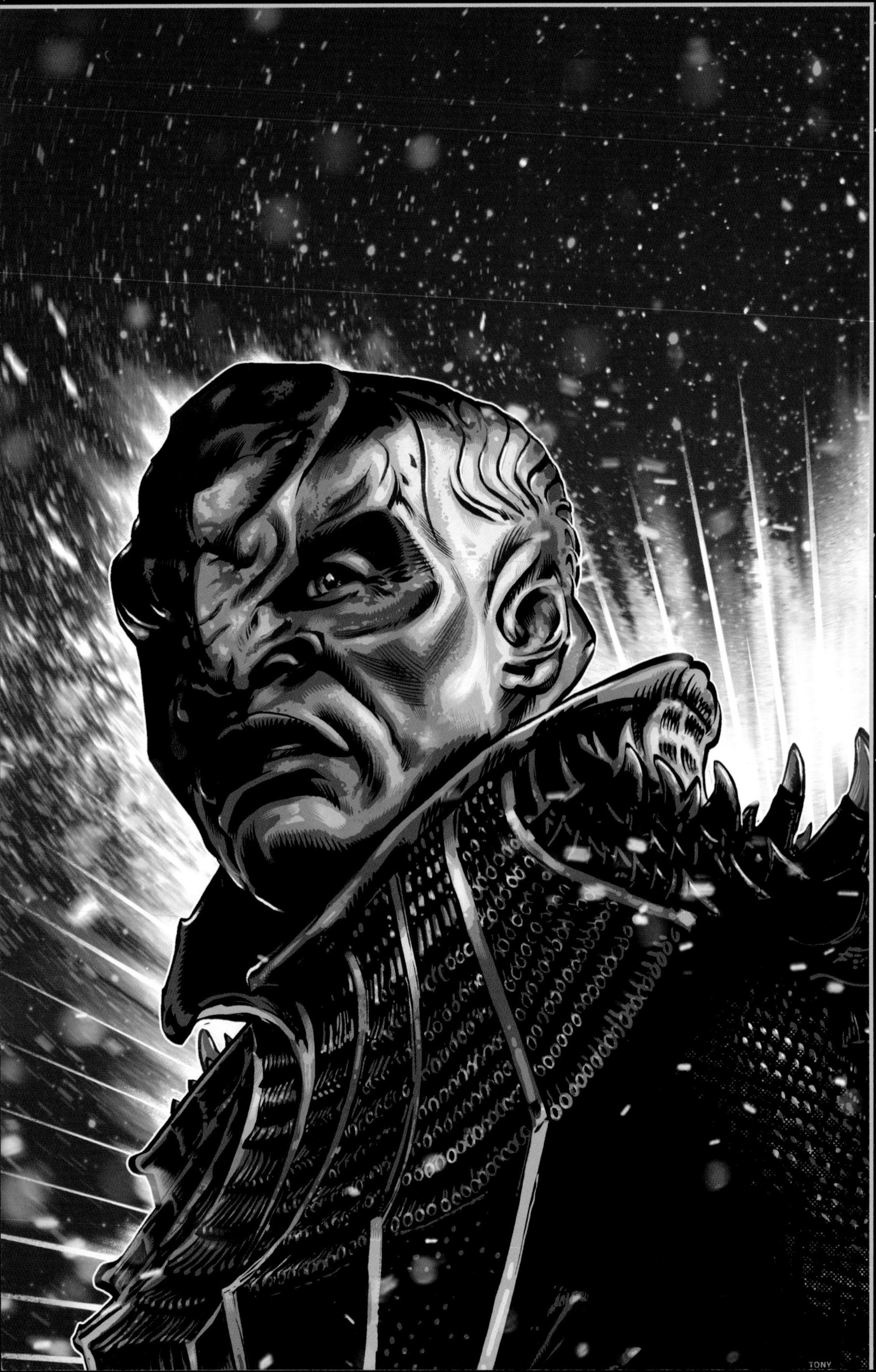

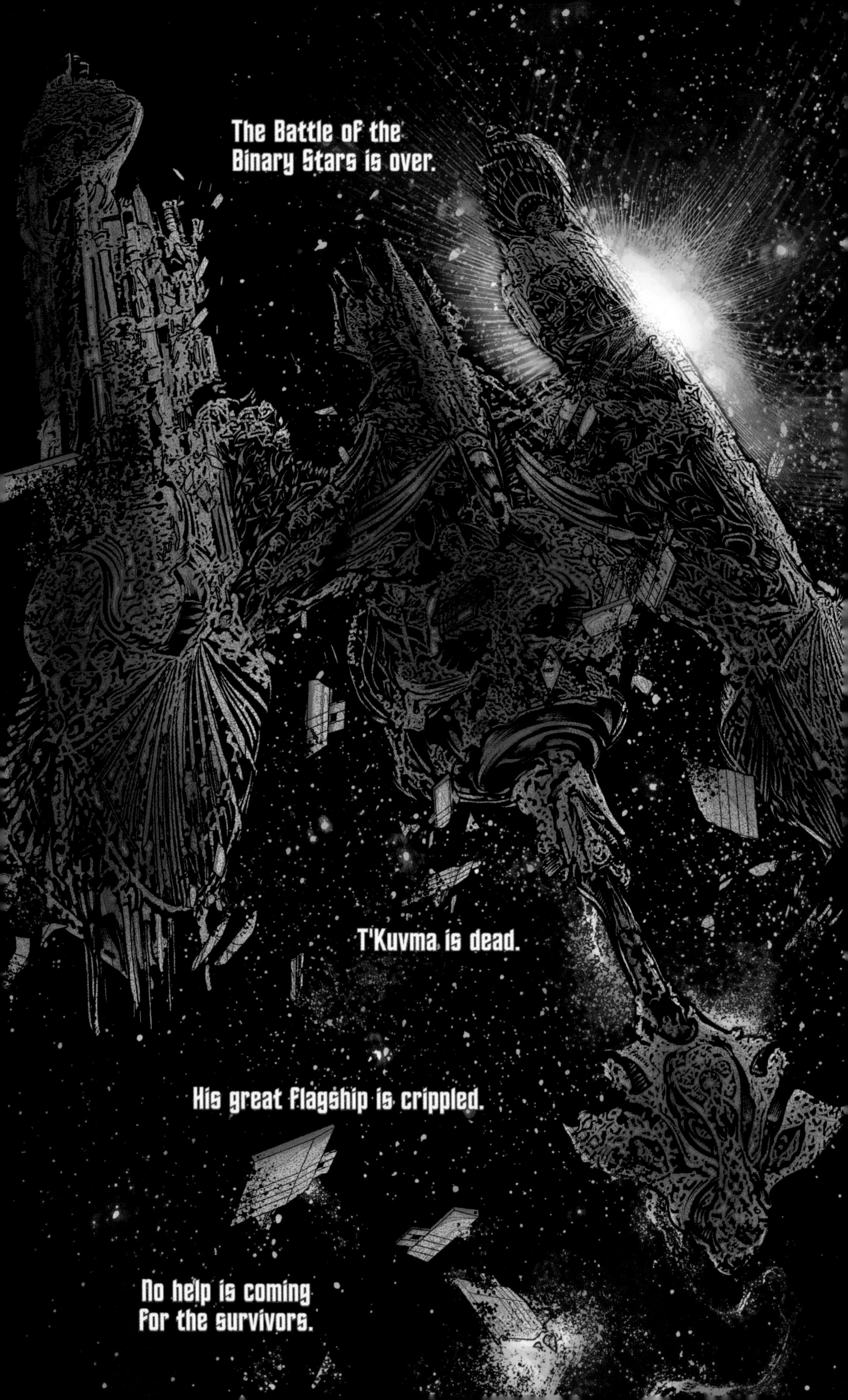
The Battle of the Binary Stars is over.
T'Kuvma is dead.
His great flagship is crippled.
No help is coming for the survivors.

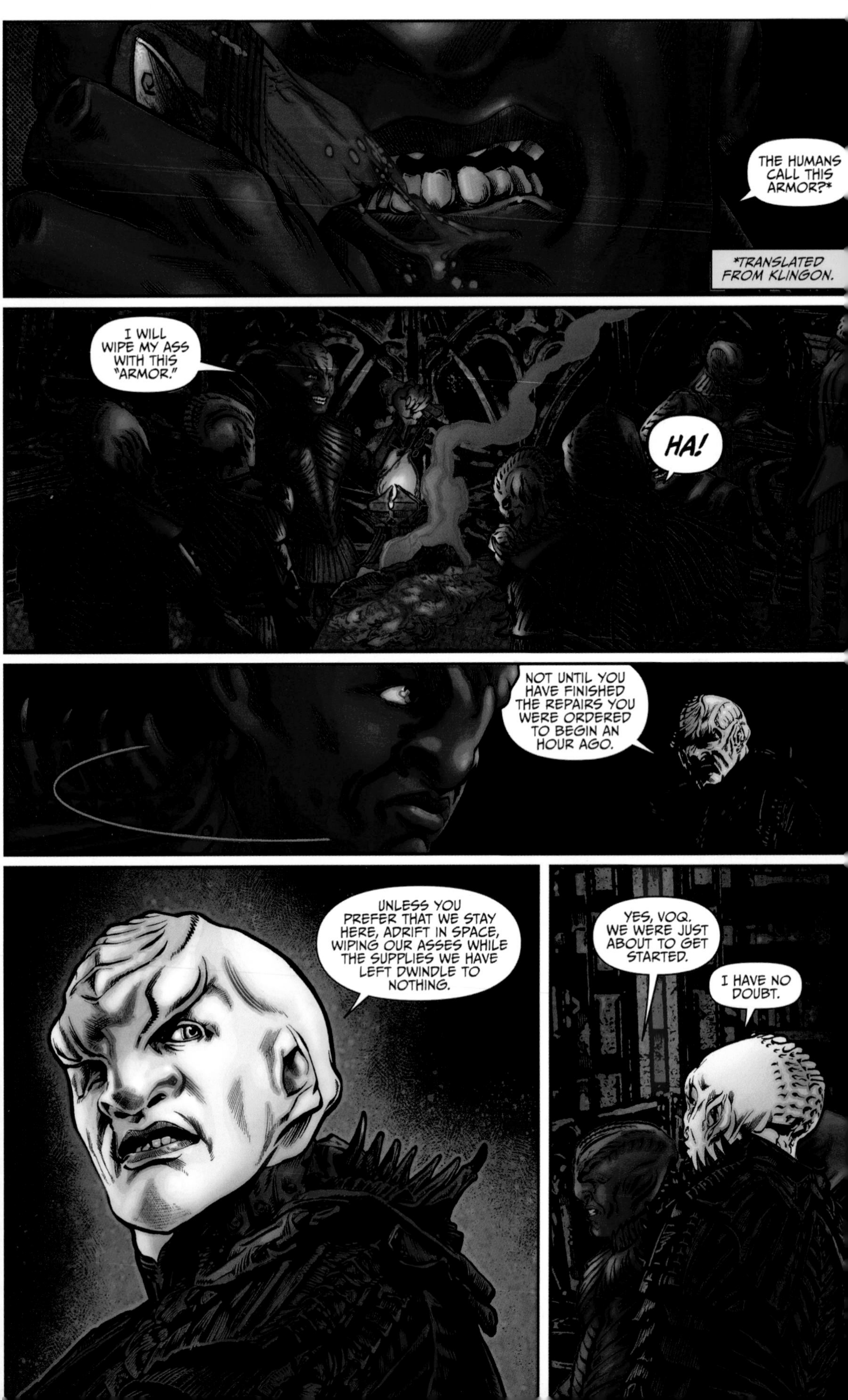
THE HUMANS CALL THIS ARMOR?*
*TRANSLATED FROM KLINGON.
I WILL WIPE MY ASS WITH THIS "ARMOR."
HA!
NOT UNTIL YOU HAVE FINISHED THE REPAIRS YOU WERE ORDERED TO BEGIN AN HOUR AGO.
UNLESS YOU PREFER THAT WE STAY HERE, ADRIFT IN SPACE, WIPING OUR ASSES WHILE THE SUPPLIES WE HAVE LEFT DWINDLE TO NOTHING.
YES, VOQ. WE WERE JUST ABOUT TO GET STARTED.
I HAVE NO DOUBT.

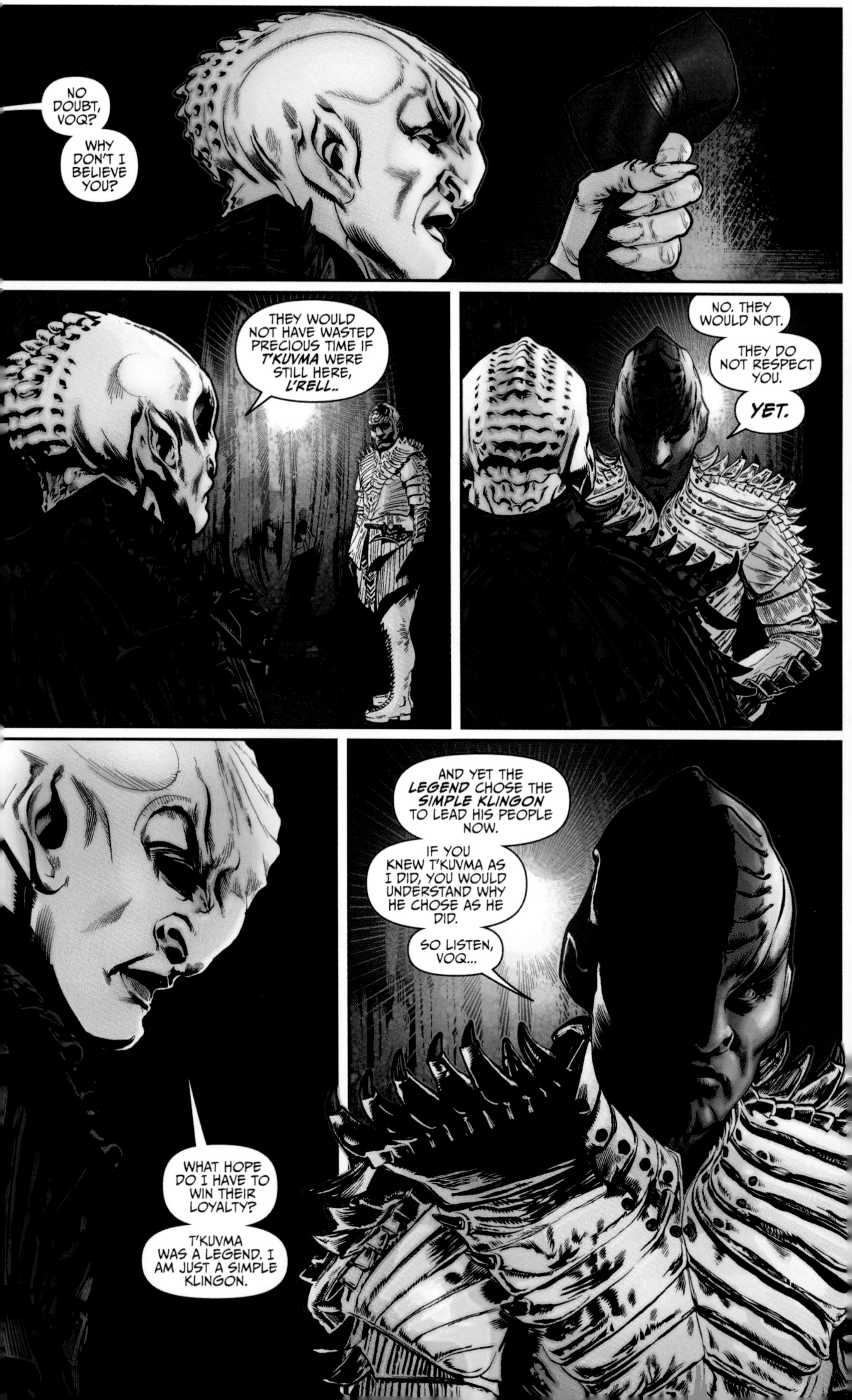
NO DOUBT, VOQ?
WHY DON'T I BELIEVE YOU?
THEY WOULD NOT HAVE WASTED PRECIOUS TIME IF *T'KUVMA* WERE STILL HERE, *L'RELL*..
NO. THEY WOULD NOT.
THEY DO NOT RESPECT YOU.
YET.
WHAT HOPE DO I HAVE TO WIN THEIR LOYALTY?
T'KUVMA WAS A LEGEND. I AM JUST A SIMPLE KLINGON.
AND YET THE *LEGEND* CHOSE THE *SIMPLE KLINGON* TO LEAD HIS PEOPLE NOW.
IF YOU KNEW T'KUVMA AS I DID, YOU WOULD UNDERSTAND WHY HE CHOSE AS HE DID.
SO LISTEN, VOQ...

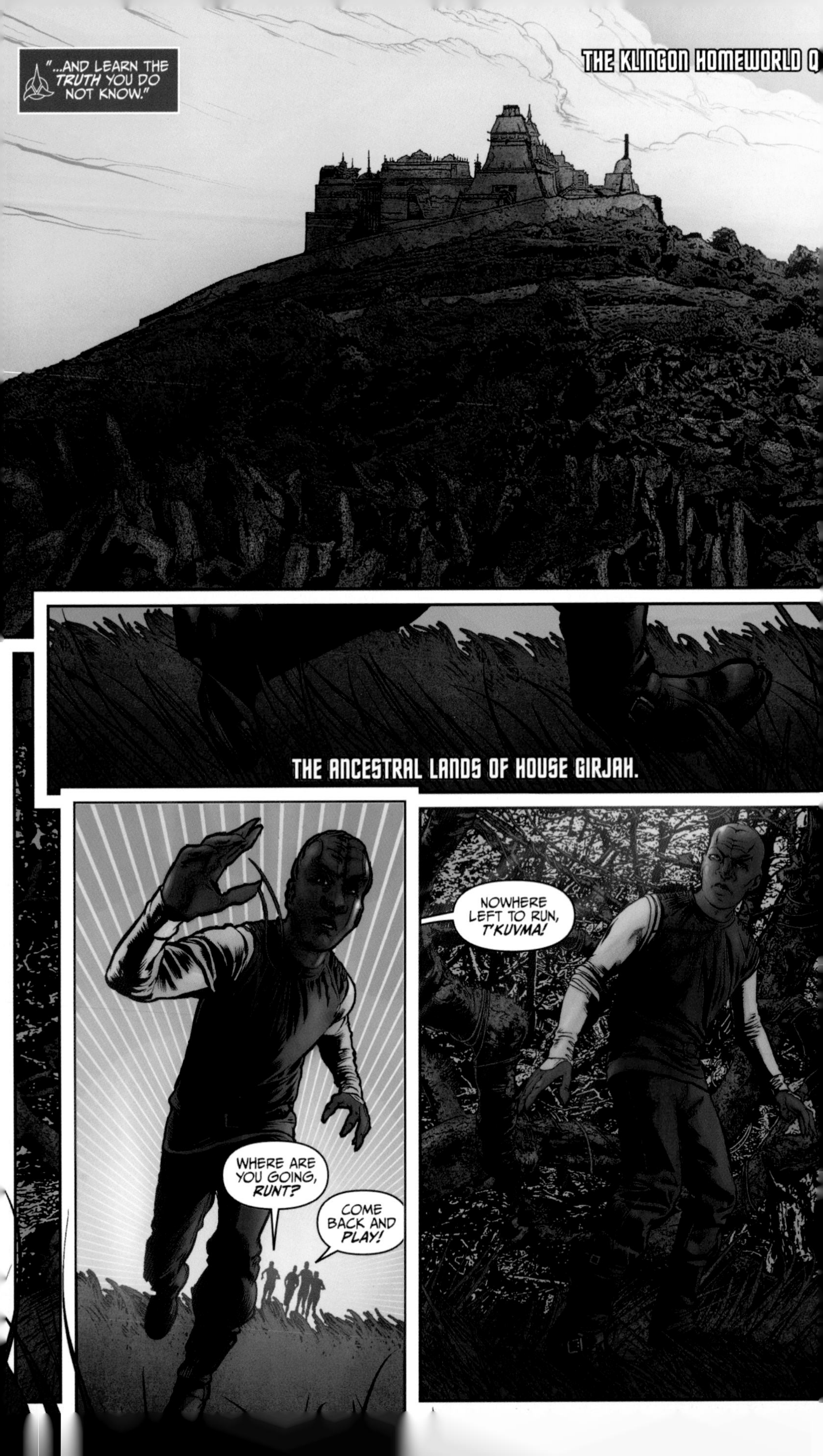
"...AND LEARN THE TRUTH YOU DO NOT KNOW."
THE KLINGON HOMEWORLD Q
THE ANCESTRAL LANDS OF HOUSE GIRJAH.
WHERE ARE YOU GOING, RUNT?
COME BACK AND PLAY!
NOWHERE LEFT TO RUN, T'KUVMA!

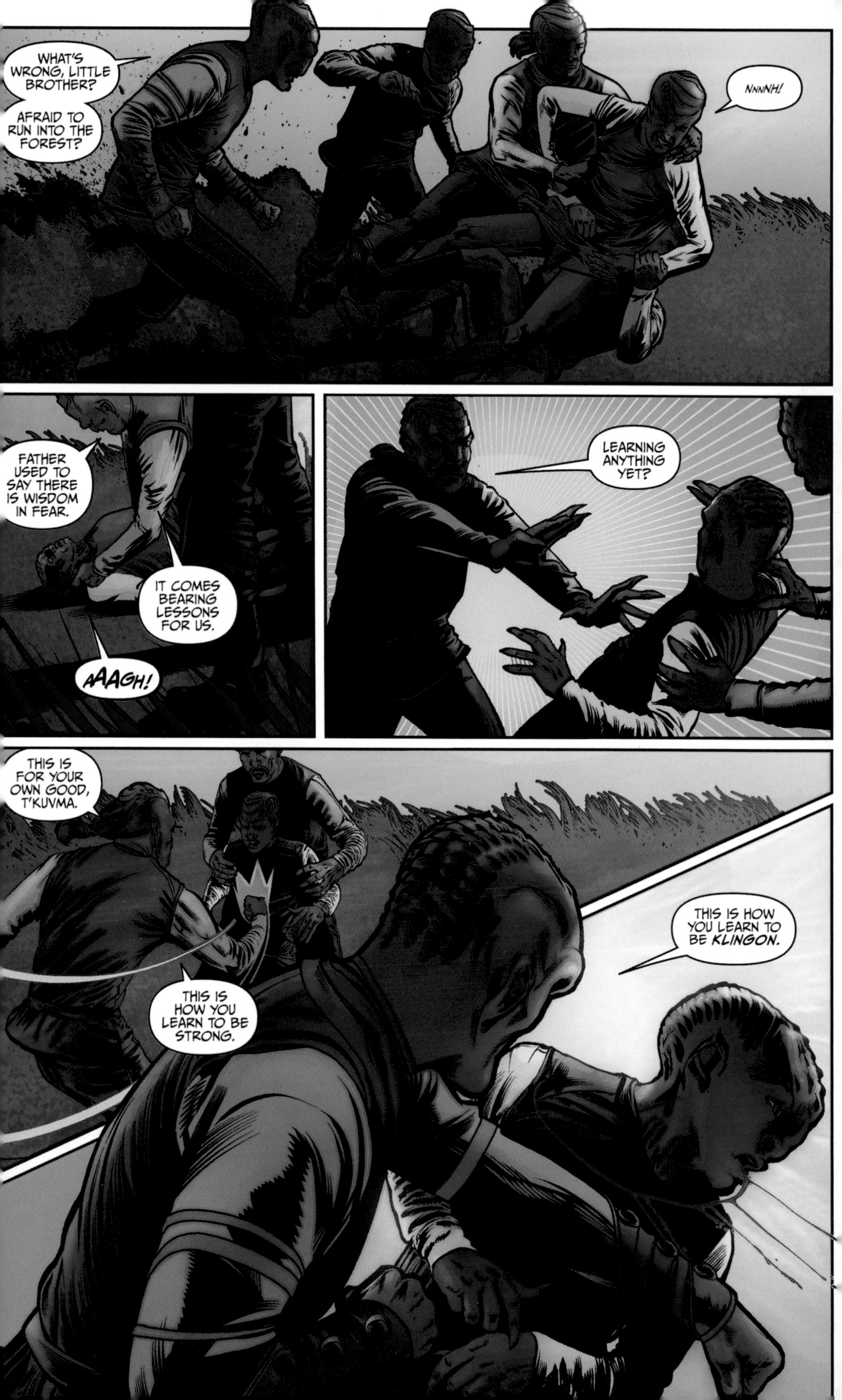
WHAT'S WRONG, LITTLE BROTHER?
AFRAID TO RUN INTO THE FOREST?
NNNNH!
FATHER USED TO SAY THERE IS WISDOM IN FEAR.
IT COMES BEARING LESSONS FOR US.
AAAGH!
LEARNING ANYTHING YET?
THIS IS FOR YOUR OWN GOOD, T'KUVMA.
THIS IS HOW YOU LEARN TO BE STRONG.
THIS IS HOW YOU LEARN TO BE KLINGON.

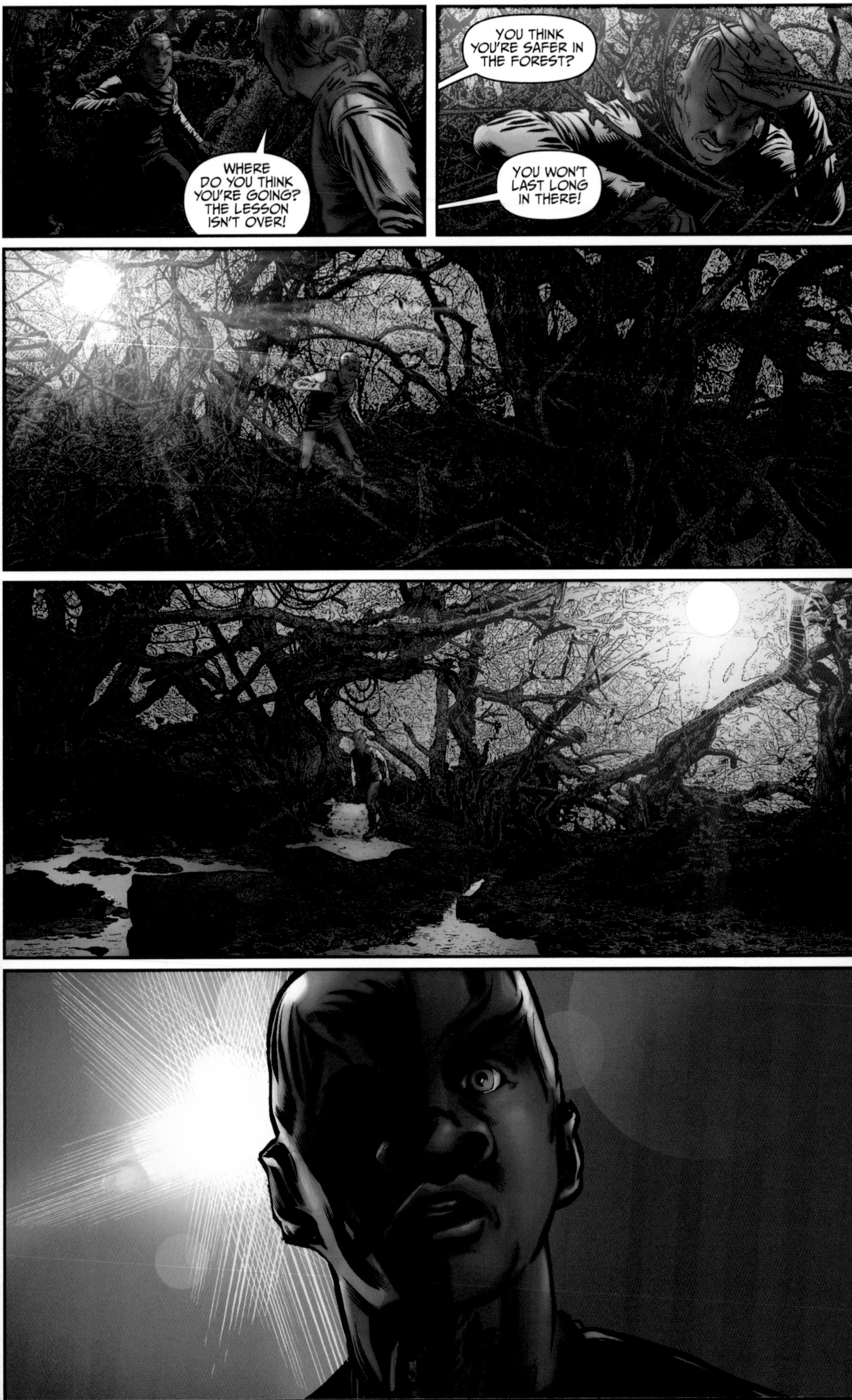
WHERE DO YOU THINK YOU'RE GOING? THE LESSON ISN'T OVER!
YOU THINK YOU'RE SAFER IN THE FOREST?
YOU WON'T LAST LONG IN THERE!

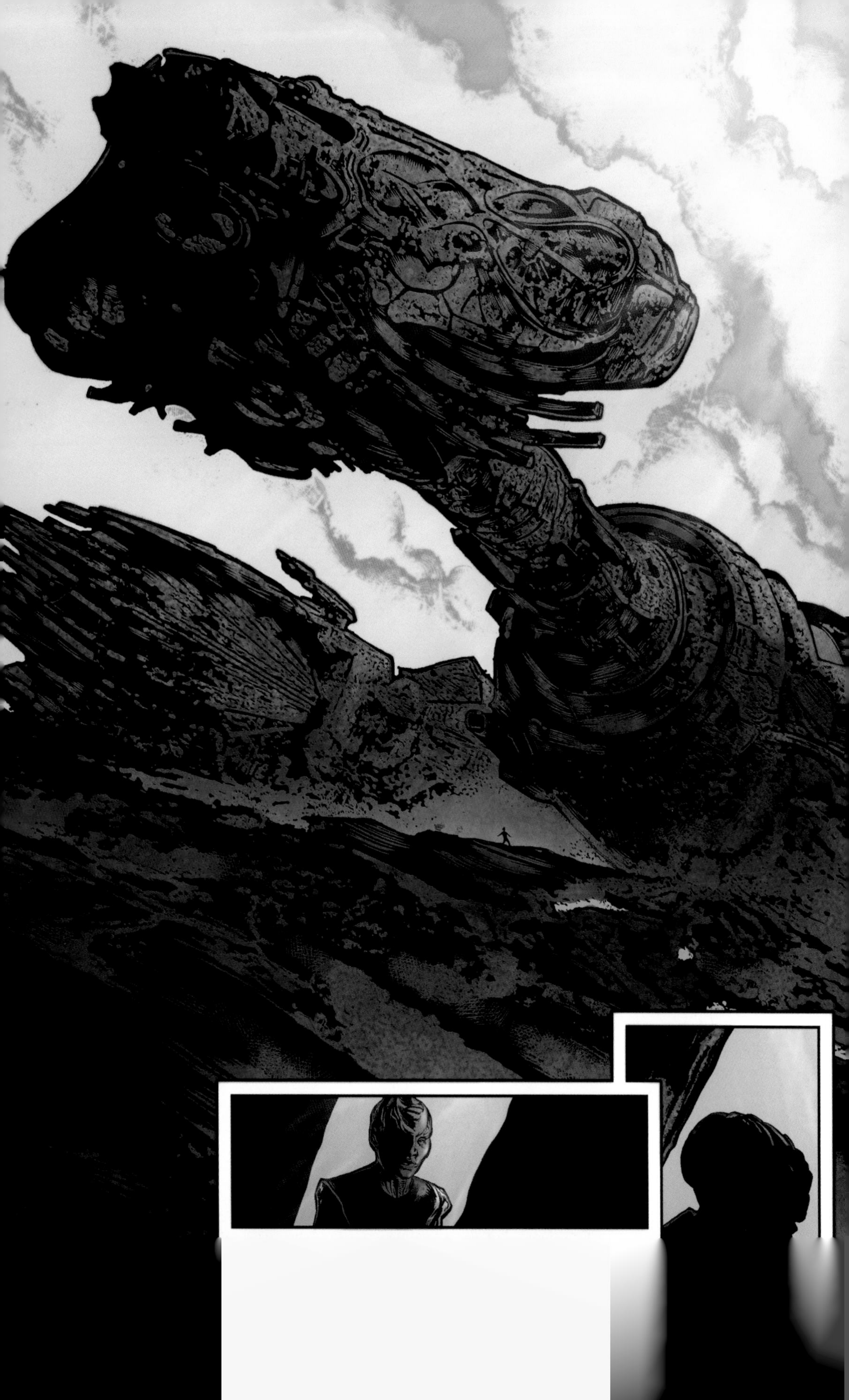

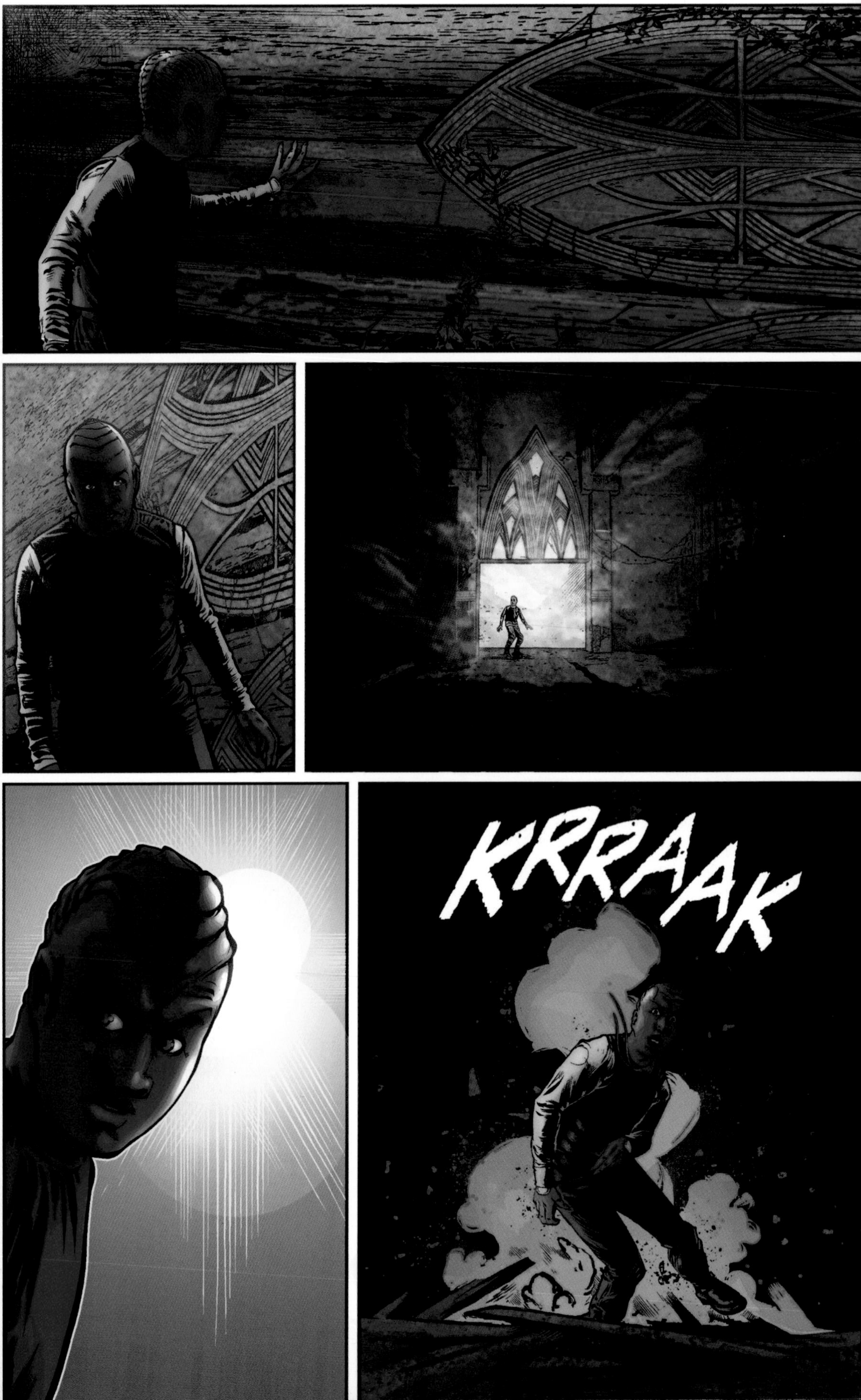
KRRAAK

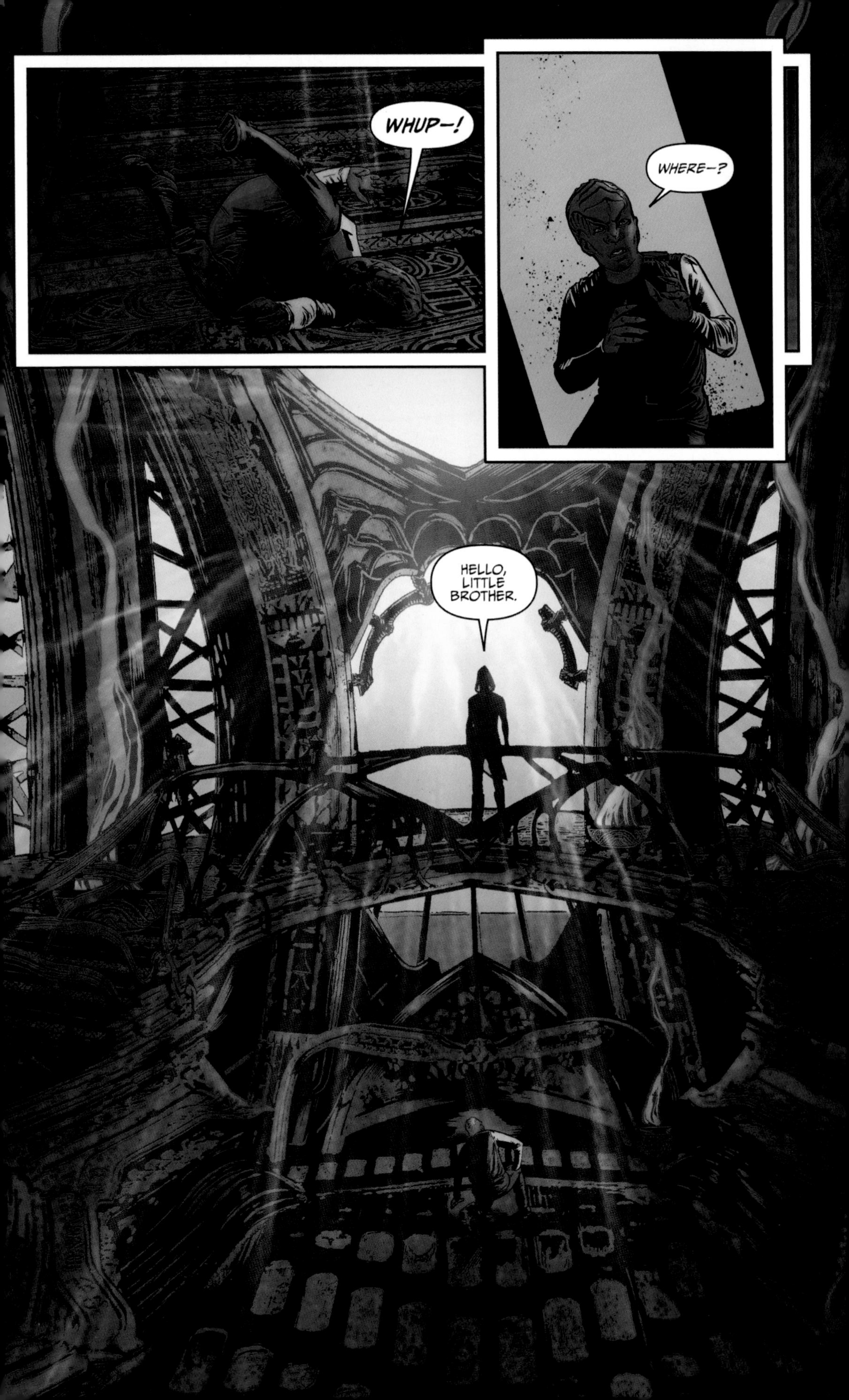
WHUP-!
WHERE-?
HELLO, LITTLE BROTHER.

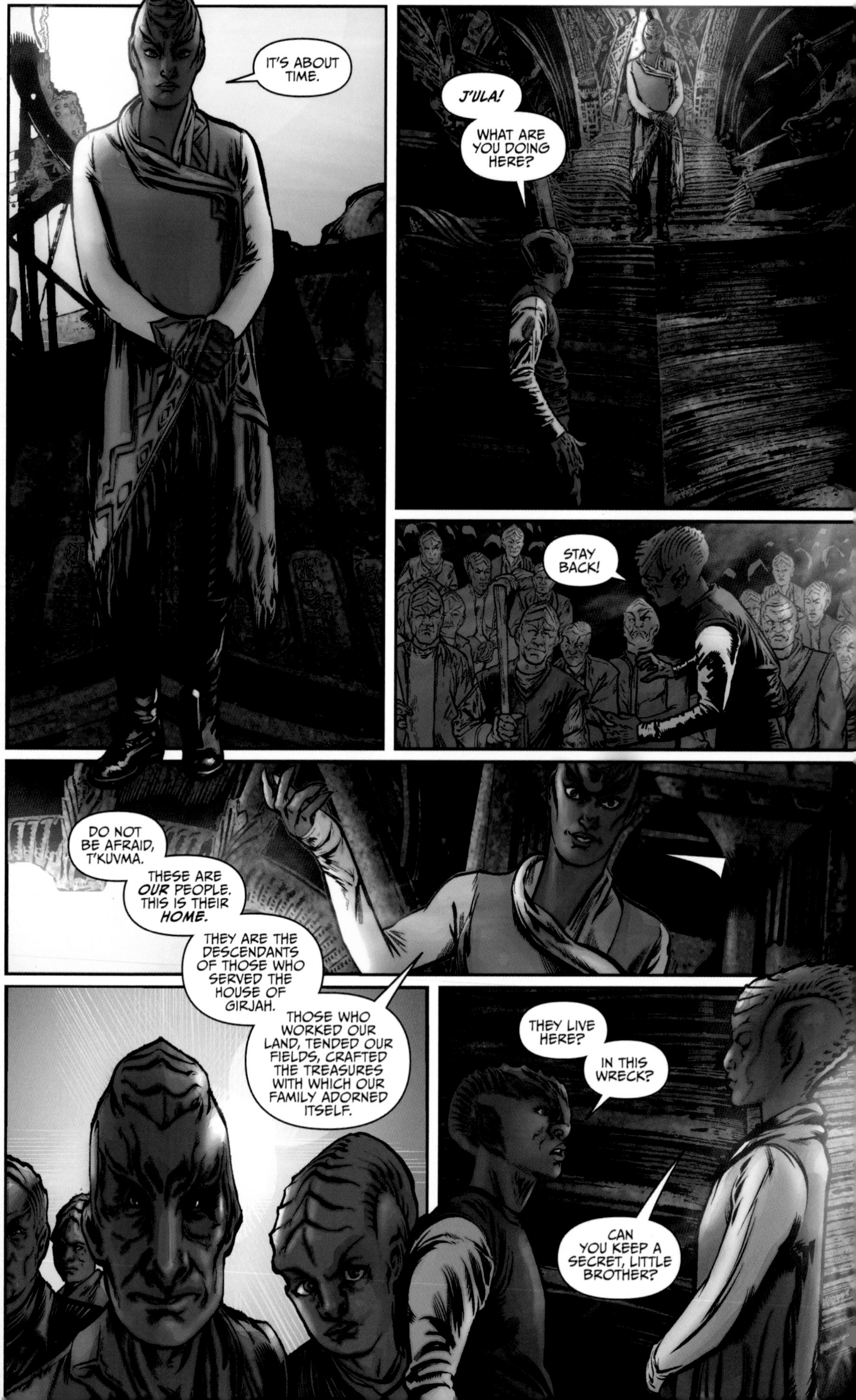
IT'S ABOUT TIME.
J'ULA!
WHAT ARE YOU DOING HERE?
STAY BACK!
DO NOT BE AFRAID, T'KUVMA.
THESE ARE OUR PEOPLE. THIS IS THEIR HOME.
THEY ARE THE DESCENDANTS OF THOSE WHO SERVED THE HOUSE OF GIRJAH.
THOSE WHO WORKED OUR LAND, TENDED OUR FIELDS, CRAFTED THE TREASURES WITH WHICH OUR FAMILY ADORNED ITSELF.
THEY LIVE HERE?
IN THIS WRECK?
CAN YOU KEEP A SECRET, LITTLE BROTHER?

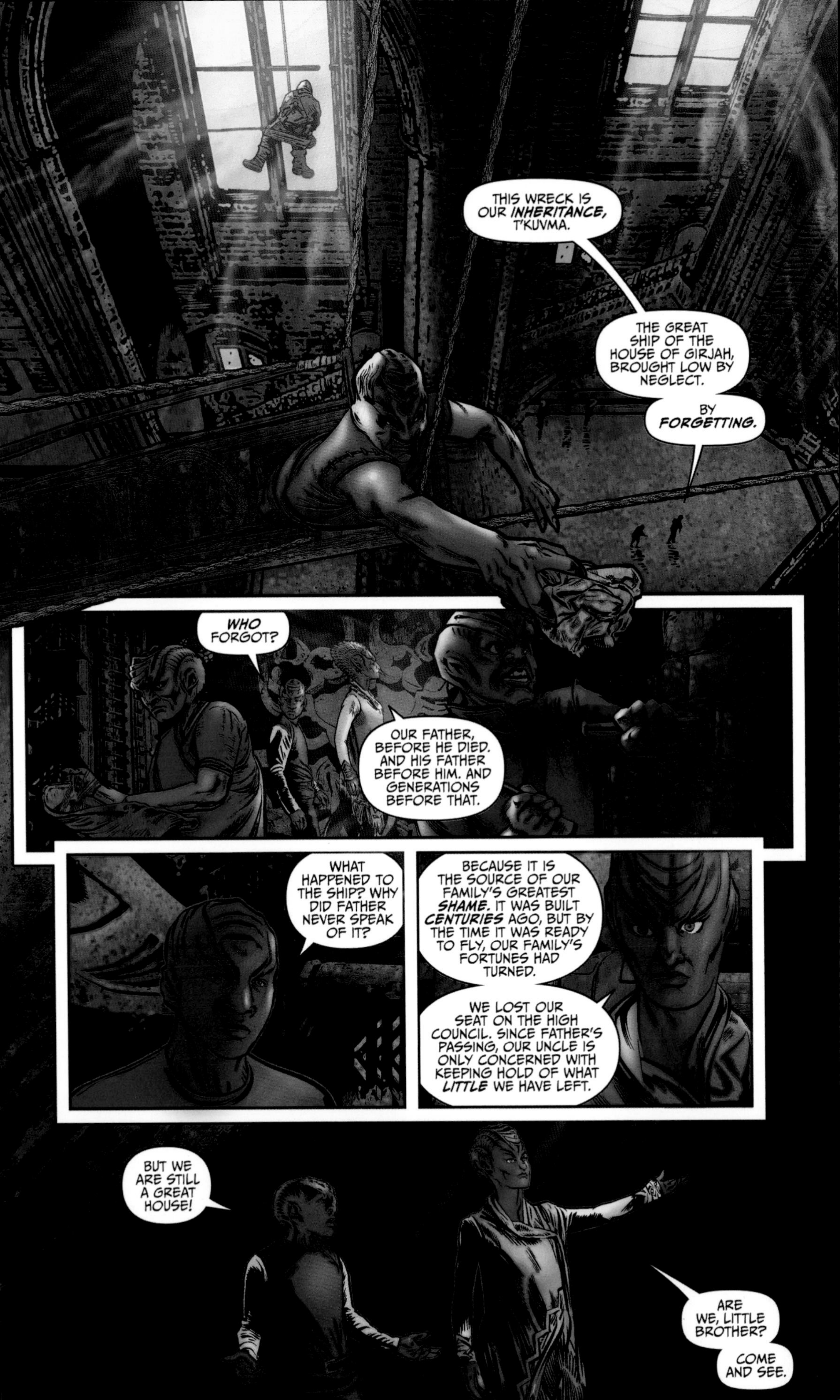
THIS WRECK IS OUR *INHERITANCE,* T'KUVMA.
THE GREAT SHIP OF THE HOUSE OF GIRJAH, BROUGHT LOW BY NEGLECT.
BY *FORGETTING.*
WHO FORGOT?
OUR FATHER, BEFORE HE DIED. AND HIS FATHER BEFORE HIM. AND GENERATIONS BEFORE THAT.
WHAT HAPPENED TO THE SHIP? WHY DID FATHER NEVER SPEAK OF IT?
BECAUSE IT IS THE SOURCE OF OUR FAMILY'S GREATEST *SHAME.* IT WAS BUILT *CENTURIES* AGO, BUT BY THE TIME IT WAS READY TO FLY, OUR FAMILY'S FORTUNES HAD TURNED.
WE LOST OUR SEAT ON THE HIGH COUNCIL. SINCE FATHER'S PASSING, OUR UNCLE IS ONLY CONCERNED WITH KEEPING HOLD OF WHAT *LITTLE* WE HAVE LEFT.
BUT WE ARE STILL A GREAT HOUSE!
ARE WE, LITTLE BROTHER?
COME AND SEE.

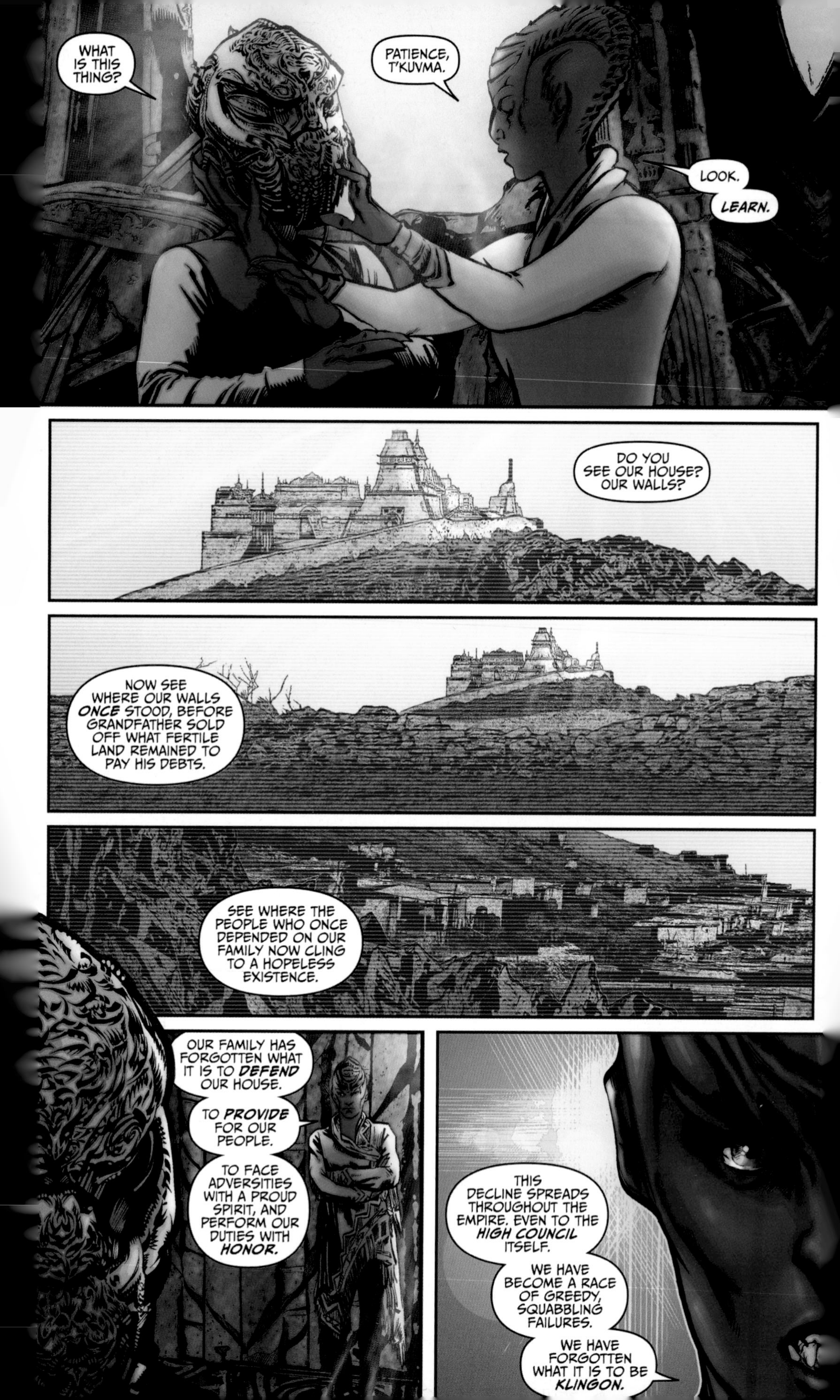
WHAT IS THIS THING?
PATIENCE, T'KUVMA.
LOOK.
LEARN.
DO YOU SEE OUR HOUSE? OUR WALLS?
NOW SEE WHERE OUR WALLS ONCE STOOD, BEFORE GRANDFATHER SOLD OFF WHAT FERTILE LAND REMAINED TO PAY HIS DEBTS.
SEE WHERE THE PEOPLE WHO ONCE DEPENDED ON OUR FAMILY NOW CLING TO A HOPELESS EXISTENCE.
OUR FAMILY HAS FORGOTTEN WHAT IT IS TO DEFEND OUR HOUSE.
TO PROVIDE FOR OUR PEOPLE.
TO FACE ADVERSITIES WITH A PROUD SPIRIT, AND PERFORM OUR DUTIES WITH HONOR.
THIS DECLINE SPREADS THROUGHOUT THE EMPIRE. EVEN TO THE HIGH COUNCIL ITSELF.
WE HAVE BECOME A RACE OF GREEDY, SQUABBLING FAILURES.
WE HAVE FORGOTTEN WHAT IT IS TO BE KLINGON.

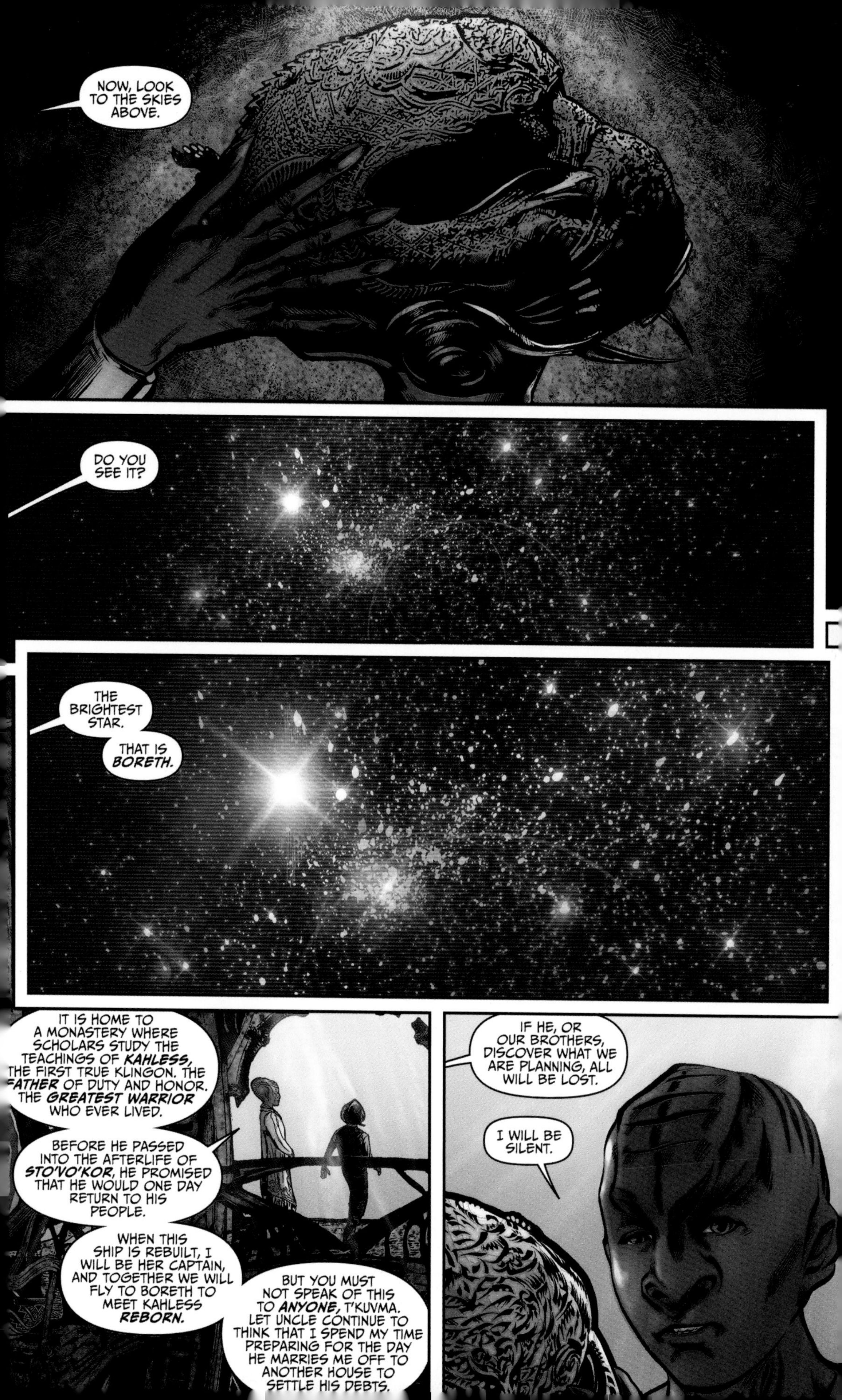
NOW, LOOK TO THE SKIES ABOVE.
DO YOU SEE IT?
THE BRIGHTEST STAR.
THAT IS *BORETH.*
IT IS HOME TO A MONASTERY WHERE SCHOLARS STUDY THE TEACHINGS OF *KAHLESS,* THE FIRST TRUE KLINGON. THE *FATHER* OF DUTY AND HONOR. THE *GREATEST WARRIOR* WHO EVER LIVED.
BEFORE HE PASSED INTO THE AFTERLIFE OF *STO'VO'KOR,* HE PROMISED THAT HE WOULD ONE DAY RETURN TO HIS PEOPLE.
WHEN THIS SHIP IS REBUILT, I WILL BE HER CAPTAIN, AND TOGETHER WE WILL FLY TO BORETH TO MEET KAHLESS *REBORN.*
BUT YOU MUST NOT SPEAK OF THIS TO *ANYONE,* T'KUVMA. LET UNCLE CONTINUE TO THINK THAT I SPEND MY TIME PREPARING FOR THE DAY HE MARRIES ME OFF TO ANOTHER HOUSE TO SETTLE HIS DEBTS.
IF HE, OR OUR BROTHERS, DISCOVER WHAT WE ARE PLANNING, ALL WILL BE LOST.
I WILL BE SILENT.

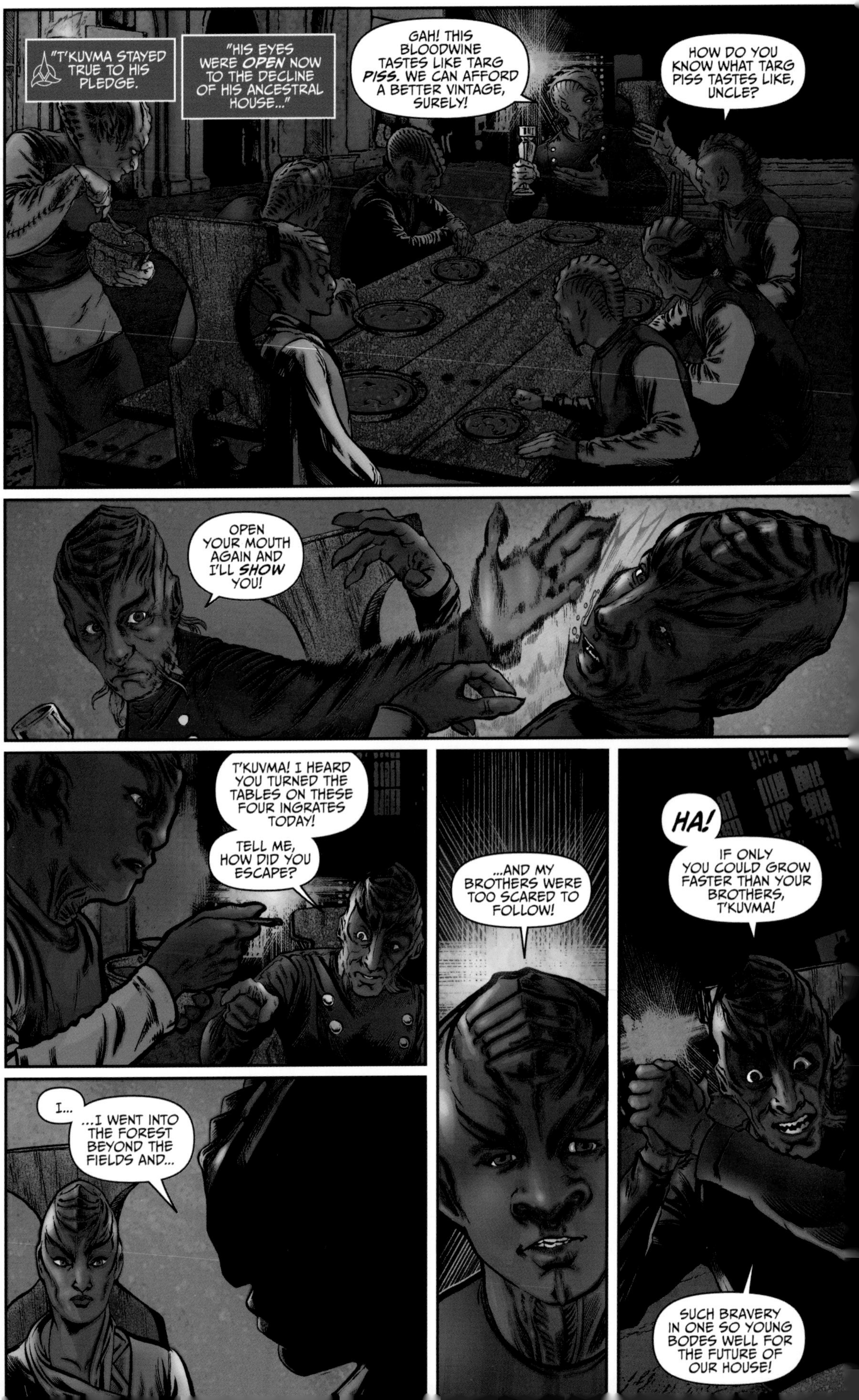
"T'KUVMA STAYED TRUE TO HIS PLEDGE.
"HIS EYES WERE *OPEN* NOW TO THE DECLINE OF HIS ANCESTRAL HOUSE..."
GAH! THIS BLOODWINE TASTES LIKE TARG ***PISS.*** WE CAN AFFORD A BETTER VINTAGE, SURELY!
HOW DO YOU KNOW WHAT TARG PISS TASTES LIKE, UNCLE?
OPEN YOUR MOUTH AGAIN AND I'LL ***SHOW*** YOU!
T'KUVMA! I HEARD YOU TURNED THE TABLES ON THESE FOUR INGRATES TODAY!
TELL ME, HOW DID YOU ESCAPE?
I...
...I WENT INTO THE FOREST BEYOND THE FIELDS AND...
...AND MY BROTHERS WERE TOO SCARED TO FOLLOW!
HA!
IF ONLY YOU COULD GROW FASTER THAN YOUR BROTHERS, T'KUVMA!
SUCH BRAVERY IN ONE SO YOUNG BODES WELL FOR THE FUTURE OF OUR HOUSE!

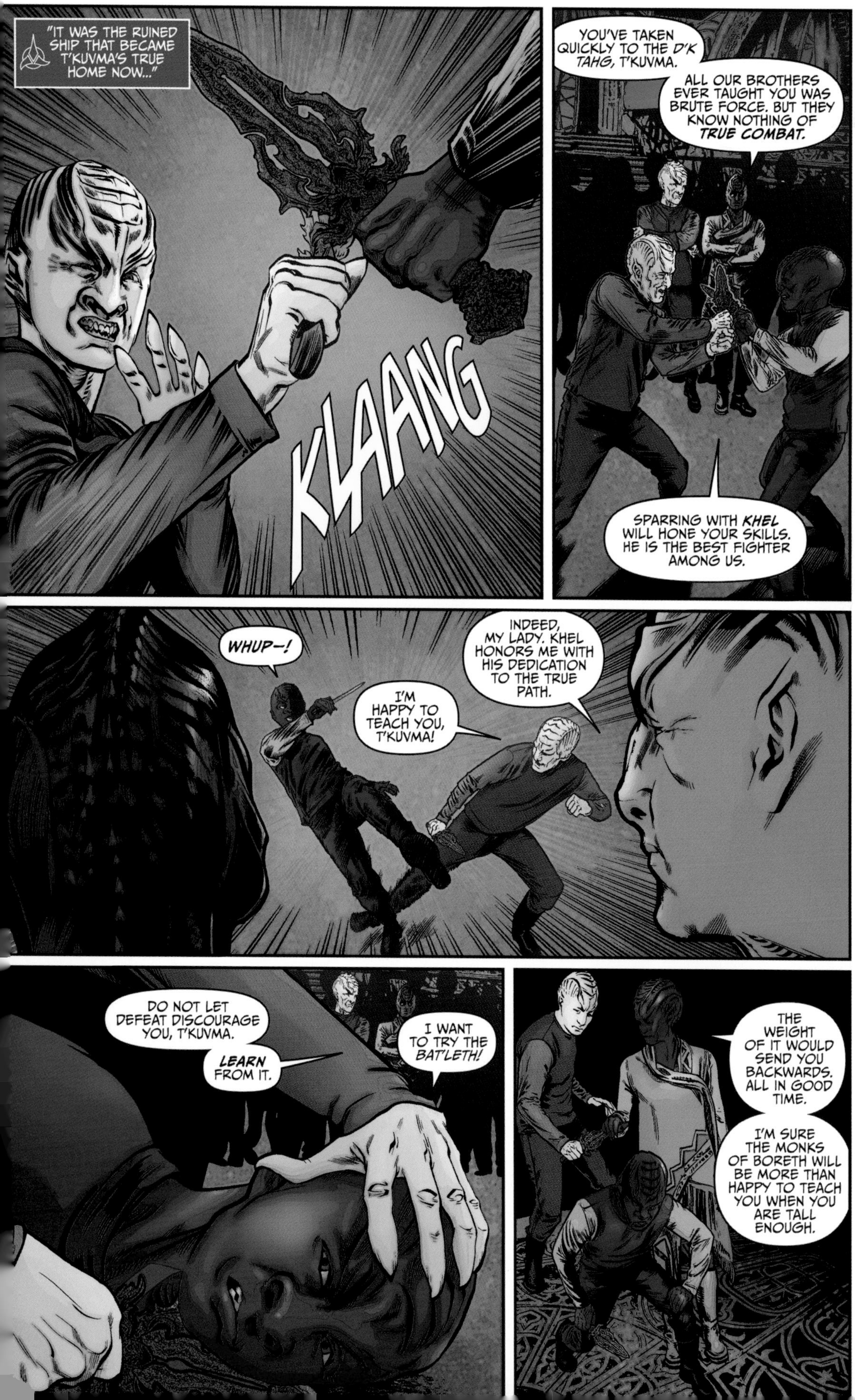
"IT WAS THE RUINED SHIP THAT BECAME T'KUVMA'S TRUE HOME NOW..."
KLAANG
YOU'VE TAKEN QUICKLY TO THE D'K TAHG, T'KUVMA.
ALL OUR BROTHERS EVER TAUGHT YOU WAS BRUTE FORCE. BUT THEY KNOW NOTHING OF TRUE COMBAT.
SPARRING WITH KHEL WILL HONE YOUR SKILLS. HE IS THE BEST FIGHTER AMONG US.
WHUP--!
I'M HAPPY TO TEACH YOU, T'KUVMA!
INDEED, MY LADY. KHEL HONORS ME WITH HIS DEDICATION TO THE TRUE PATH.
DO NOT LET DEFEAT DISCOURAGE YOU, T'KUVMA.
LEARN FROM IT.
I WANT TO TRY THE BAT'LETH!
THE WEIGHT OF IT WOULD SEND YOU BACKWARDS. ALL IN GOOD TIME.
I'M SURE THE MONKS OF BORETH WILL BE MORE THAN HAPPY TO TEACH YOU WHEN YOU ARE TALL ENOUGH.

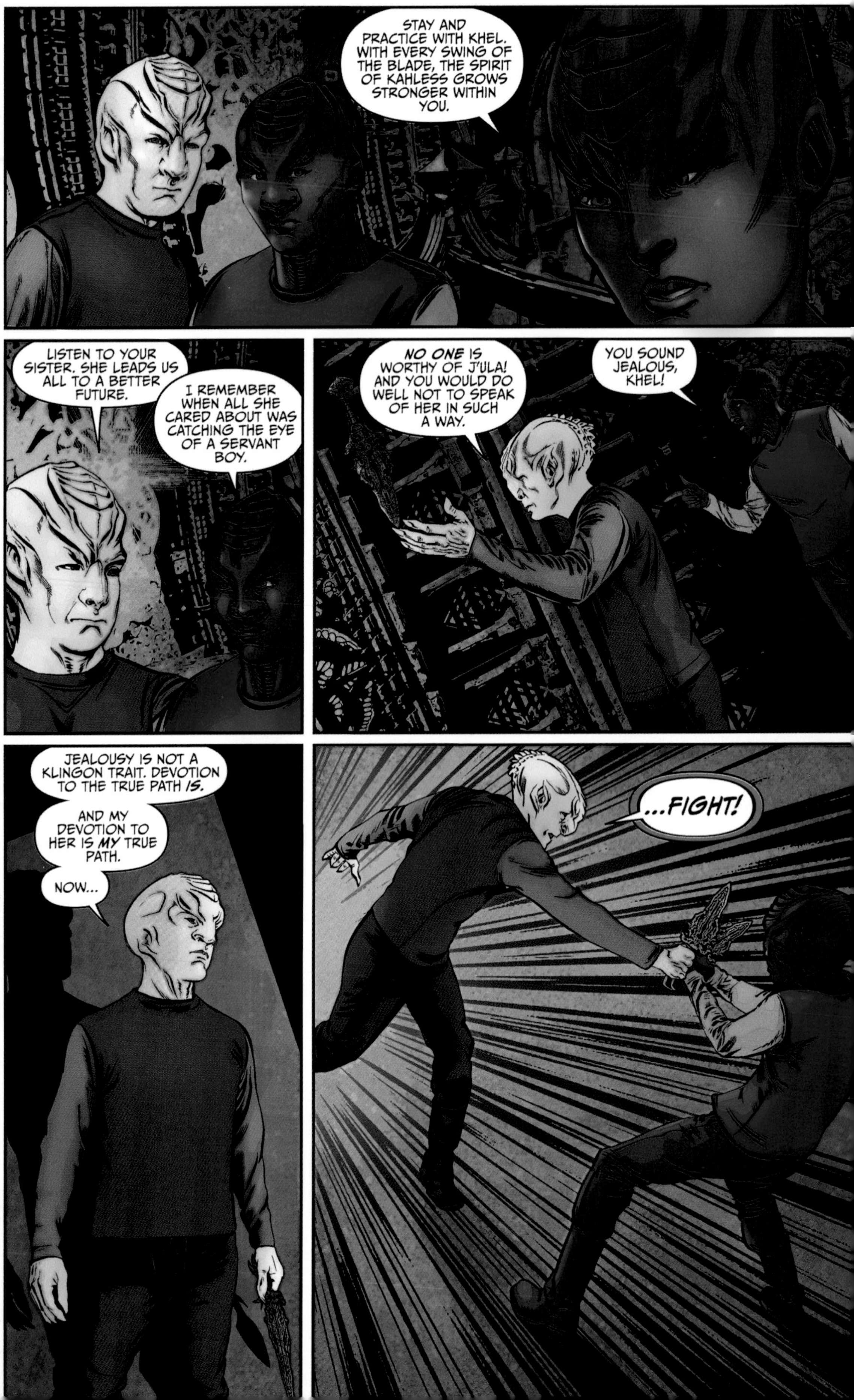

STAY AND PRACTICE WITH KHEL. WITH EVERY SWING OF THE BLADE, THE SPIRIT OF KAHLESS GROWS STRONGER WITHIN YOU.
LISTEN TO YOUR SISTER. SHE LEADS US ALL TO A BETTER FUTURE.
I REMEMBER WHEN ALL SHE CARED ABOUT WAS CATCHING THE EYE OF A SERVANT BOY.
NO ONE IS WORTHY OF J'ULA! AND YOU WOULD DO WELL NOT TO SPEAK OF HER IN SUCH A WAY.
YOU SOUND JEALOUS, KHEL!
JEALOUSY IS NOT A KLINGON TRAIT. DEVOTION TO THE TRUE PATH *IS.*
AND MY DEVOTION TO HER IS *MY* TRUE PATH.
NOW...
...FIGHT!

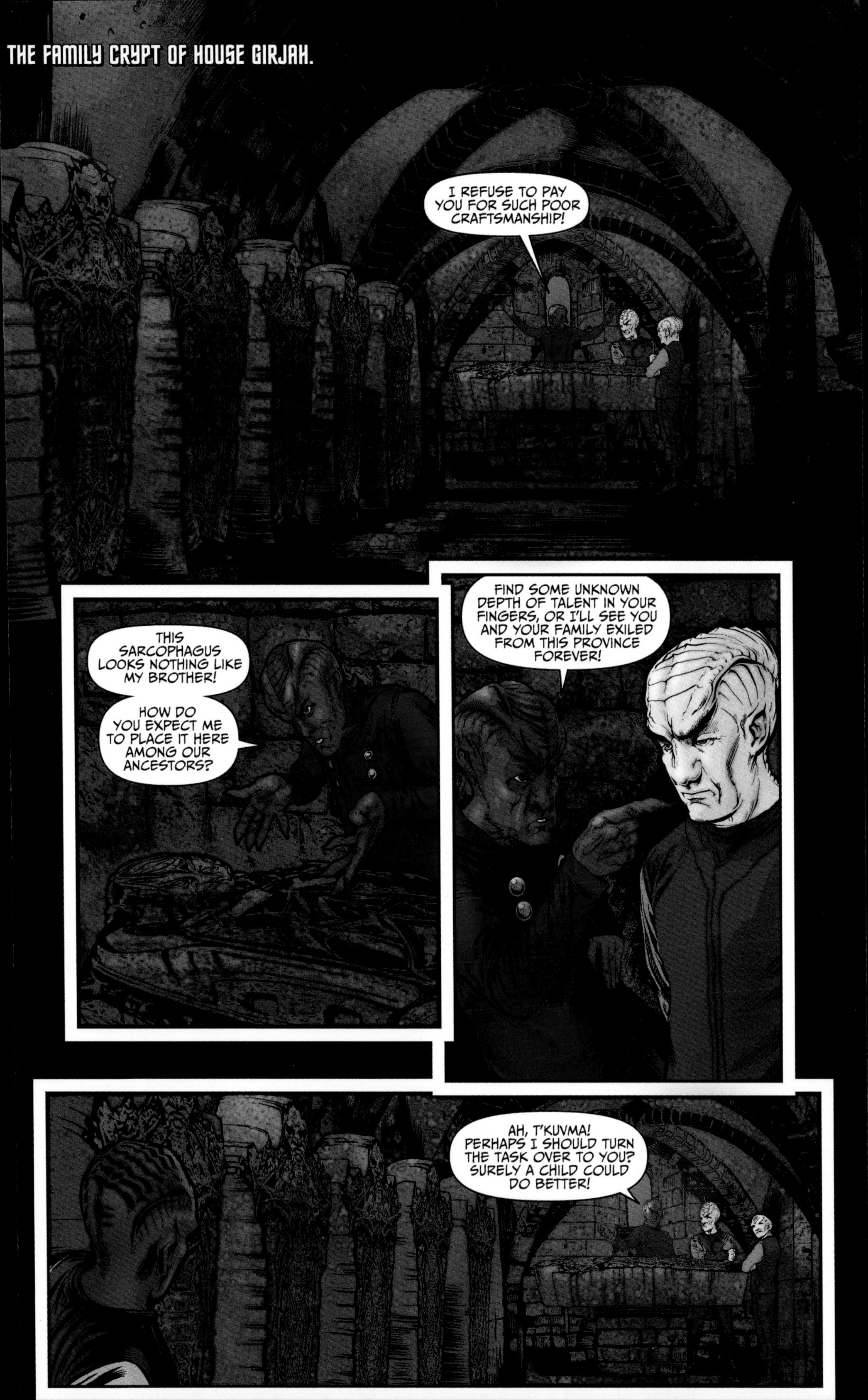
THE FAMILY CRYPT OF HOUSE GIRJAH.
I REFUSE TO PAY YOU FOR SUCH POOR CRAFTSMANSHIP!
THIS SARCOPHAGUS LOOKS NOTHING LIKE MY BROTHER!
HOW DO YOU EXPECT ME TO PLACE IT HERE AMONG OUR ANCESTORS?
FIND SOME UNKNOWN DEPTH OF TALENT IN YOUR FINGERS, OR I'LL SEE YOU AND YOUR FAMILY EXILED FROM THIS PROVINCE FOREVER!
AH, T'KUVMA! PERHAPS I SHOULD TURN THE TASK OVER TO YOU? SURELY A CHILD COULD DO BETTER!

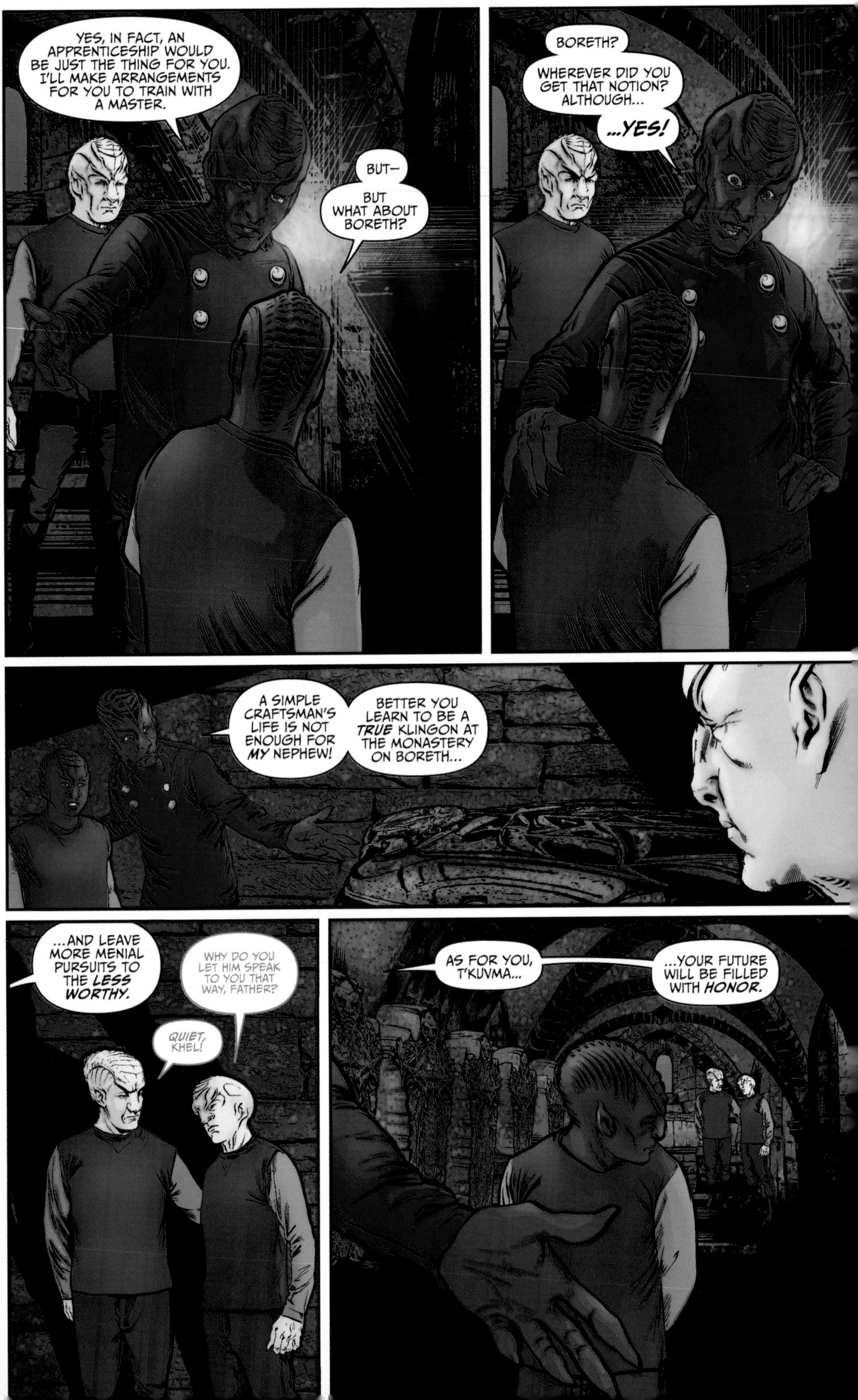

YES, IN FACT, AN APPRENTICESHIP WOULD BE JUST THE THING FOR YOU. I'LL MAKE ARRANGEMENTS FOR YOU TO TRAIN WITH A MASTER.
BUT—
BUT WHAT ABOUT BORETH?
BORETH?
WHEREVER DID YOU GET THAT NOTION? ALTHOUGH...
...YES!
A SIMPLE CRAFTSMAN'S LIFE IS NOT ENOUGH FOR MY NEPHEW!
BETTER YOU LEARN TO BE A TRUE KLINGON AT THE MONASTERY ON BORETH...
...AND LEAVE MORE MENIAL PURSUITS TO THE LESS WORTHY.
WHY DO YOU LET HIM SPEAK TO YOU THAT WAY, FATHER?
QUIET, KHEL!
AS FOR YOU, T'KUVMA...
...YOUR FUTURE WILL BE FILLED WITH HONOR.

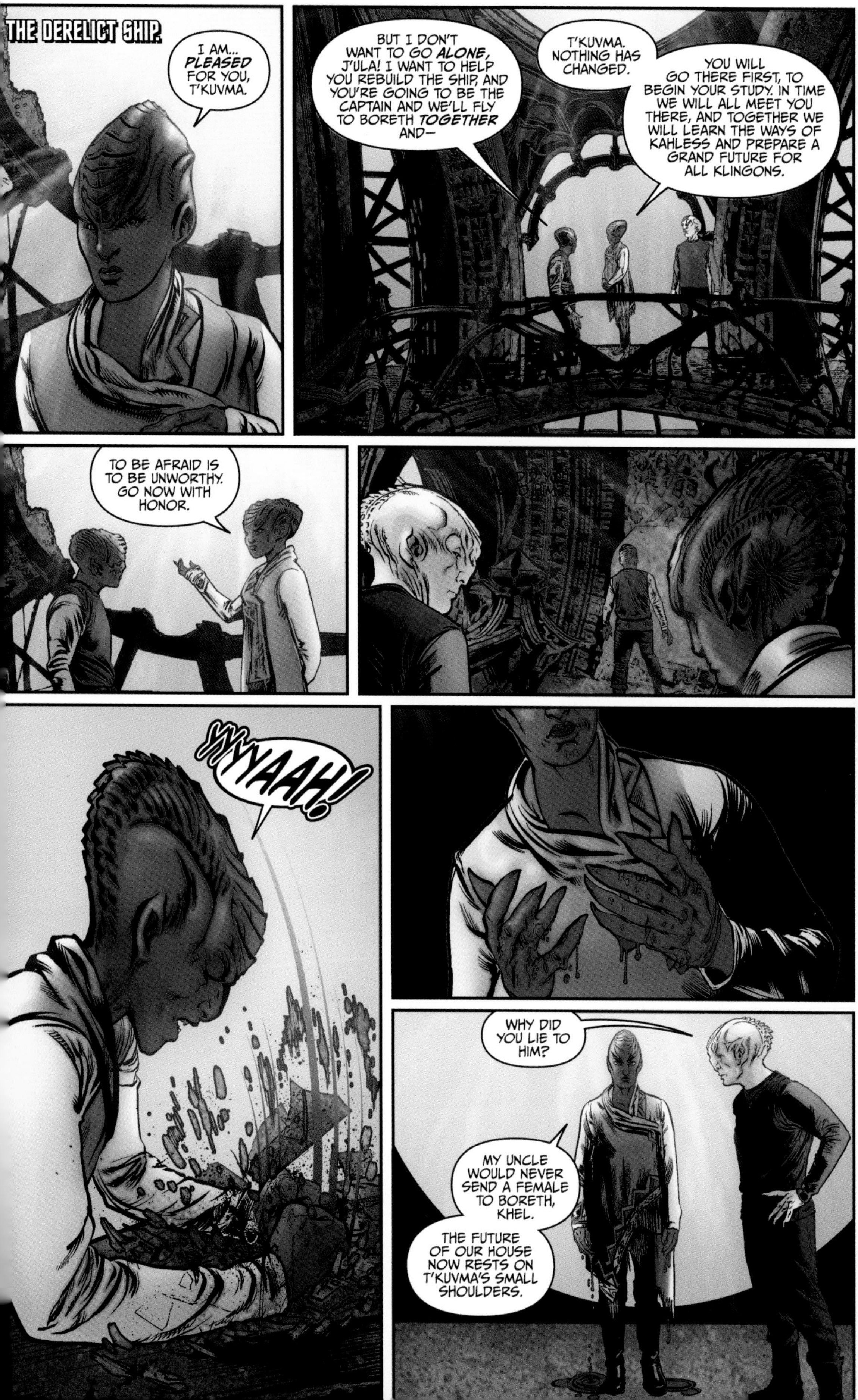
THE DERELICT SHIP.
I AM... *PLEASED* FOR YOU, T'KUVMA.
BUT I DON'T WANT TO GO *ALONE,* J'ULA! I WANT TO HELP YOU REBUILD THE SHIP, AND YOU'RE GOING TO BE THE CAPTAIN AND WE'LL FLY TO BORETH *TOGETHER* AND—
T'KUVMA. NOTHING HAS CHANGED.
YOU WILL GO THERE FIRST, TO BEGIN YOUR STUDY. IN TIME WE WILL ALL MEET YOU THERE, AND TOGETHER WE WILL LEARN THE WAYS OF KAHLESS AND PREPARE A GRAND FUTURE FOR ALL KLINGONS.
TO BE AFRAID IS TO BE UNWORTHY. GO NOW WITH HONOR.
YYYAAAH!
WHY DID YOU LIE TO HIM?
MY UNCLE WOULD NEVER SEND A FEMALE TO BORETH, KHEL.
THE FUTURE OF OUR HOUSE NOW RESTS ON T'KUVMA'S SMALL SHOULDERS.

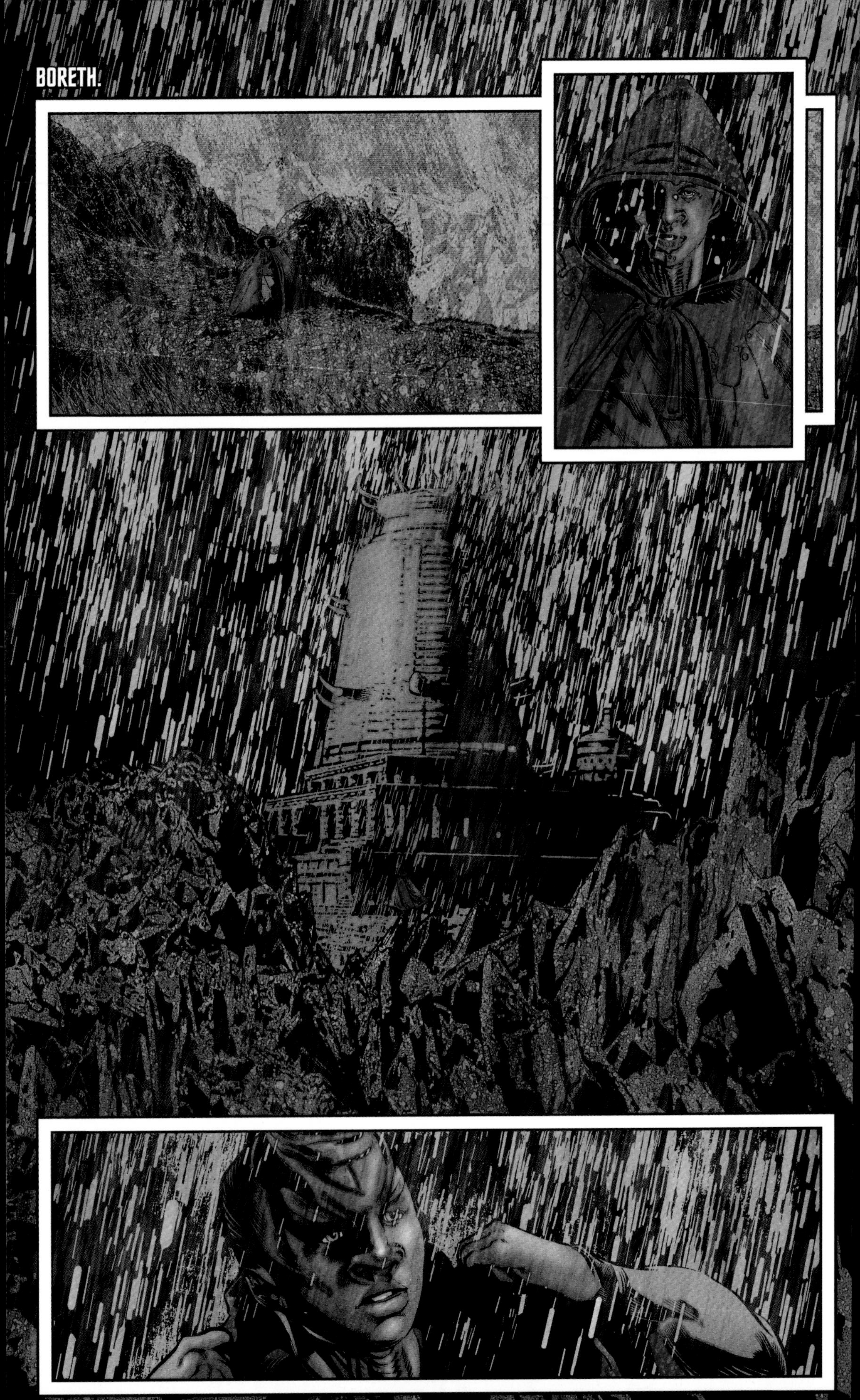
BORETH.

ART BY **J.K. WOODWARD**

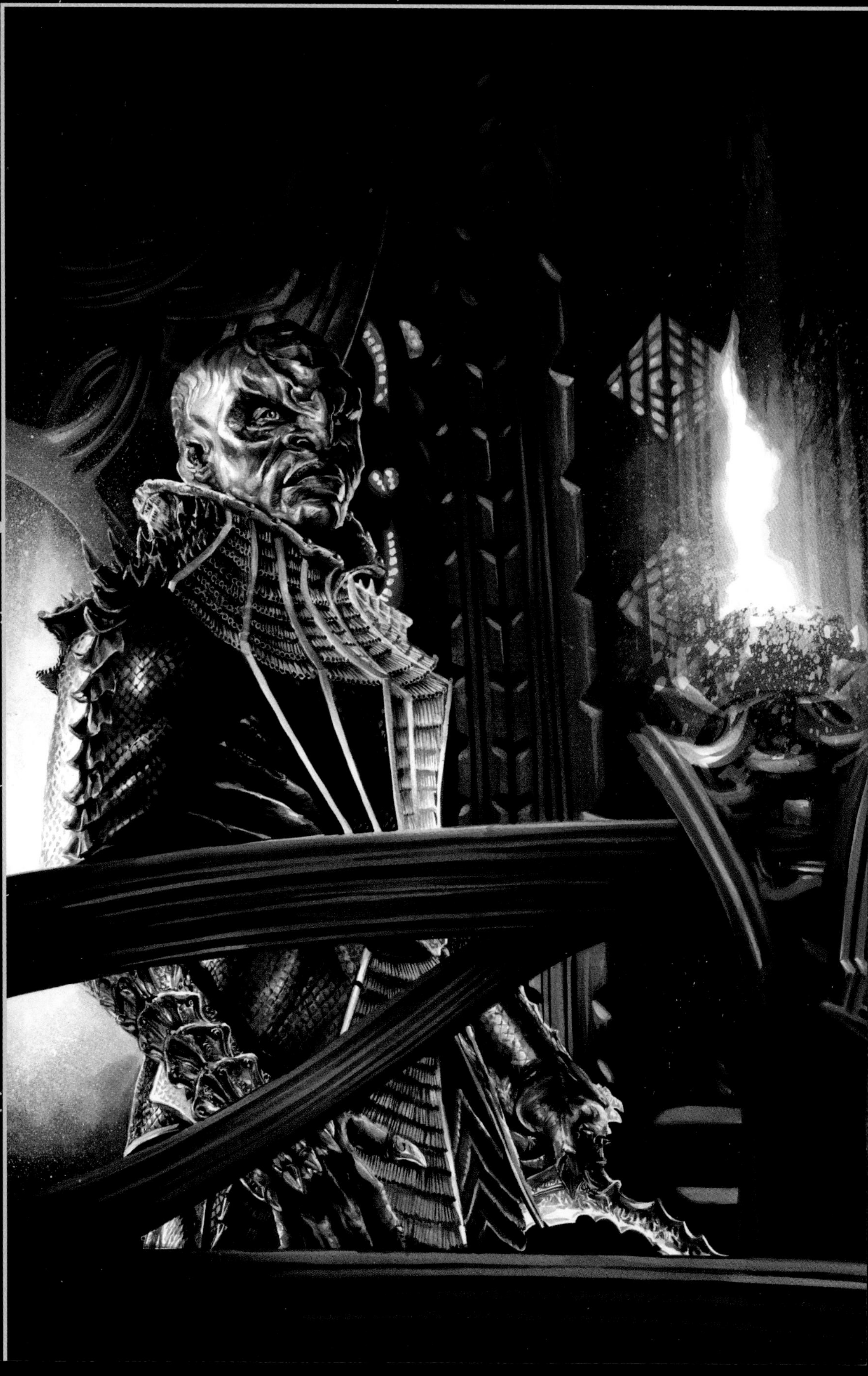

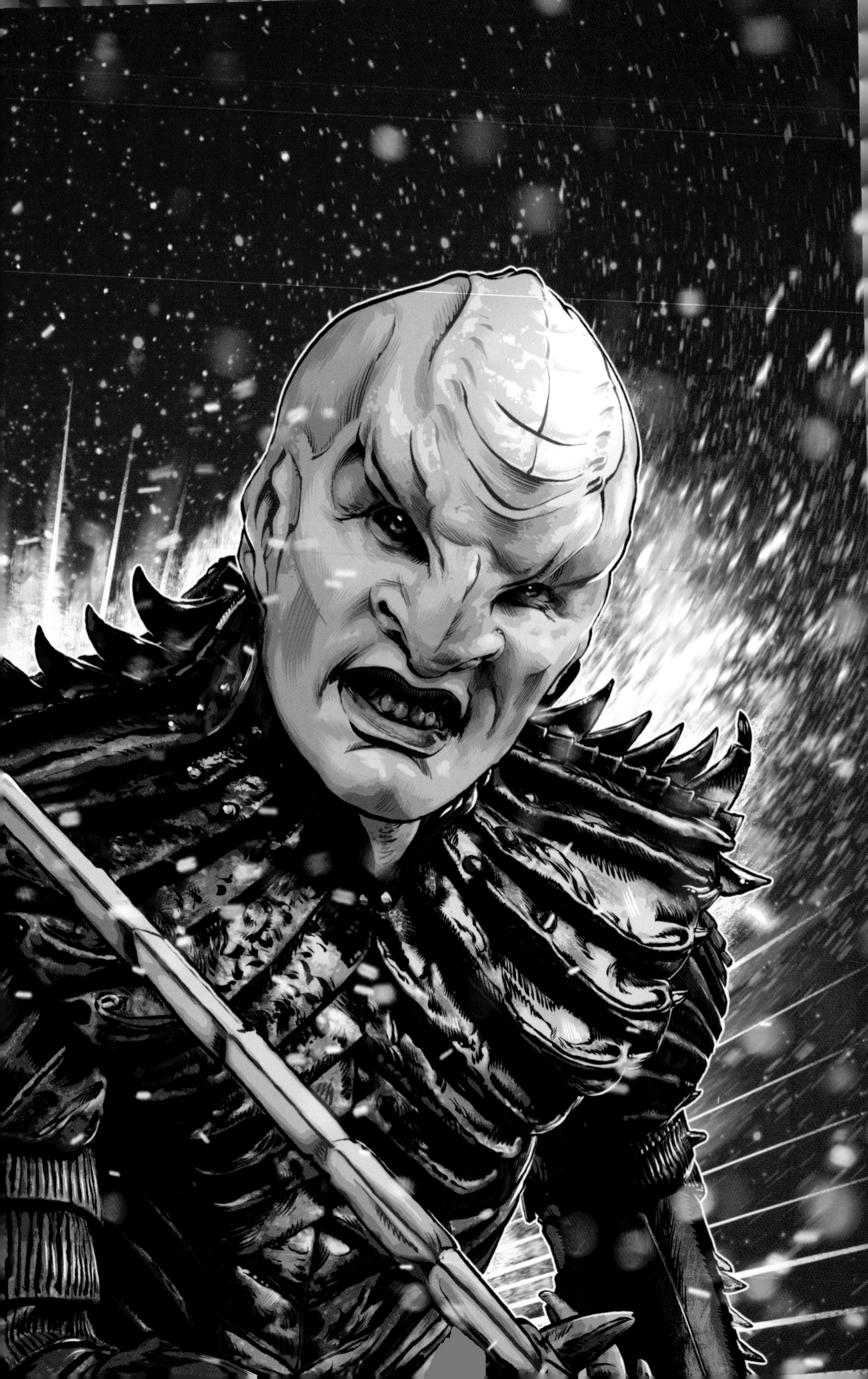

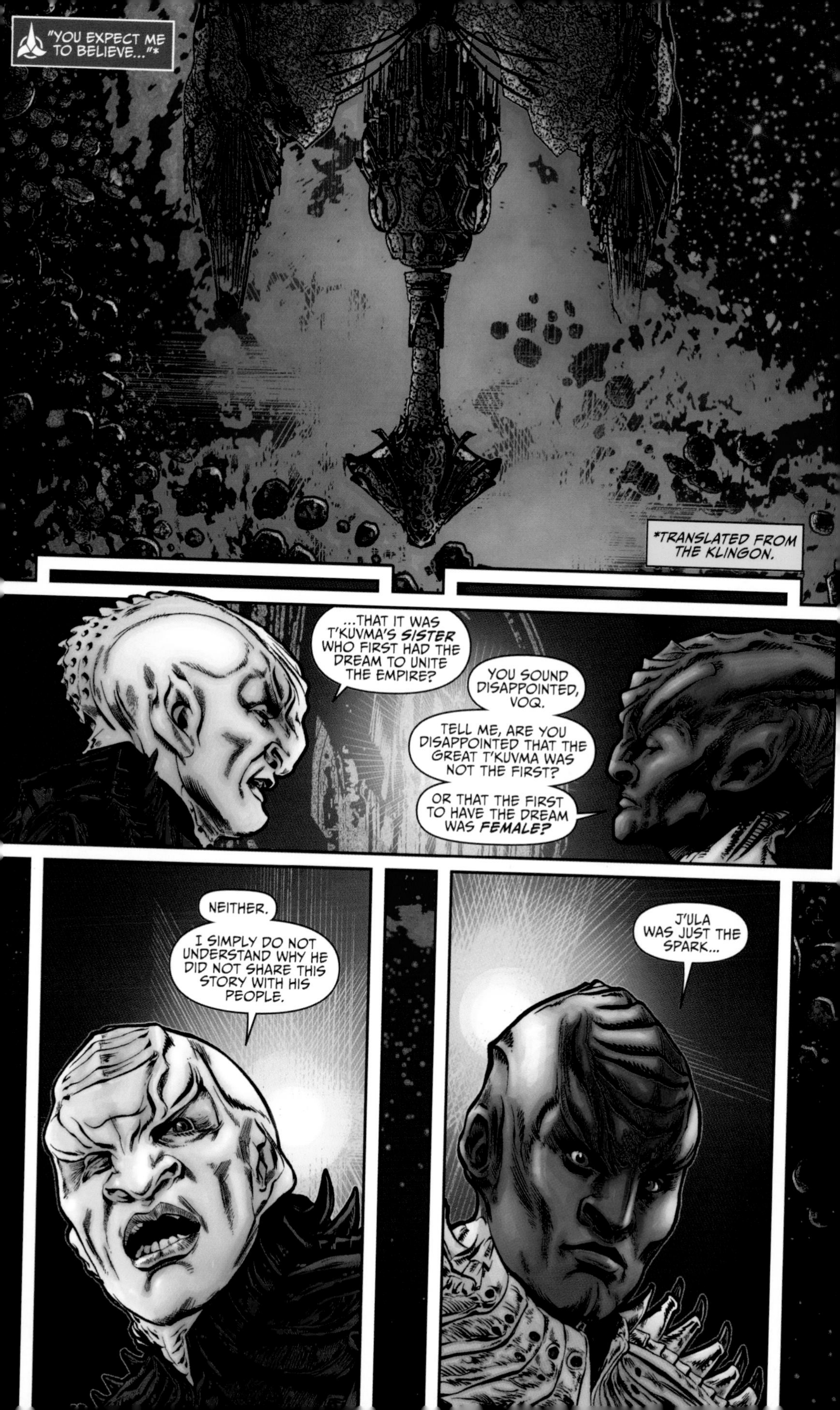
"YOU EXPECT ME TO BELIEVE..."*
*TRANSLATED FROM THE KLINGON.
...THAT IT WAS T'KUVMA'S SISTER WHO FIRST HAD THE DREAM TO UNITE THE EMPIRE?
YOU SOUND DISAPPOINTED, VOQ.
TELL ME, ARE YOU DISAPPOINTED THAT THE GREAT T'KUVMA WAS NOT THE FIRST?
OR THAT THE FIRST TO HAVE THE DREAM WAS FEMALE?
NEITHER.
I SIMPLY DO NOT UNDERSTAND WHY HE DID NOT SHARE THIS STORY WITH HIS PEOPLE.
J'ULA WAS JUST THE SPARK...

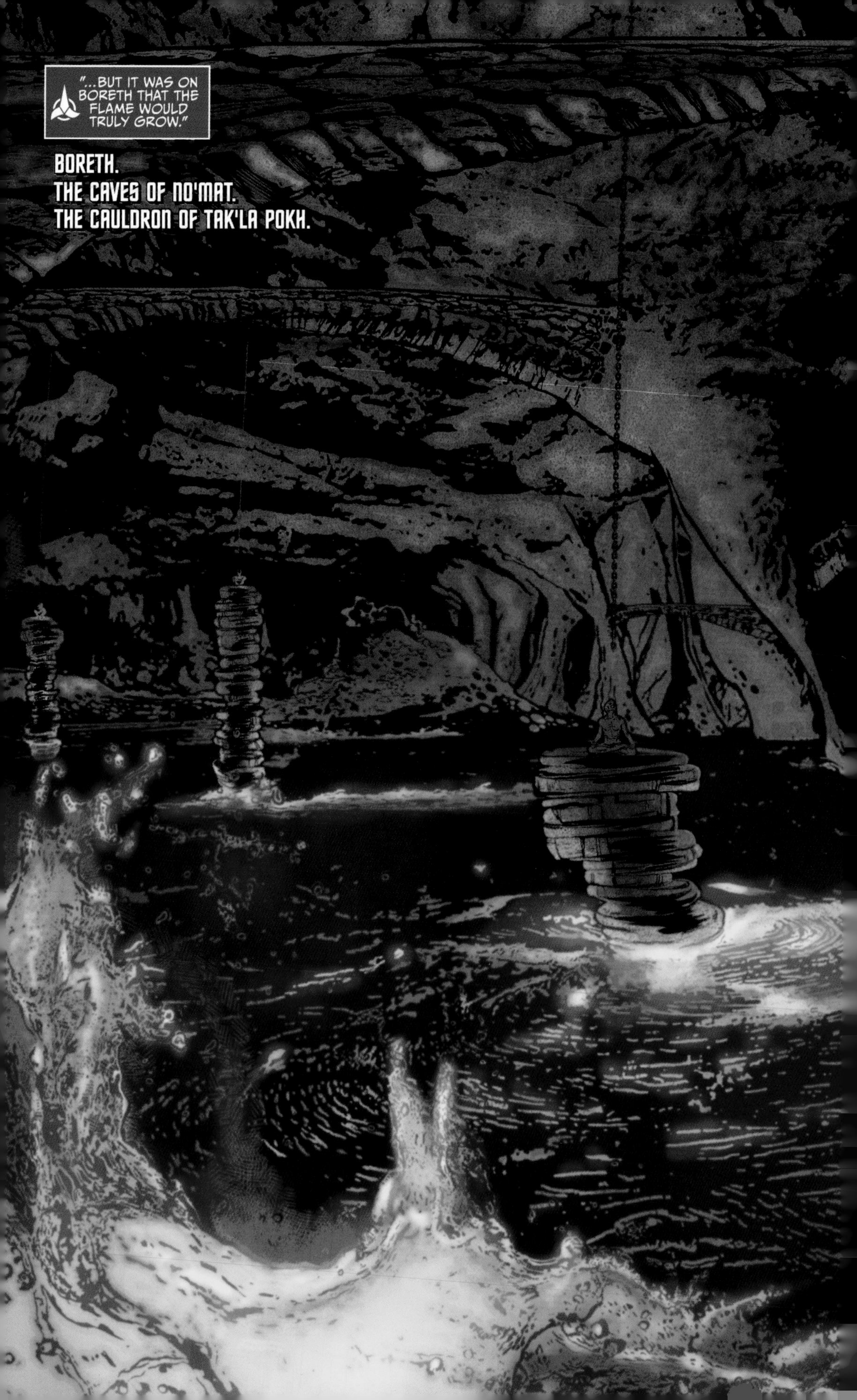
"...BUT IT WAS ON BORETH THAT THE FLAME WOULD TRULY GROW."
BORETH.
THE CAVES OF NO'MAT.
THE CAULDRON OF TAK'LA POKH.

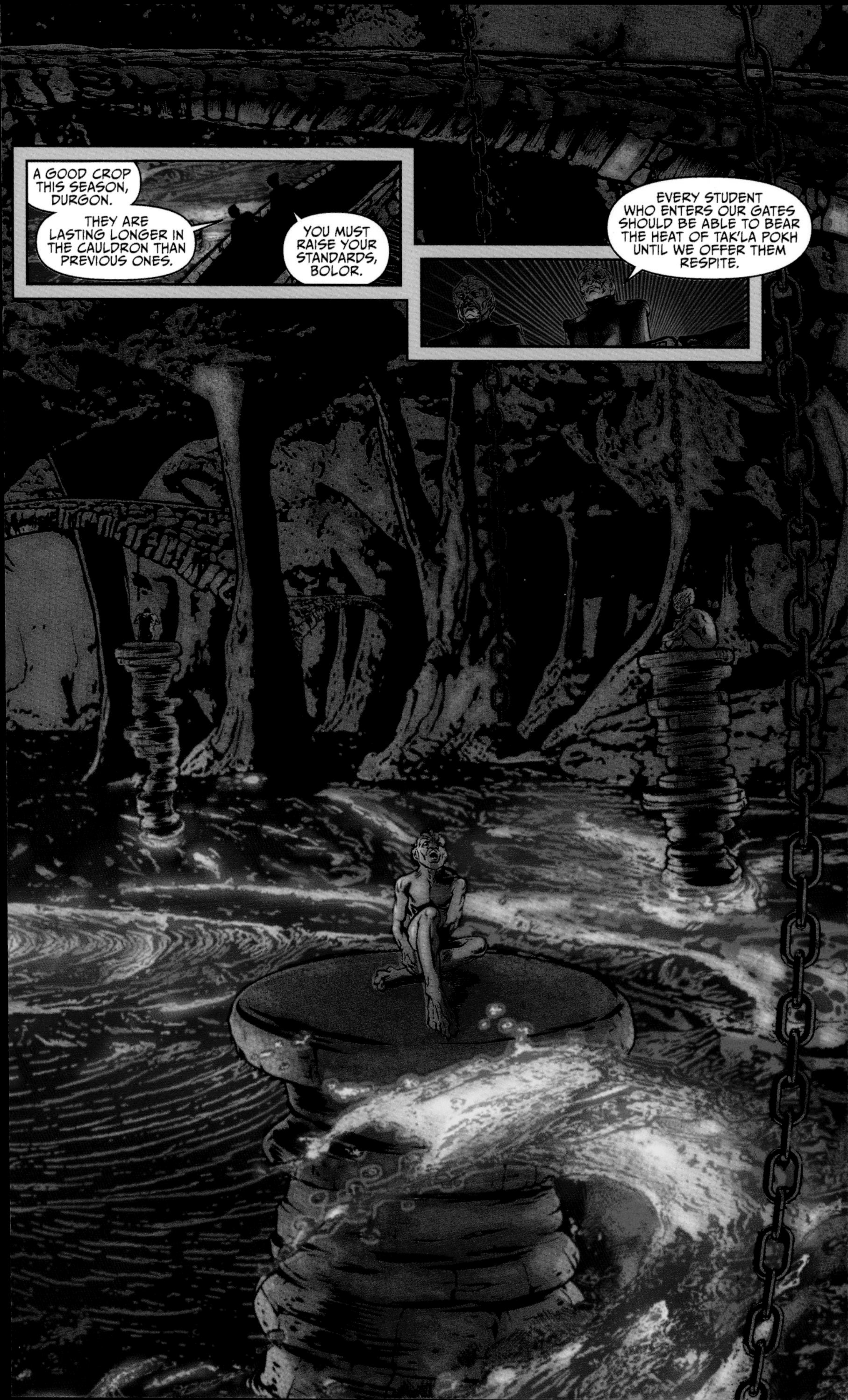
A GOOD CROP THIS SEASON, DURGON.
THEY ARE LASTING LONGER IN THE CAULDRON THAN PREVIOUS ONES.
YOU MUST RAISE YOUR STANDARDS, BOLOR.
EVERY STUDENT WHO ENTERS OUR GATES SHOULD BE ABLE TO BEAR THE HEAT OF TAK'LA POKH UNTIL WE OFFER THEM RESPITE.

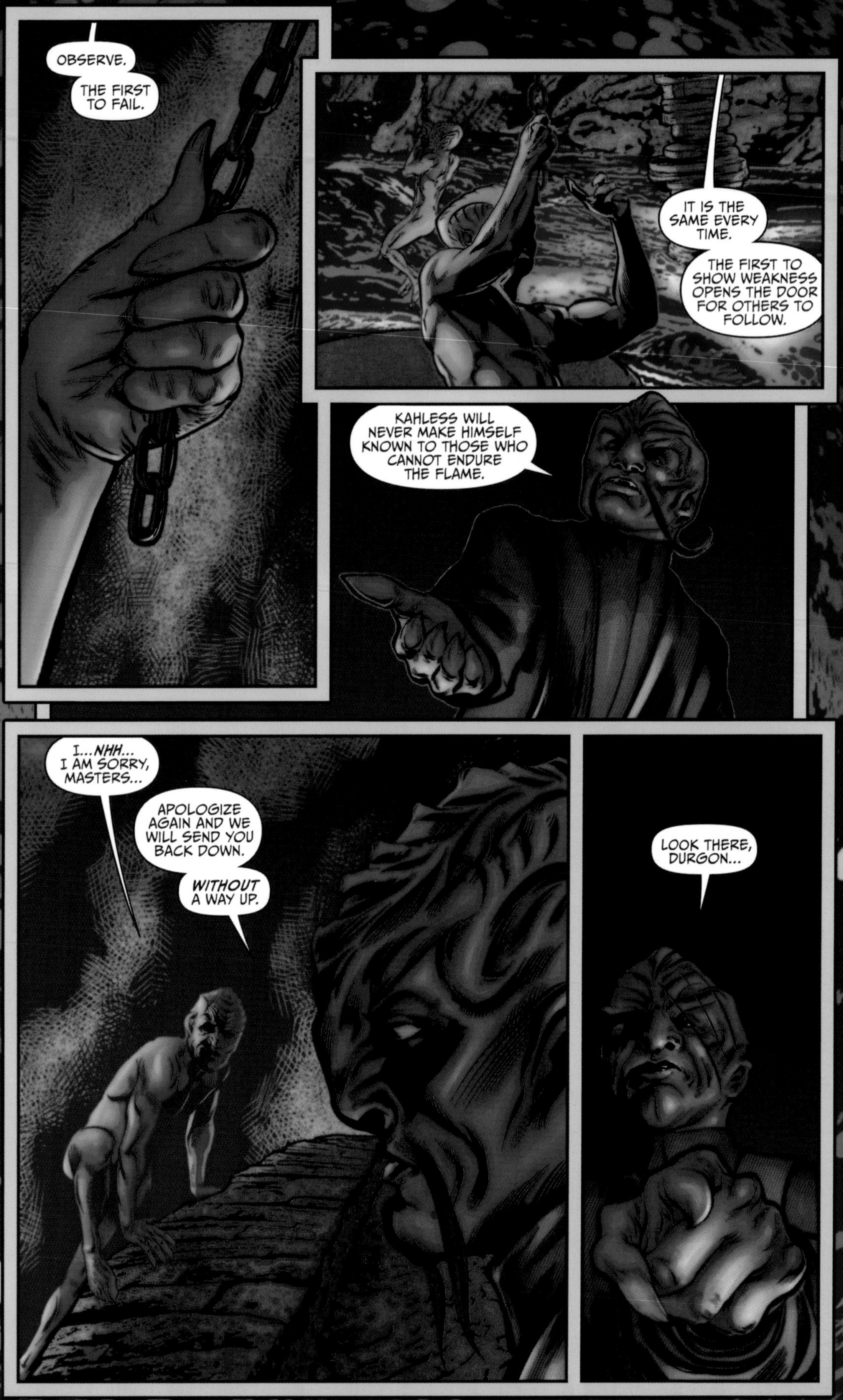
OBSERVE.
THE FIRST TO FAIL.
IT IS THE SAME EVERY TIME.
THE FIRST TO SHOW WEAKNESS OPENS THE DOOR FOR OTHERS TO FOLLOW.
KAHLESS WILL NEVER MAKE HIMSELF KNOWN TO THOSE WHO CANNOT ENDURE THE FLAME.
I... *NHH*... I AM SORRY, MASTERS...
APOLOGIZE AGAIN AND WE WILL SEND YOU BACK DOWN.
WITHOUT A WAY UP.
LOOK THERE, DURGON...

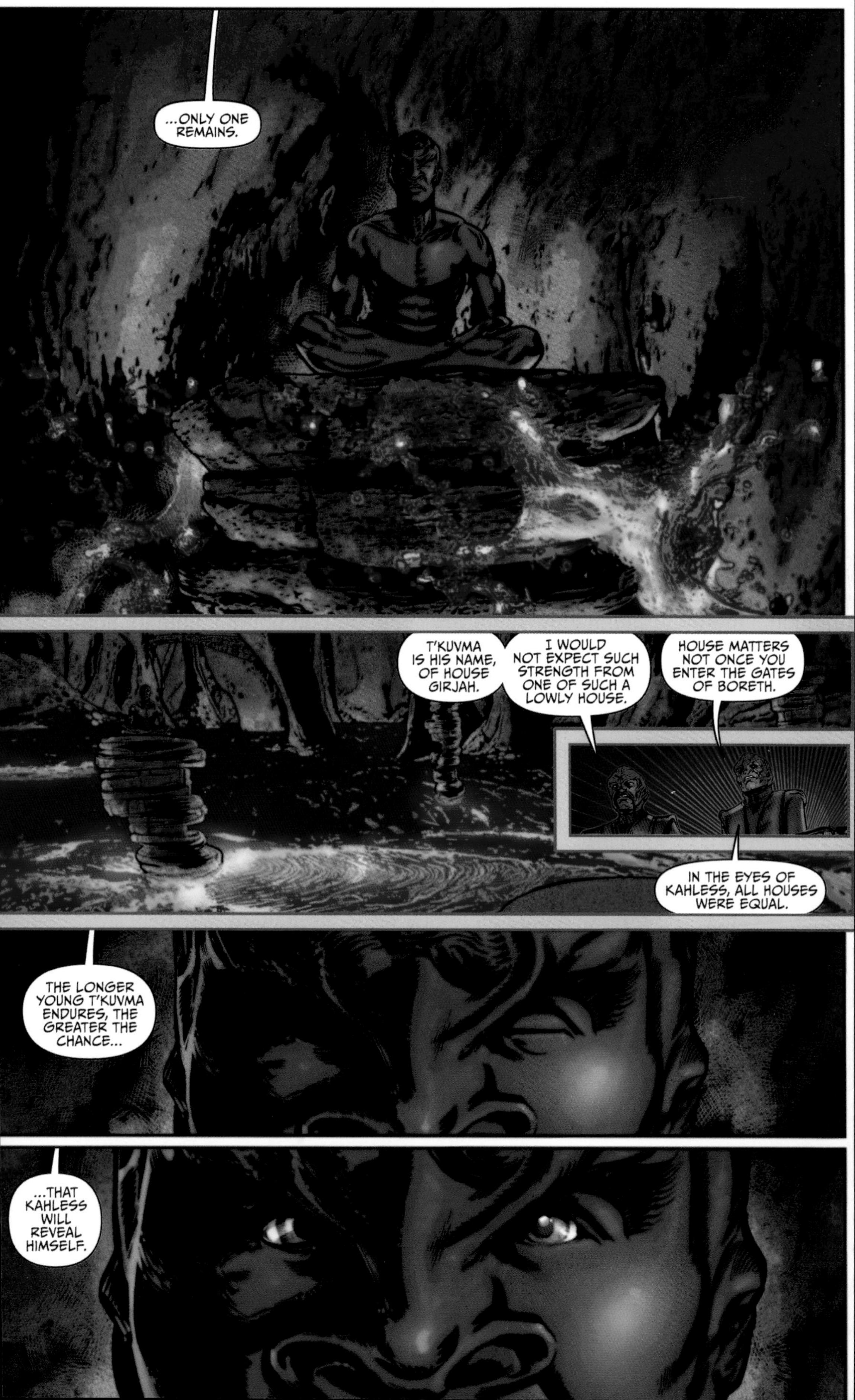
...ONLY ONE REMAINS.
T'KUVMA IS HIS NAME, OF HOUSE GIRJAH.
I WOULD NOT EXPECT SUCH STRENGTH FROM ONE OF SUCH A LOWLY HOUSE.
HOUSE MATTERS NOT ONCE YOU ENTER THE GATES OF BORETH.
IN THE EYES OF KAHLESS, ALL HOUSES WERE EQUAL.
THE LONGER YOUNG T'KUVMA ENDURES, THE GREATER THE CHANCE...
...THAT KAHLESS WILL REVEAL HIMSELF.

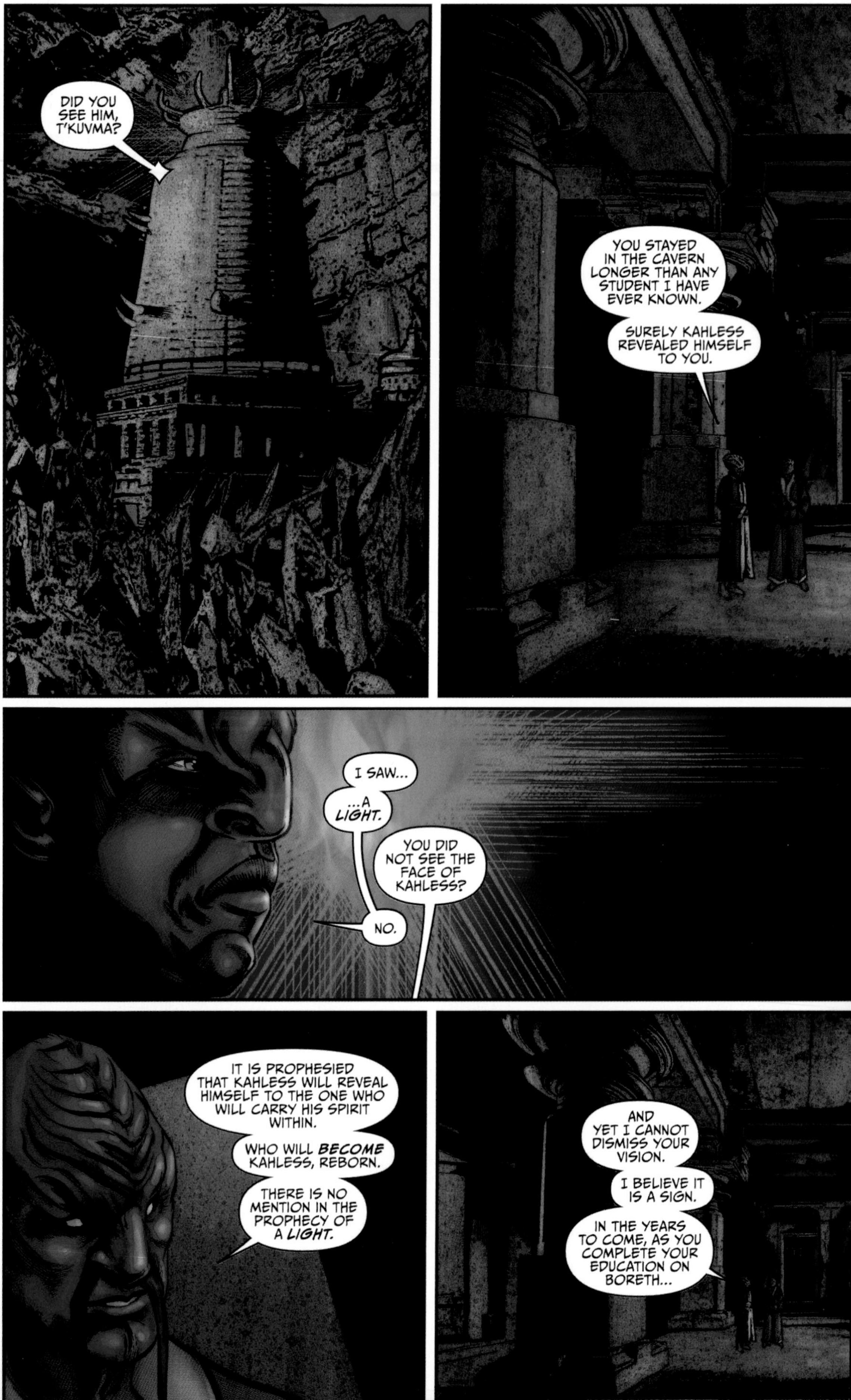
DID YOU SEE HIM, T'KUVMA?
YOU STAYED IN THE CAVERN LONGER THAN ANY STUDENT I HAVE EVER KNOWN.
SURELY KAHLESS REVEALED HIMSELF TO YOU.
I SAW...
...A *LIGHT*.
YOU DID NOT SEE THE FACE OF KAHLESS?
NO.
IT IS PROPHESIED THAT KAHLESS WILL REVEAL HIMSELF TO THE ONE WHO WILL CARRY HIS SPIRIT WITHIN.
WHO WILL *BECOME* KAHLESS, REBORN.
THERE IS NO MENTION IN THE PROPHECY OF A *LIGHT*.
AND YET I CANNOT DISMISS YOUR VISION.
I BELIEVE IT IS A SIGN.
IN THE YEARS TO COME, AS YOU COMPLETE YOUR EDUCATION ON BORETH...

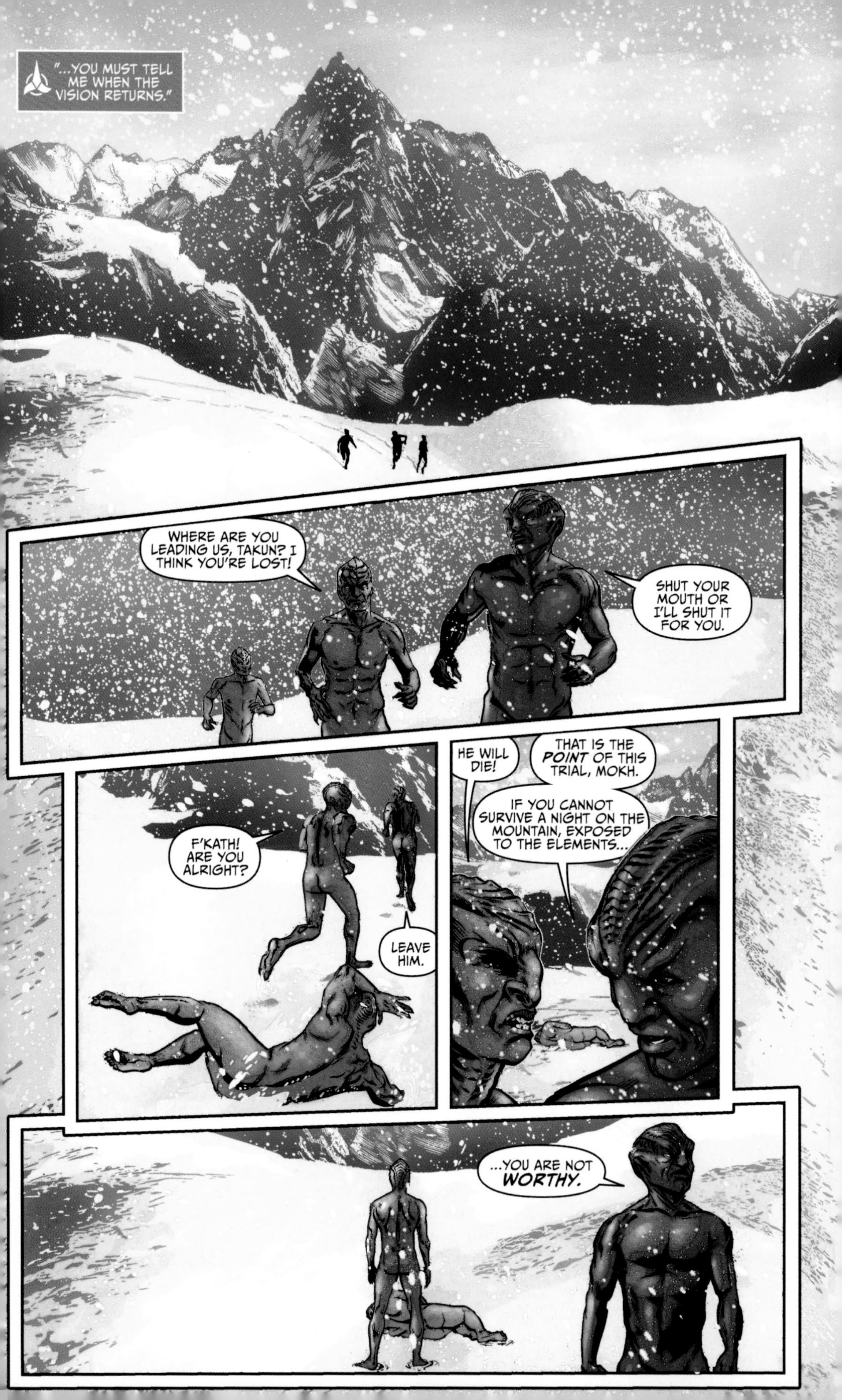

"...YOU MUST TELL ME WHEN THE VISION RETURNS."
WHERE ARE YOU LEADING US, TAKUN? I THINK YOU'RE LOST!
SHUT YOUR MOUTH OR I'LL SHUT IT FOR YOU.
F'KATH! ARE YOU ALRIGHT?
LEAVE HIM.
HE WILL DIE!
THAT IS THE *POINT* OF THIS TRIAL, MOKH.
IF YOU CANNOT SURVIVE A NIGHT ON THE MOUNTAIN, EXPOSED TO THE ELEMENTS...
...YOU ARE NOT *WORTHY.*

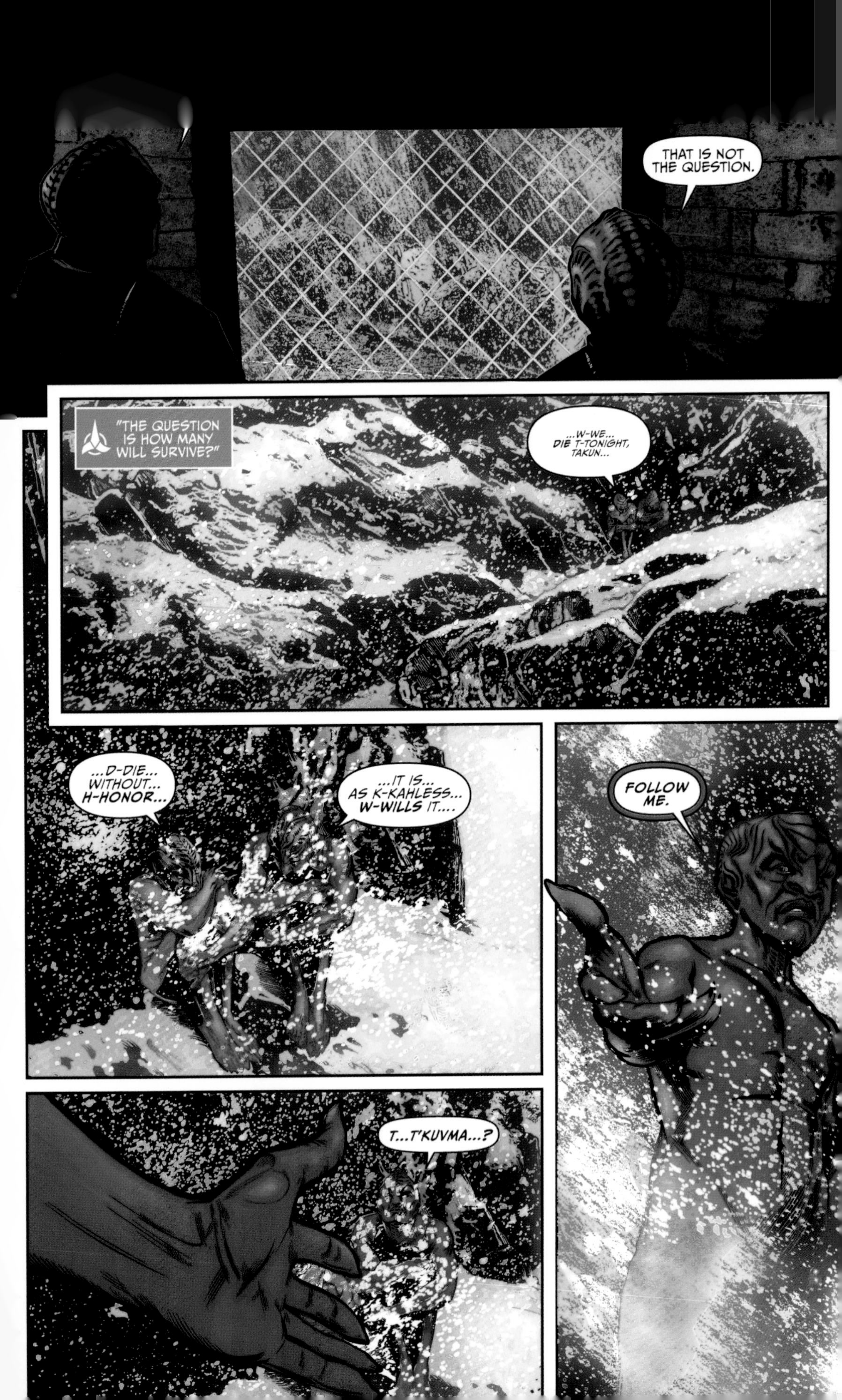
THAT IS NOT THE QUESTION.
"THE QUESTION IS HOW MANY WILL SURVIVE?"
...W-WE... DIE T-TONIGHT, TAKUN...
...D-DIE... WITHOUT... H-HONOR...
...IT IS... AS K-KAHLESS... W-WILLS IT....
FOLLOW ME.
T...T'KUVMA...?

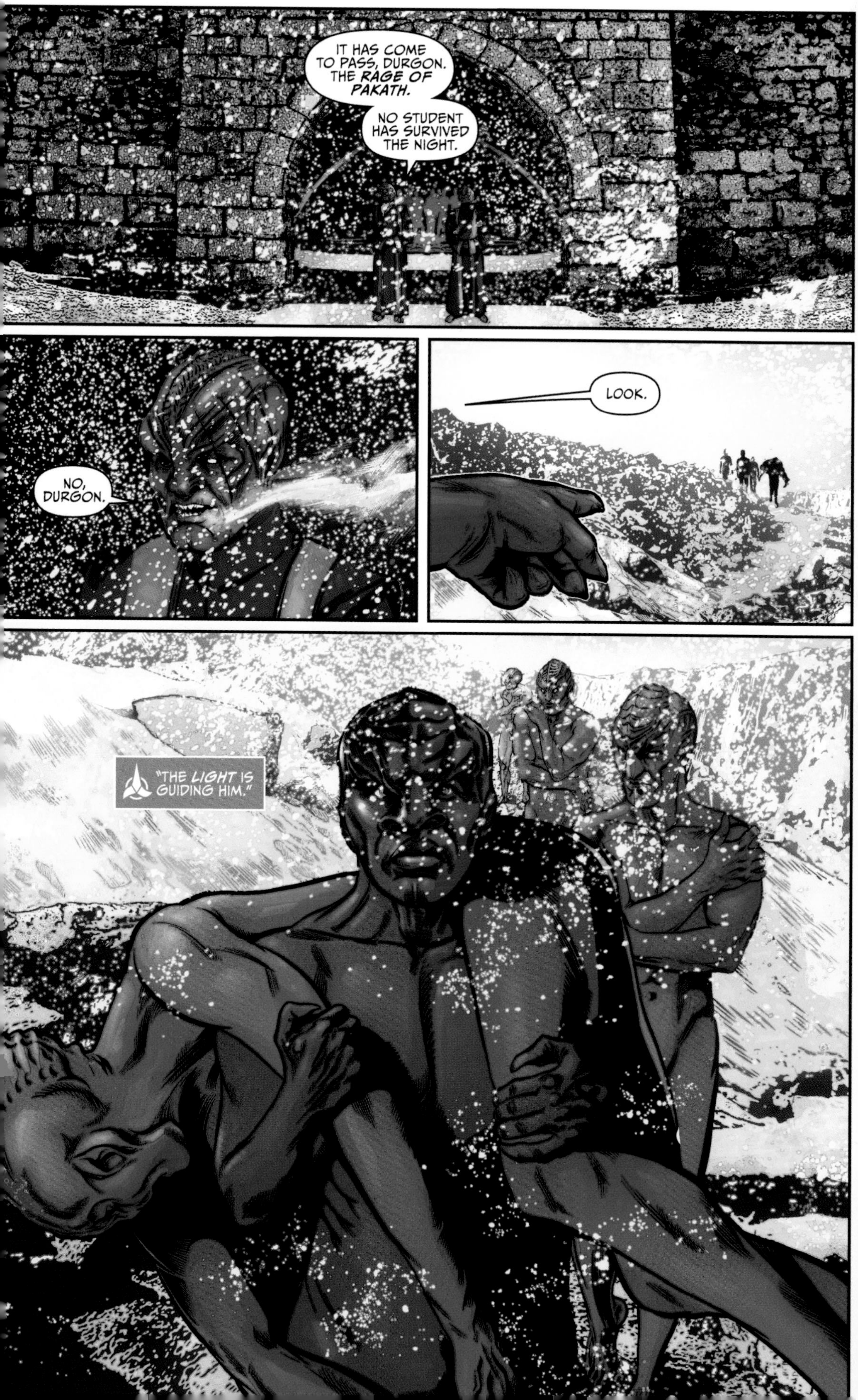
IT HAS COME TO PASS, DURGON. THE RAGE OF PAKATH.
NO STUDENT HAS SURVIVED THE NIGHT.
NO, DURGON.
LOOK.
"THE LIGHT IS GUIDING HIM."

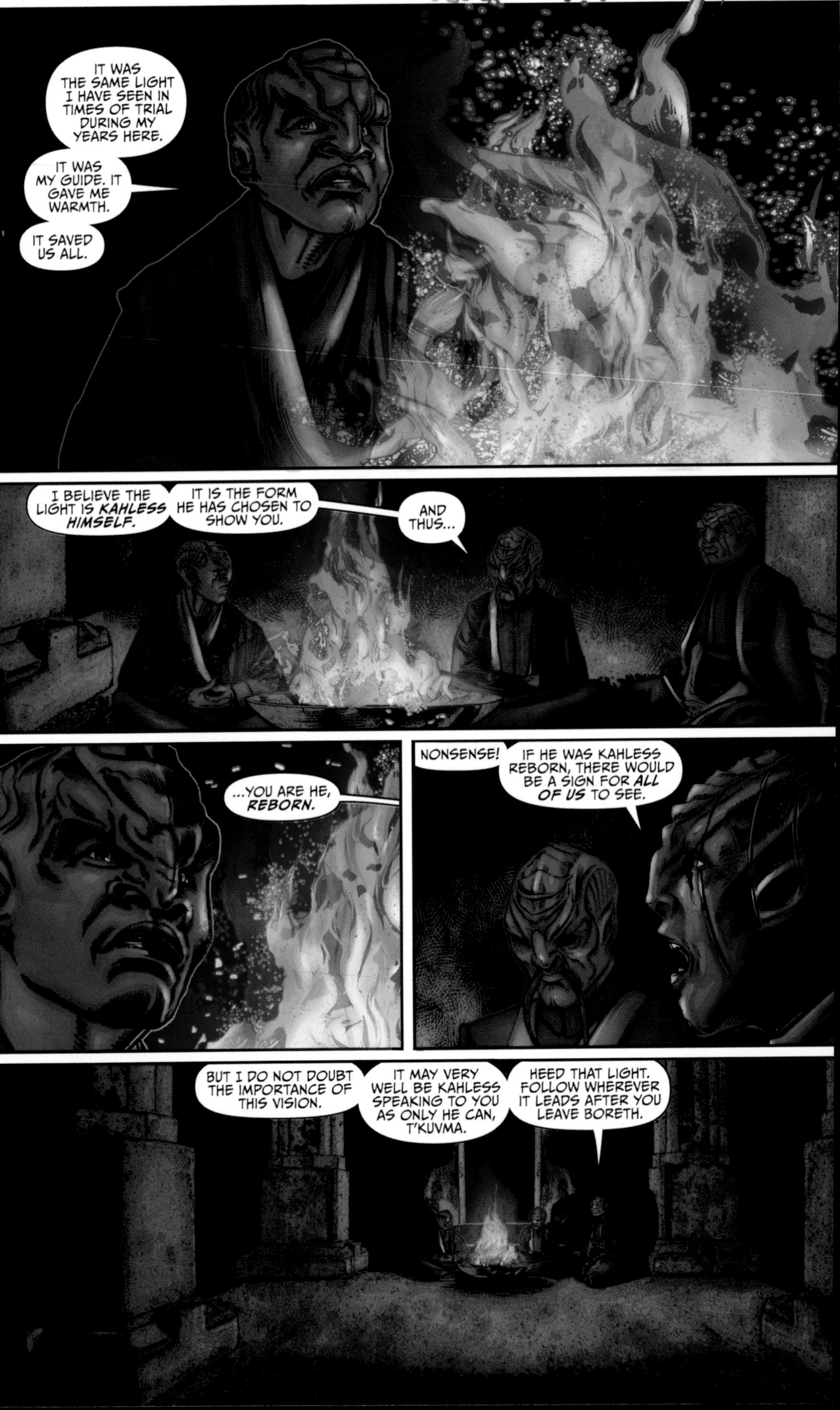
IT WAS THE SAME LIGHT I HAVE SEEN IN TIMES OF TRIAL DURING MY YEARS HERE.
IT WAS MY GUIDE. IT GAVE ME WARMTH.
IT SAVED US ALL.
I BELIEVE THE LIGHT IS KAHLESS HIMSELF.
IT IS THE FORM HE HAS CHOSEN TO SHOW YOU.
AND THUS...
...YOU ARE HE, REBORN.
NONSENSE!
IF HE WAS KAHLESS REBORN, THERE WOULD BE A SIGN FOR ALL OF US TO SEE.
BUT I DO NOT DOUBT THE IMPORTANCE OF THIS VISION.
IT MAY VERY WELL BE KAHLESS SPEAKING TO YOU AS ONLY HE CAN, T'KUVMA.
HEED THAT LIGHT. FOLLOW WHEREVER IT LEADS AFTER YOU LEAVE BORETH.

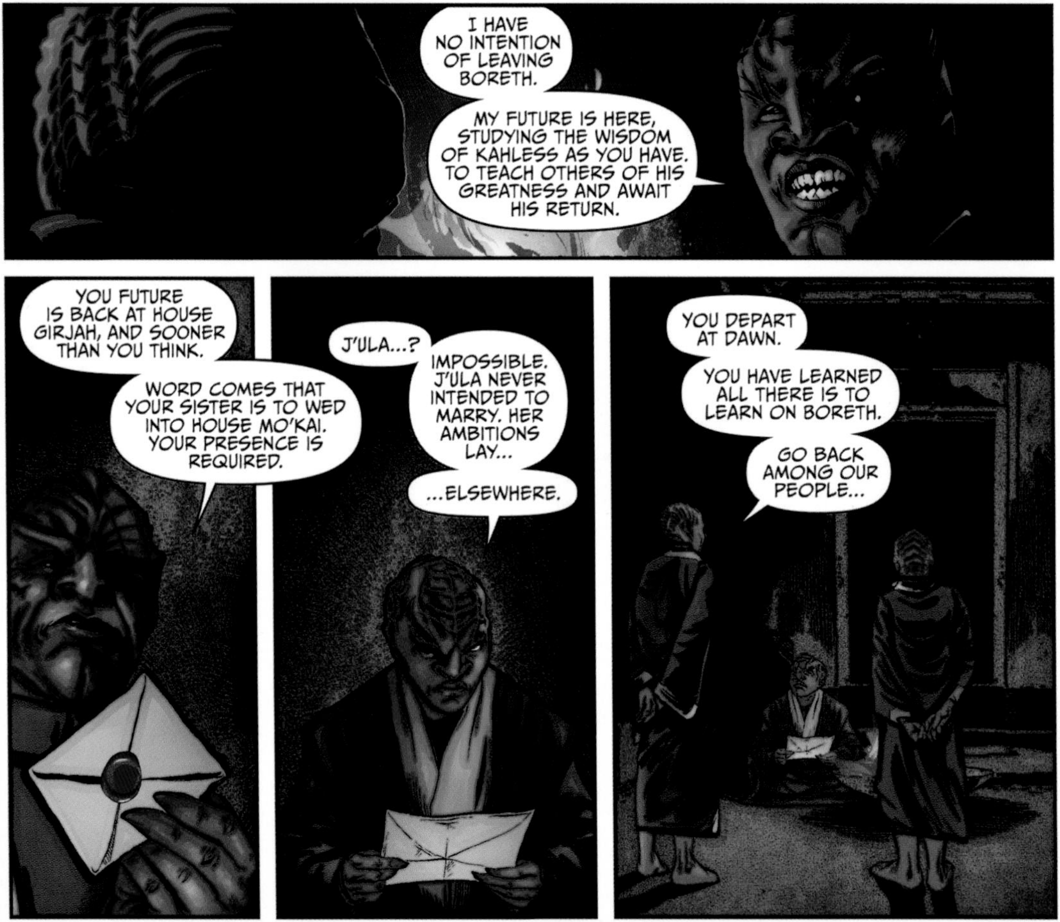
I HAVE NO INTENTION OF LEAVING BORETH.
MY FUTURE IS HERE, STUDYING THE WISDOM OF KAHLESS AS YOU HAVE. TO TEACH OTHERS OF HIS GREATNESS AND AWAIT HIS RETURN.
YOU FUTURE IS BACK AT HOUSE GIRJAH, AND SOONER THAN YOU THINK.
WORD COMES THAT YOUR SISTER IS TO WED INTO HOUSE MO'KAI. YOUR PRESENCE IS REQUIRED.
J'ULA...?
IMPOSSIBLE. J'ULA NEVER INTENDED TO MARRY. HER AMBITIONS LAY...
...ELSEWHERE.
YOU DEPART AT DAWN.
YOU HAVE LEARNED ALL THERE IS TO LEARN ON BORETH.
GO BACK AMONG OUR PEOPLE...

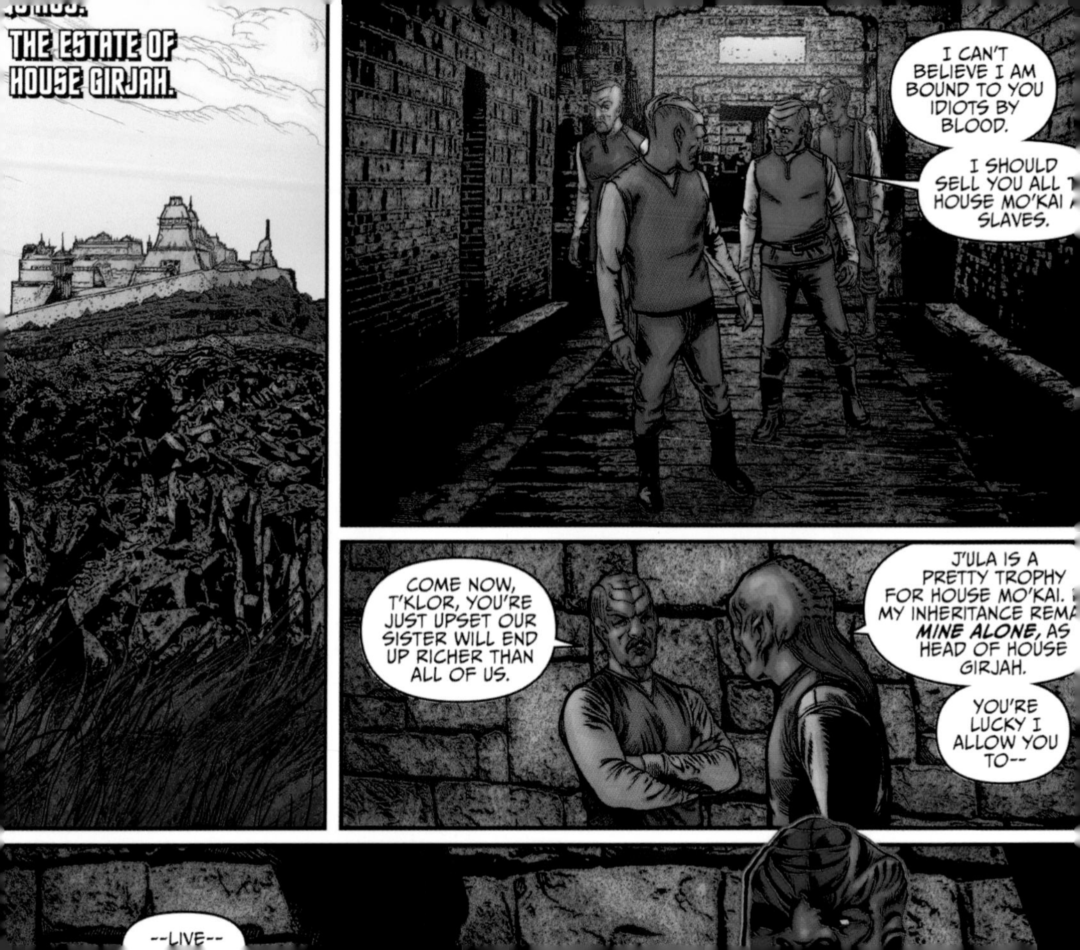
THE ESTATE OF HOUSE GIRJAH.
I CAN'T BELIEVE I AM BOUND TO YOU IDIOTS BY BLOOD.
I SHOULD SELL YOU ALL T HOUSE MO'KAI SLAVES.
COME NOW, T'KLOR, YOU'RE JUST UPSET OUR SISTER WILL END UP RICHER THAN ALL OF US.
J'ULA IS A PRETTY TROPHY FOR HOUSE MO'KAI. MY INHERITANCE REMA MINE ALONE, AS HEAD OF HOUSE GIRJAH.
YOU'RE LUCKY I ALLOW YOU TO--
--LIVE--

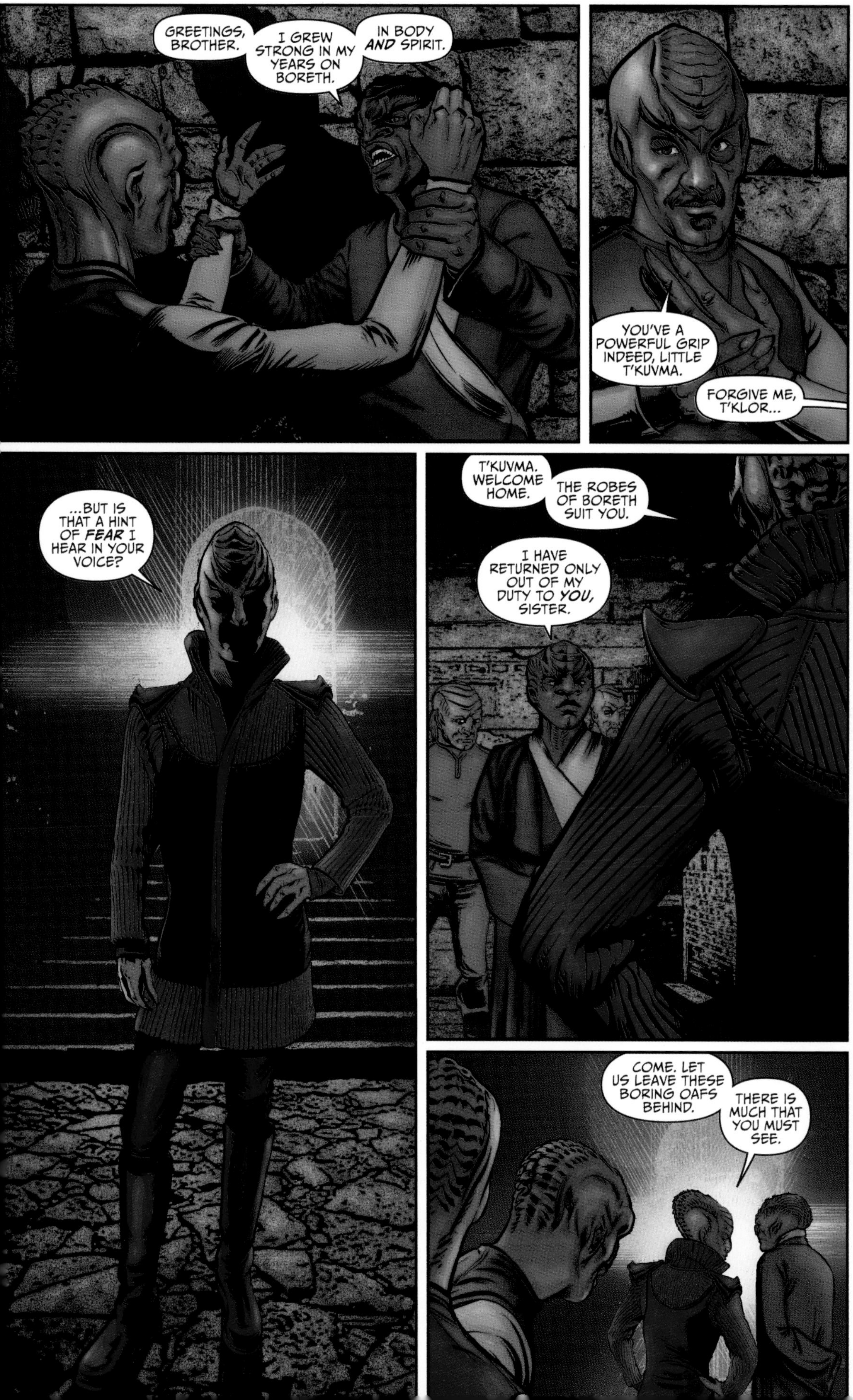
GREETINGS, BROTHER.
I GREW STRONG IN MY YEARS ON BORETH.
IN BODY AND SPIRIT.
YOU'VE A POWERFUL GRIP INDEED, LITTLE T'KUVMA.
FORGIVE ME, T'KLOR...
...BUT IS THAT A HINT OF FEAR I HEAR IN YOUR VOICE?
T'KUVMA. WELCOME HOME.
THE ROBES OF BORETH SUIT YOU.
I HAVE RETURNED ONLY OUT OF MY DUTY TO YOU, SISTER.
COME. LET US LEAVE THESE BORING OAFS BEHIND.
THERE IS MUCH THAT YOU MUST SEE.

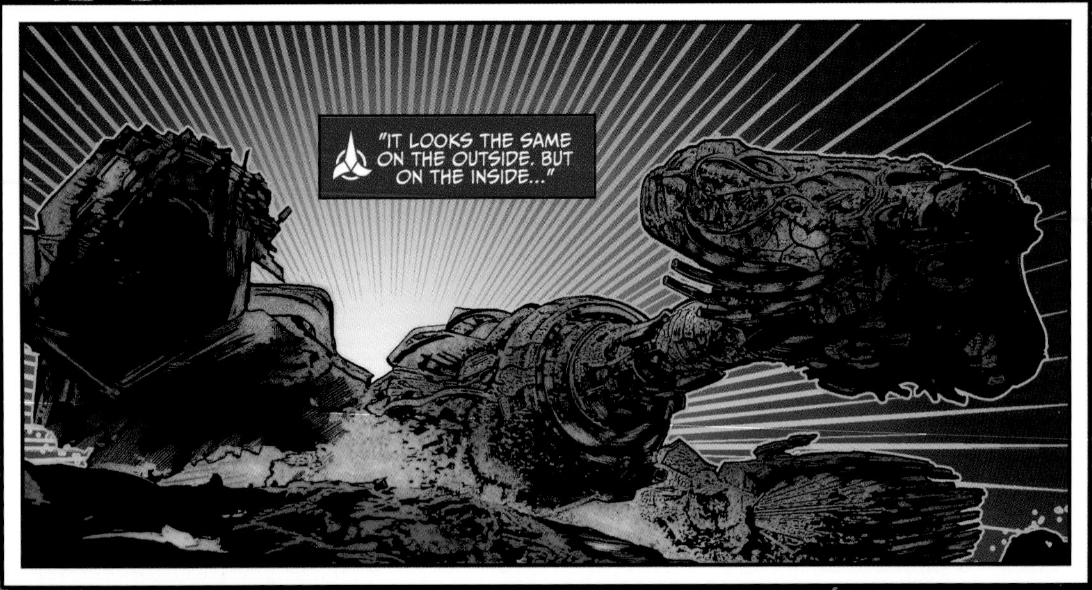
"IT LOOKS THE SAME ON THE OUTSIDE. BUT ON THE INSIDE..."

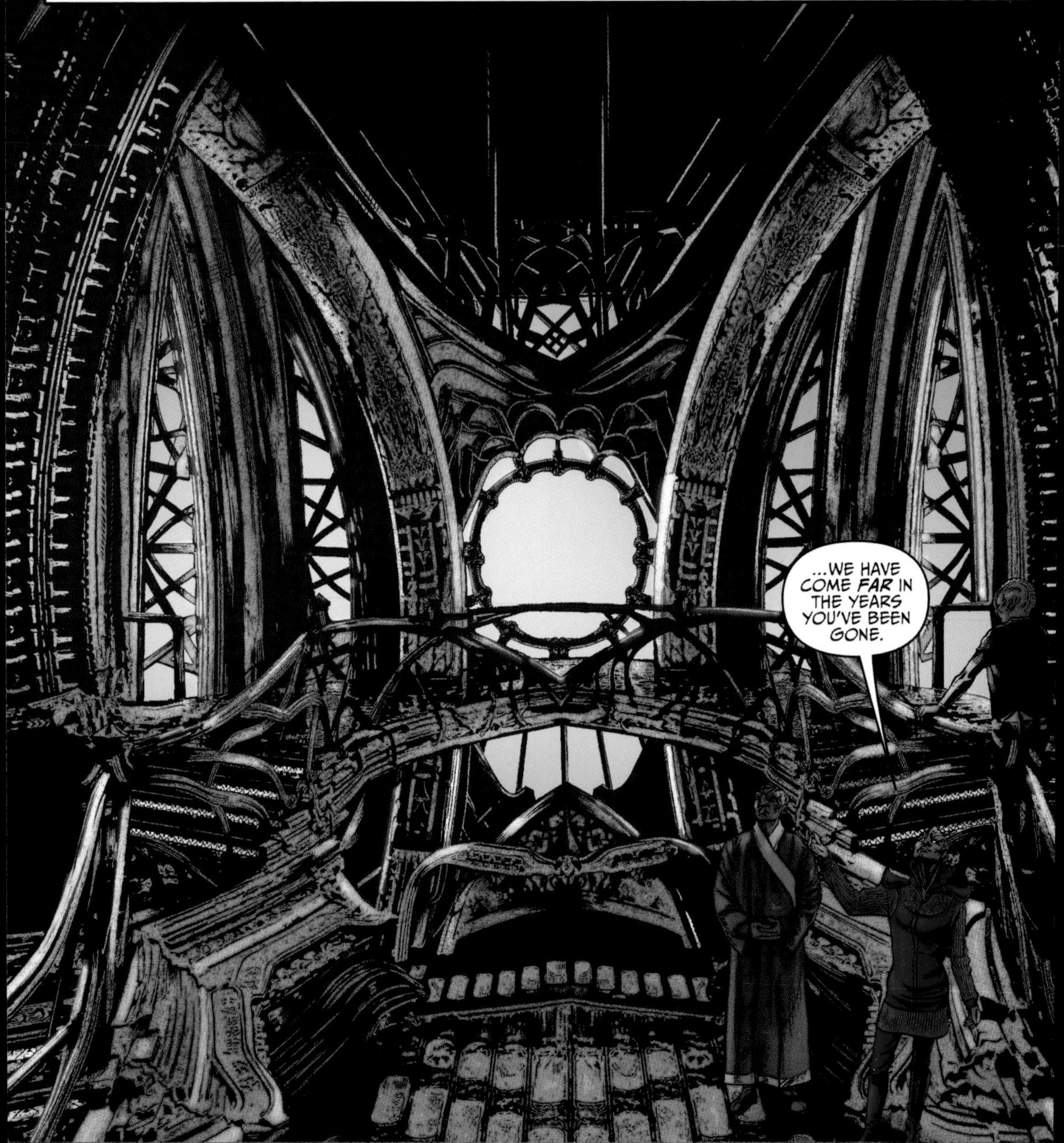
...WE HAVE COME FAR IN THE YEARS YOU'VE BEEN GONE.

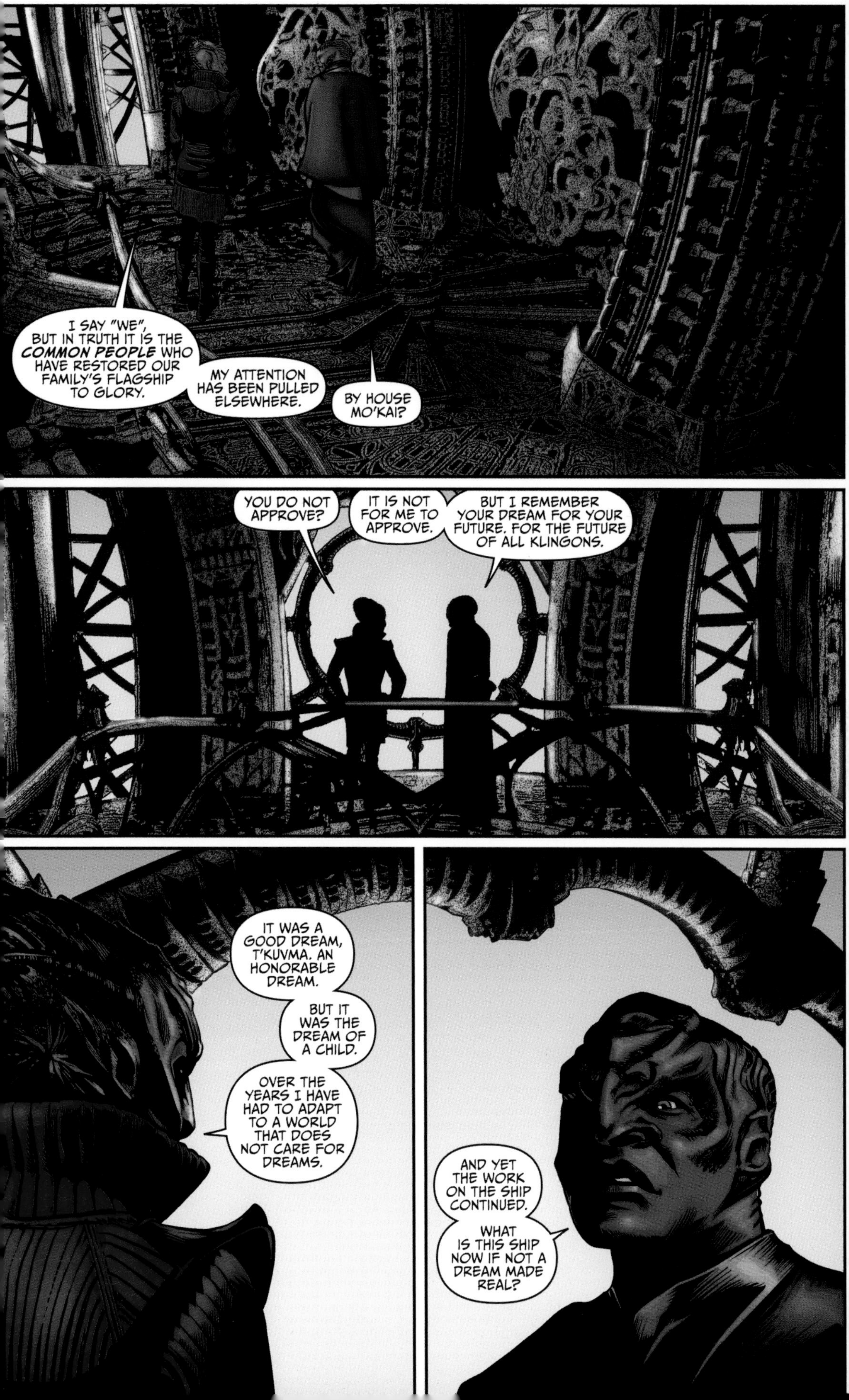
I SAY "WE", BUT IN TRUTH IT IS THE *COMMON PEOPLE* WHO HAVE RESTORED OUR FAMILY'S FLAGSHIP TO GLORY.
MY ATTENTION HAS BEEN PULLED ELSEWHERE.
BY HOUSE MO'KAI?
YOU DO NOT APPROVE?
IT IS NOT FOR ME TO APPROVE.
BUT I REMEMBER YOUR DREAM FOR YOUR FUTURE. FOR THE FUTURE OF ALL KLINGONS.
IT WAS A GOOD DREAM, T'KUVMA. AN HONORABLE DREAM.
BUT IT WAS THE DREAM OF A CHILD.
OVER THE YEARS I HAVE HAD TO ADAPT TO A WORLD THAT DOES NOT CARE FOR DREAMS.
AND YET THE WORK ON THE SHIP CONTINUED.
WHAT IS THIS SHIP NOW IF NOT A DREAM MADE REAL?

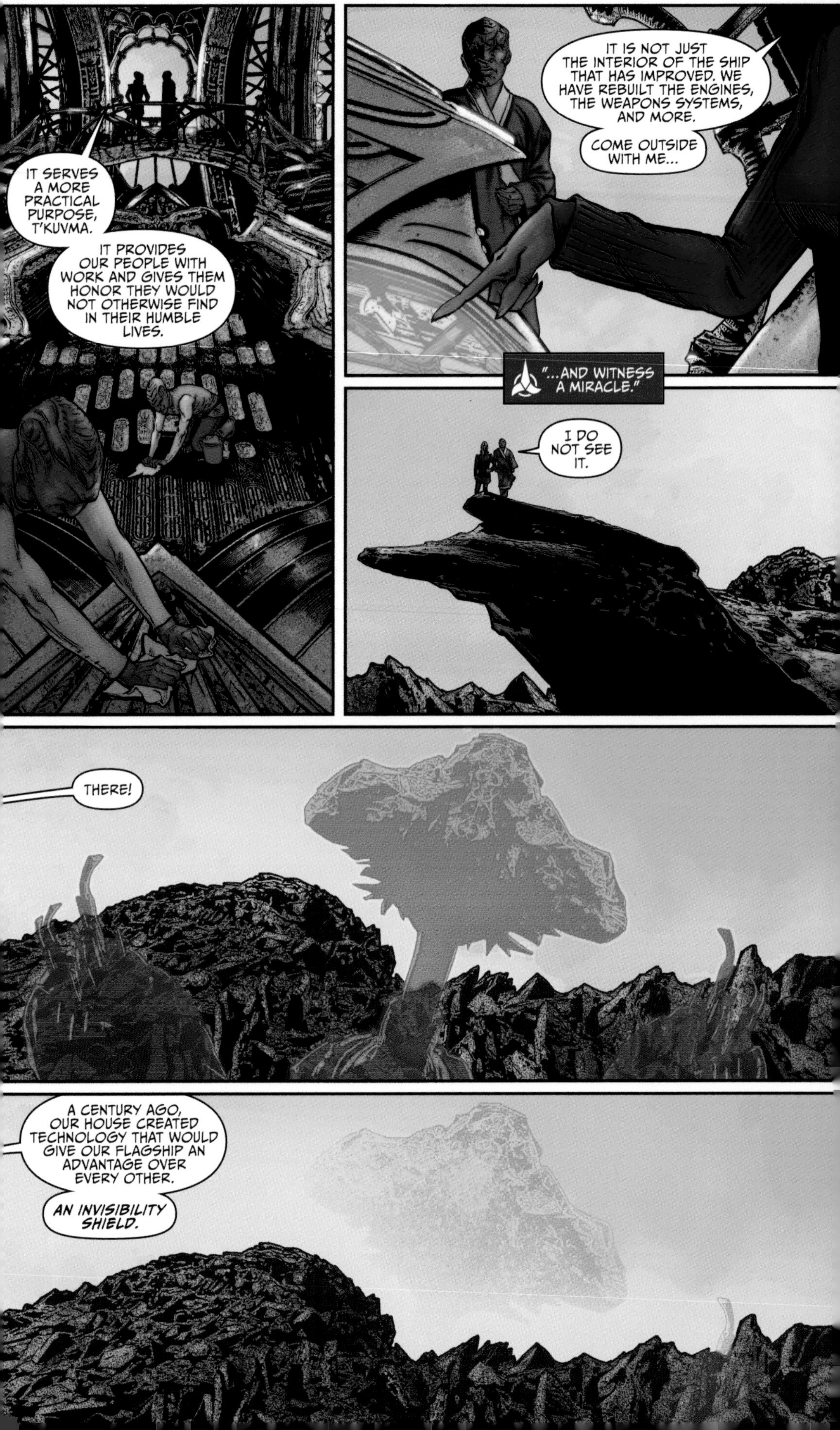

IT SERVES A MORE PRACTICAL PURPOSE, T'KUVMA.
IT PROVIDES OUR PEOPLE WITH WORK AND GIVES THEM HONOR THEY WOULD NOT OTHERWISE FIND IN THEIR HUMBLE LIVES.
IT IS NOT JUST THE INTERIOR OF THE SHIP THAT HAS IMPROVED. WE HAVE REBUILT THE ENGINES, THE WEAPONS SYSTEMS, AND MORE.
COME OUTSIDE WITH ME...
"...AND WITNESS A MIRACLE."
I DO NOT SEE IT.
THERE!
A CENTURY AGO, OUR HOUSE CREATED TECHNOLOGY THAT WOULD GIVE OUR FLAGSHIP AN ADVANTAGE OVER EVERY OTHER.
AN INVISIBILITY SHIELD.

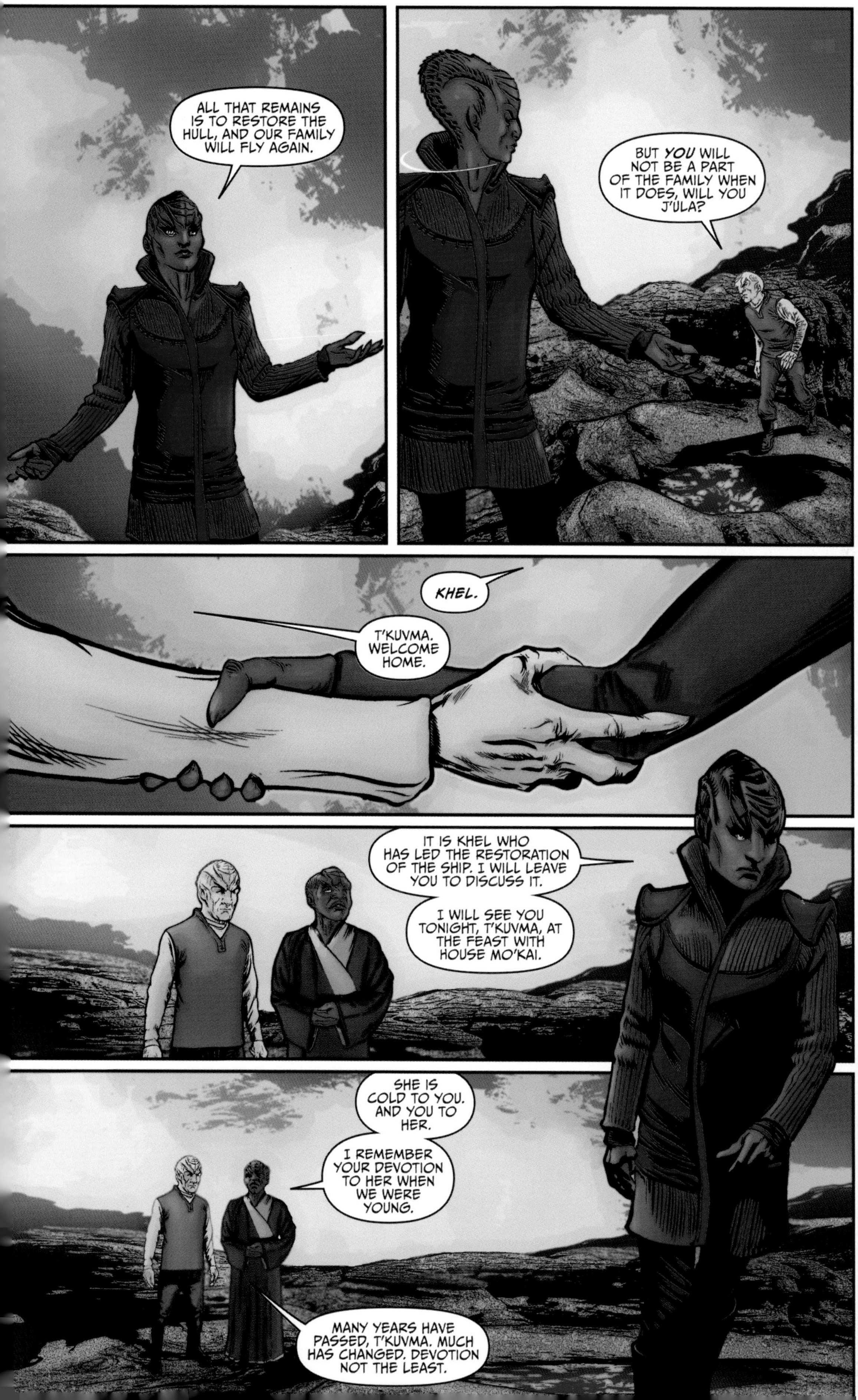
ALL THAT REMAINS IS TO RESTORE THE HULL, AND OUR FAMILY WILL FLY AGAIN.
BUT *YOU* WILL NOT BE A PART OF THE FAMILY WHEN IT DOES, WILL YOU J'ULA?
KHEL.
T'KUVMA. WELCOME HOME.
IT IS KHEL WHO HAS LED THE RESTORATION OF THE SHIP. I WILL LEAVE YOU TO DISCUSS IT.
I WILL SEE YOU TONIGHT, T'KUVMA, AT THE FEAST WITH HOUSE MO'KAI.
SHE IS COLD TO YOU. AND YOU TO HER.
I REMEMBER YOUR DEVOTION TO HER WHEN WE WERE YOUNG.
MANY YEARS HAVE PASSED, T'KUVMA. MUCH HAS CHANGED. DEVOTION NOT THE LEAST.

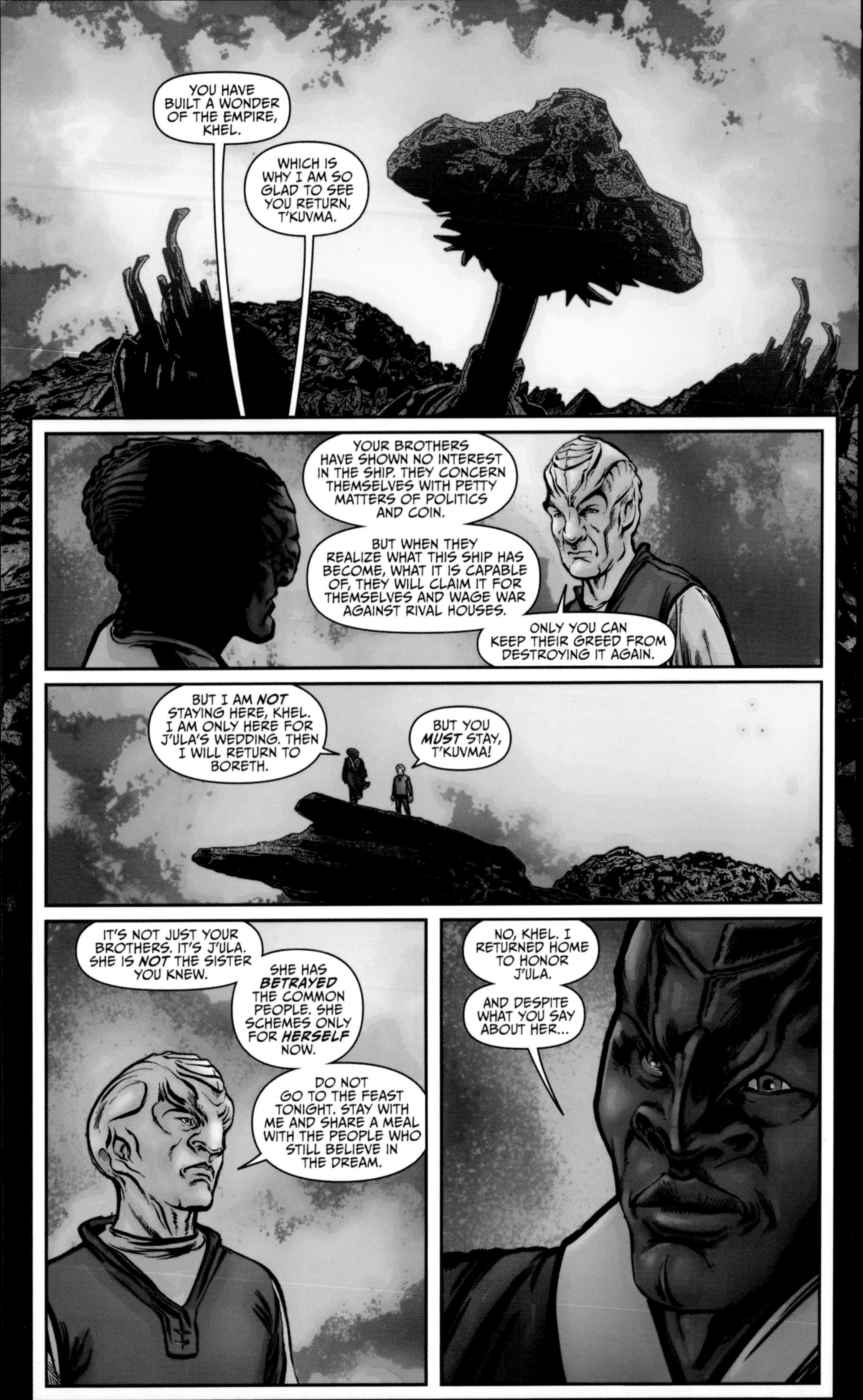
YOU HAVE BUILT A WONDER OF THE EMPIRE, KHEL.
WHICH IS WHY I AM SO GLAD TO SEE YOU RETURN, T'KUVMA.
YOUR BROTHERS HAVE SHOWN NO INTEREST IN THE SHIP. THEY CONCERN THEMSELVES WITH PETTY MATTERS OF POLITICS AND COIN.
BUT WHEN THEY REALIZE WHAT THIS SHIP HAS BECOME, WHAT IT IS CAPABLE OF, THEY WILL CLAIM IT FOR THEMSELVES AND WAGE WAR AGAINST RIVAL HOUSES.
ONLY YOU CAN KEEP THEIR GREED FROM DESTROYING IT AGAIN.
BUT I AM *NOT* STAYING HERE, KHEL. I AM ONLY HERE FOR J'ULA'S WEDDING. THEN I WILL RETURN TO BORETH.
BUT YOU *MUST* STAY, T'KUVMA!
IT'S NOT JUST YOUR BROTHERS. IT'S J'ULA. SHE IS *NOT* THE SISTER YOU KNEW.
SHE HAS *BETRAYED* THE COMMON PEOPLE. SHE SCHEMES ONLY FOR *HERSELF* NOW.
DO NOT GO TO THE FEAST TONIGHT. STAY WITH ME AND SHARE A MEAL WITH THE PEOPLE WHO STILL BELIEVE IN THE DREAM.
NO, KHEL. I RETURNED HOME TO HONOR J'ULA.
AND DESPITE WHAT YOU SAY ABOUT HER...

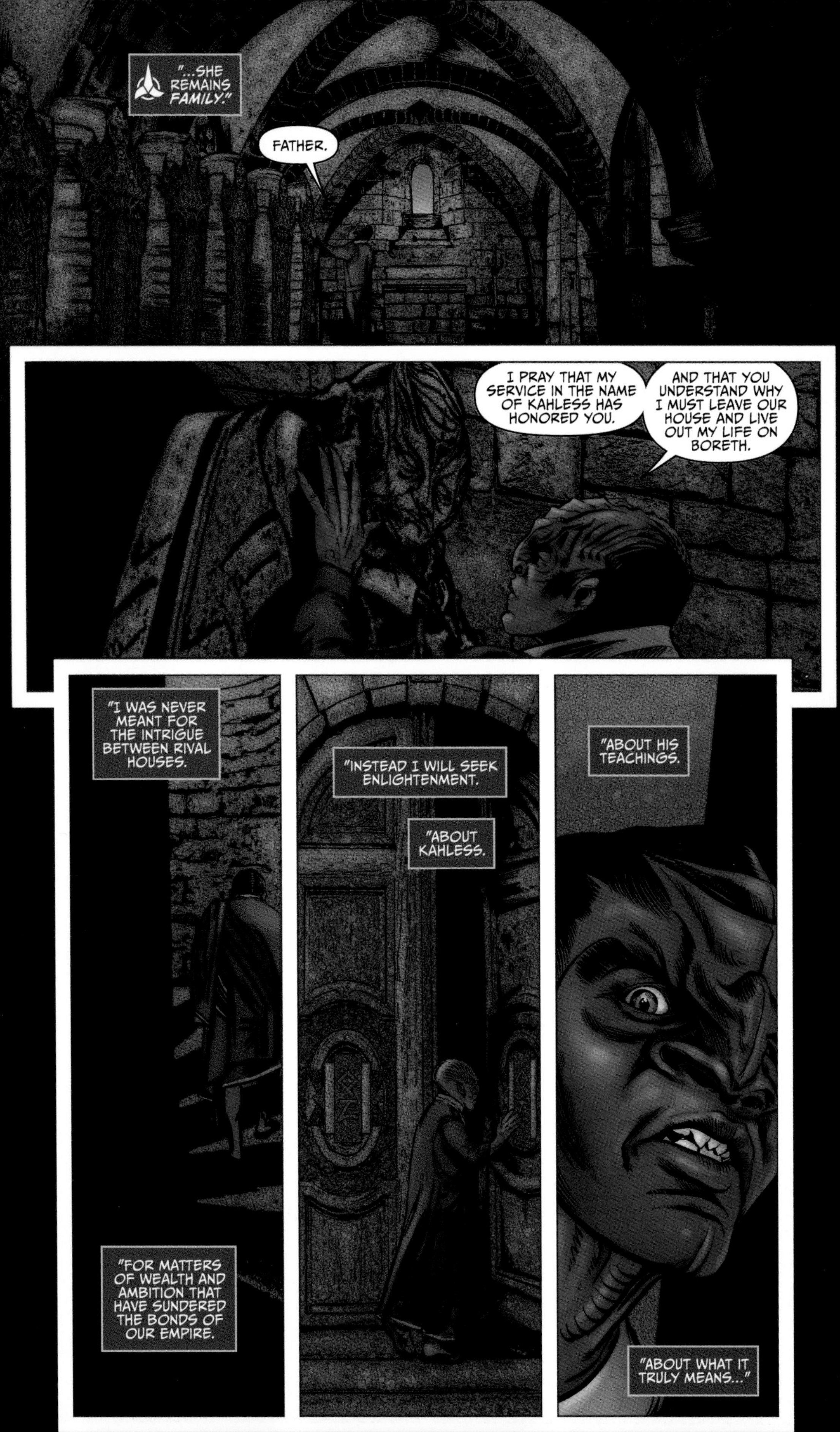
"...SHE REMAINS *FAMILY.*"
FATHER.
I PRAY THAT MY SERVICE IN THE NAME OF KAHLESS HAS HONORED YOU.
AND THAT YOU UNDERSTAND WHY I MUST LEAVE OUR HOUSE AND LIVE OUT MY LIFE ON BORETH.
"I WAS NEVER MEANT FOR THE INTRIGUE BETWEEN RIVAL HOUSES.
"FOR MATTERS OF WEALTH AND AMBITION THAT HAVE SUNDERED THE BONDS OF OUR EMPIRE.
"INSTEAD I WILL SEEK ENLIGHTENMENT.
"ABOUT KAHLESS.
"ABOUT HIS TEACHINGS.
"ABOUT WHAT IT TRULY MEANS..."

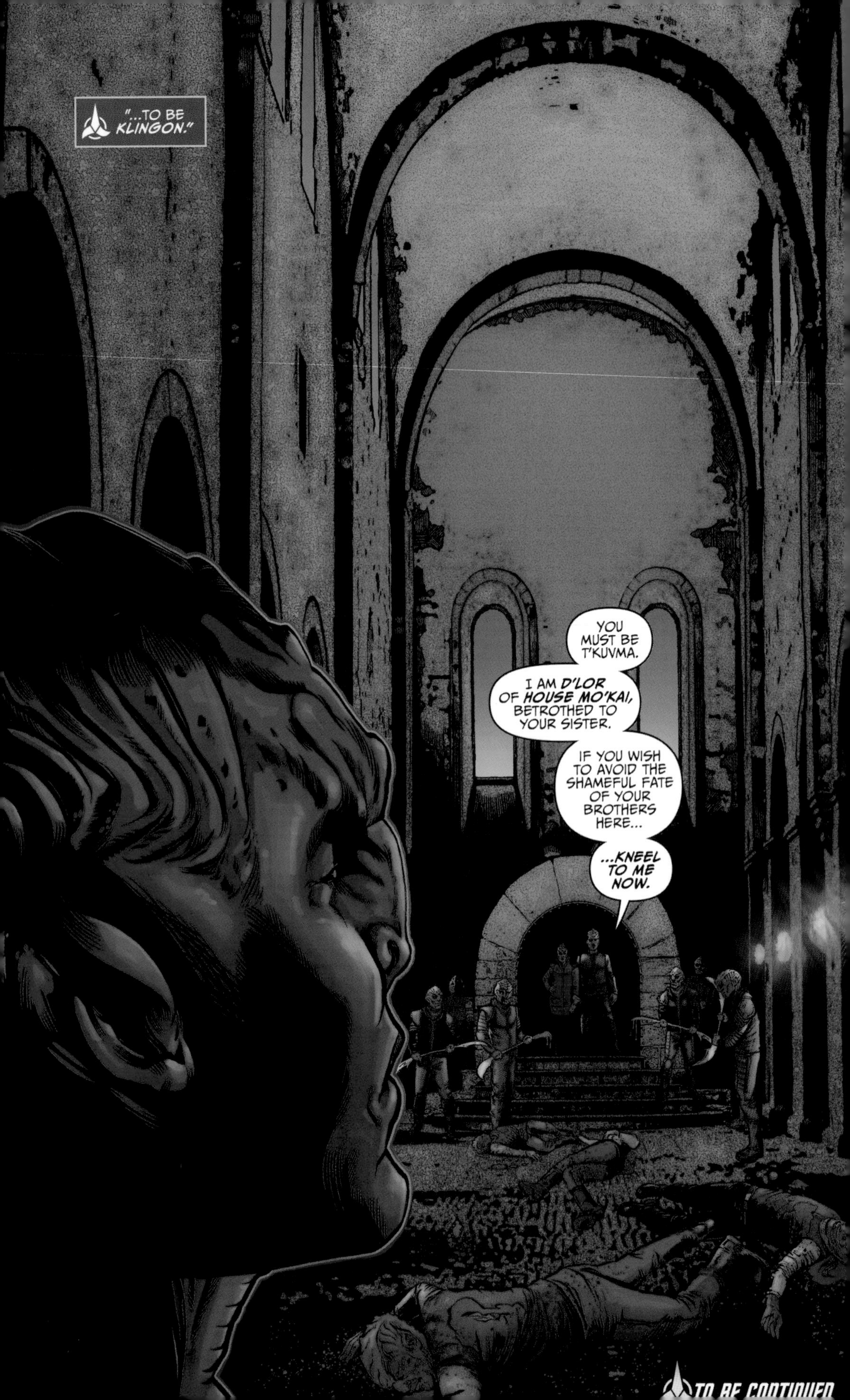
"...TO BE KLINGON."
YOU MUST BE T'KUVMA.
I AM D'LOR OF HOUSE MO'KAI, BETROTHED TO YOUR SISTER.
IF YOU WISH TO AVOID THE SHAMEFUL FATE OF YOUR BROTHERS HERE...
...KNEEL TO ME NOW.
TO BE CONTINUED

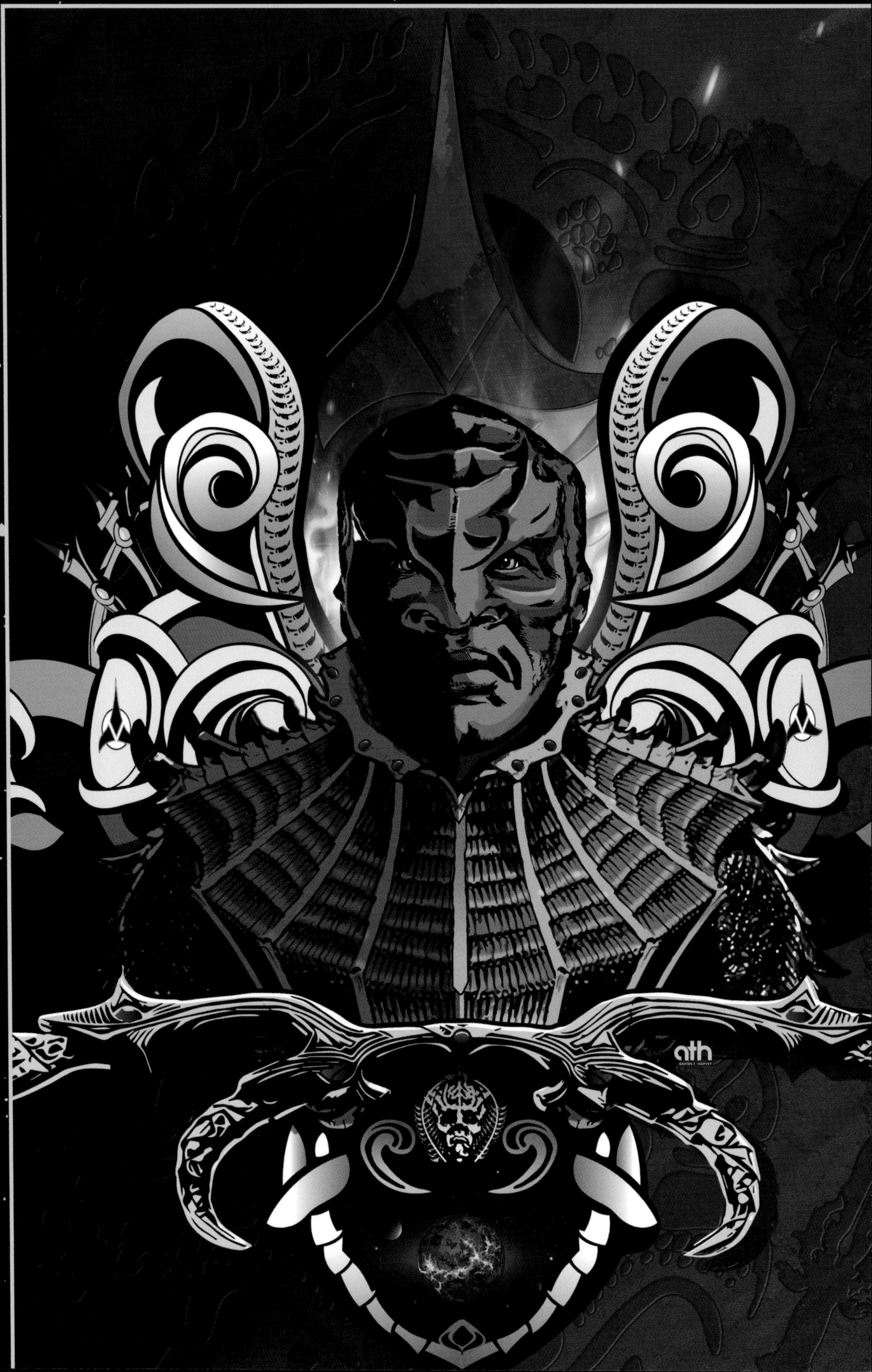
ath
AARON T. HARVEY

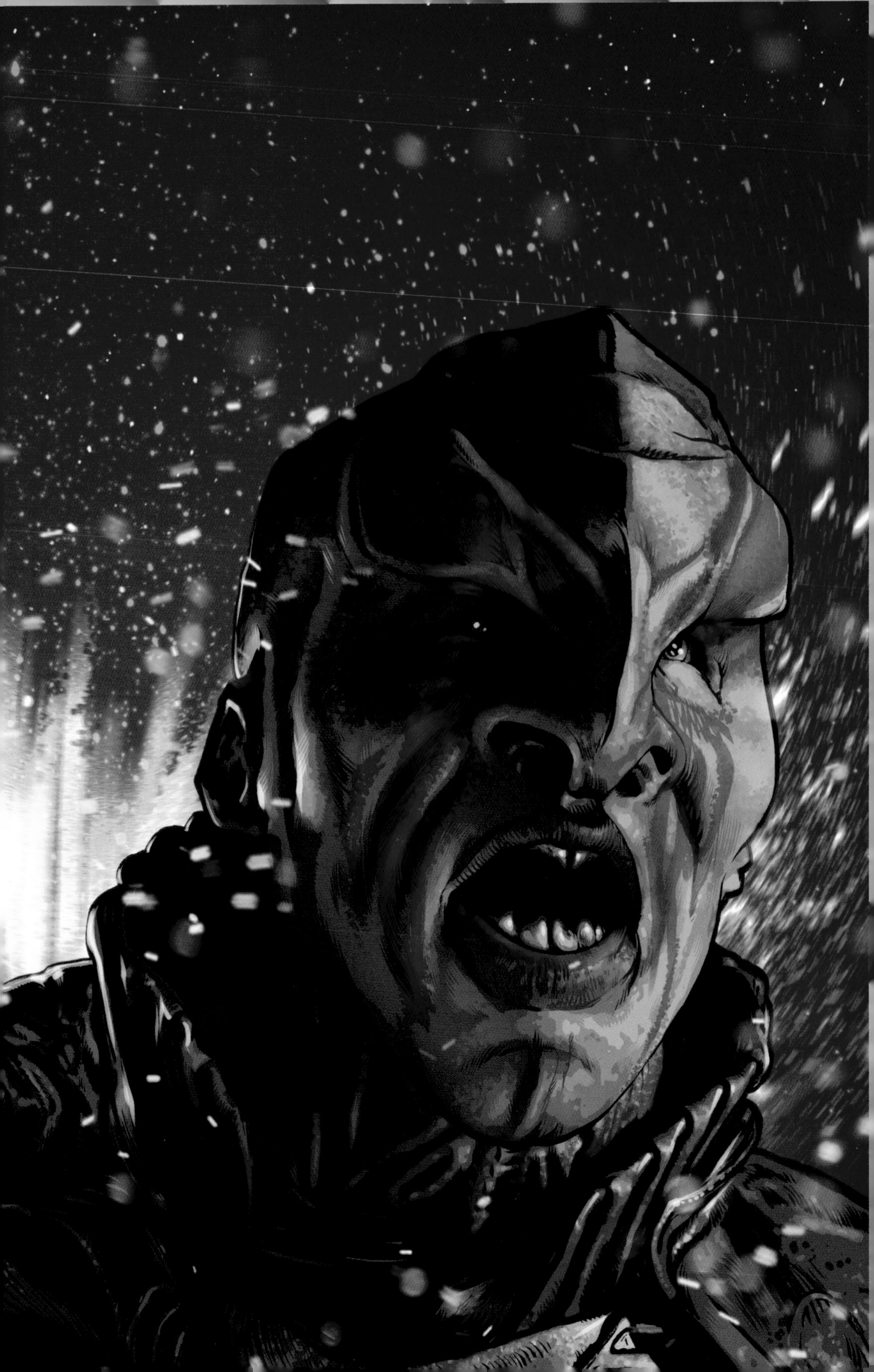

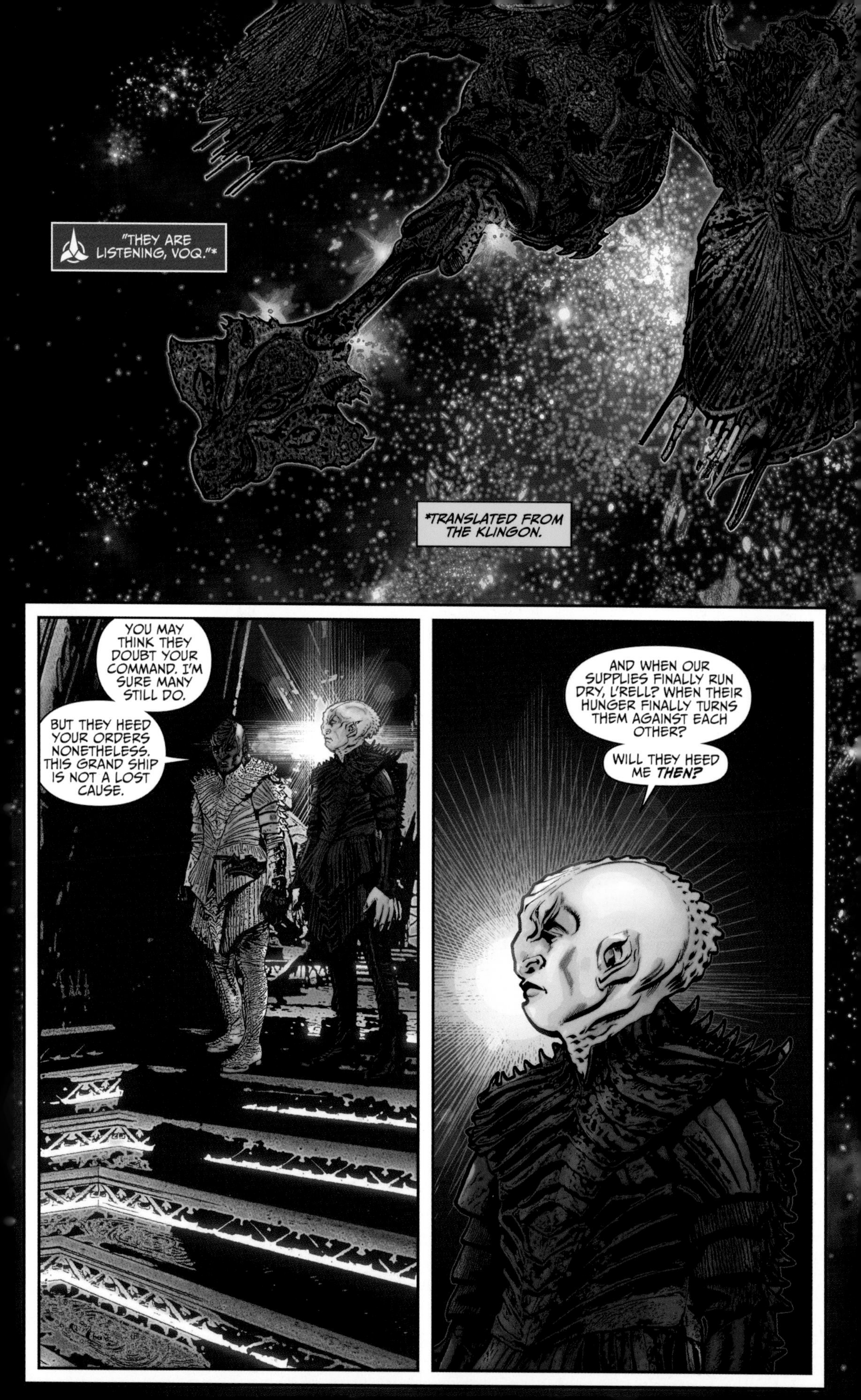
"THEY ARE LISTENING, VOQ."*
*TRANSLATED FROM THE KLINGON.
YOU MAY THINK THEY DOUBT YOUR COMMAND. I'M SURE MANY STILL DO.
BUT THEY HEED YOUR ORDERS NONETHELESS. THIS GRAND SHIP IS NOT A LOST CAUSE.
AND WHEN OUR SUPPLIES FINALLY RUN DRY, L'RELL? WHEN THEIR HUNGER FINALLY TURNS THEM AGAINST EACH OTHER?
WILL THEY HEED ME *THEN?*

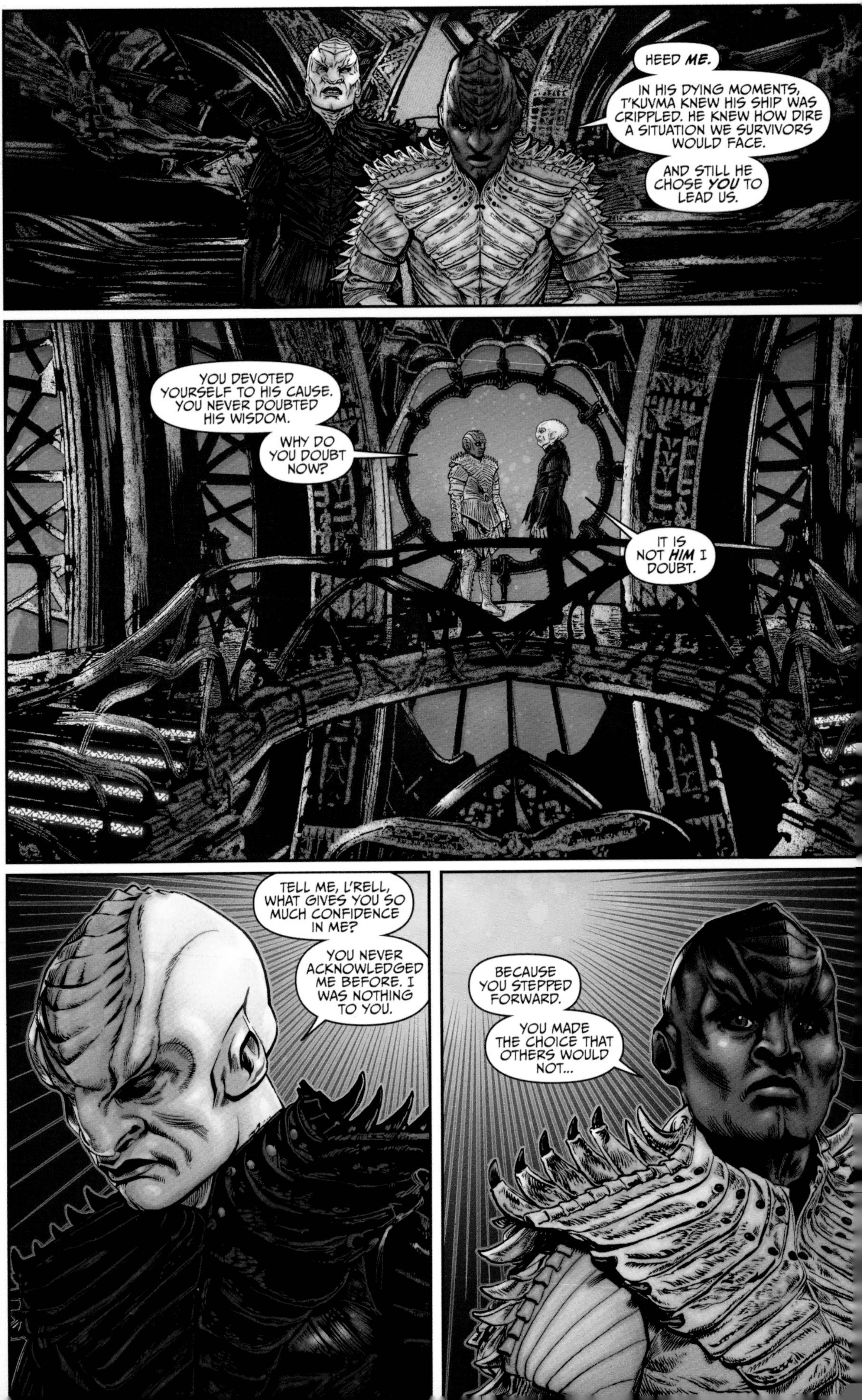
HEED *ME.*
IN HIS DYING MOMENTS, T'KUVMA KNEW HIS SHIP WAS CRIPPLED. HE KNEW HOW DIRE A SITUATION WE SURVIVORS WOULD FACE.
AND STILL HE CHOSE *YOU* TO LEAD US.
YOU DEVOTED YOURSELF TO HIS CAUSE. YOU NEVER DOUBTED HIS WISDOM.
WHY DO YOU DOUBT NOW?
IT IS NOT *HIM* I DOUBT.
TELL ME, L'RELL, WHAT GIVES YOU SO MUCH CONFIDENCE IN ME?
YOU NEVER ACKNOWLEDGED ME BEFORE. I WAS NOTHING TO YOU.
BECAUSE YOU STEPPED FORWARD.
YOU MADE THE CHOICE THAT OTHERS WOULD NOT...

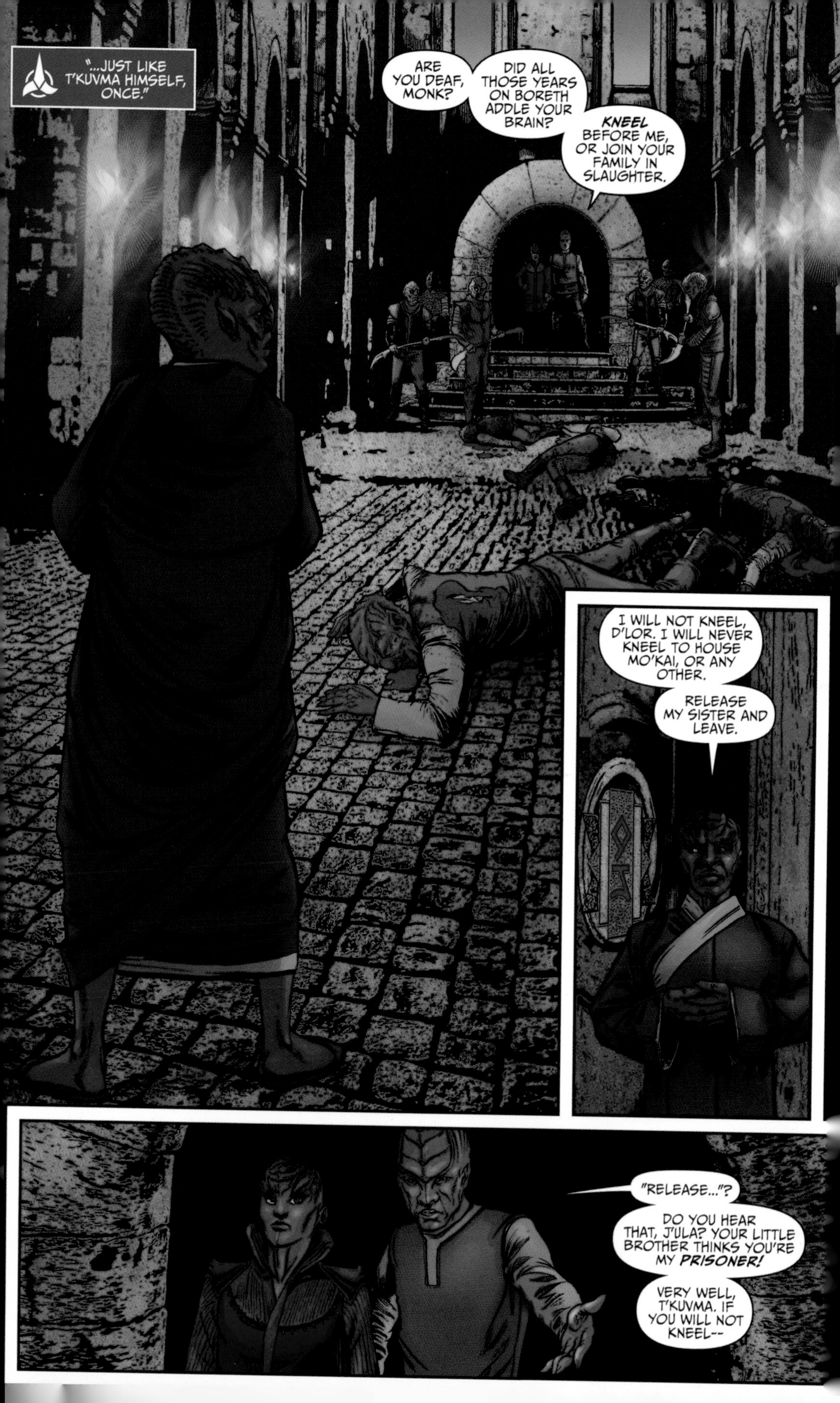
"...JUST LIKE T'KUVMA HIMSELF, ONCE."
ARE YOU DEAF, MONK?
DID ALL THOSE YEARS ON BORETH ADDLE YOUR BRAIN?
KNEEL BEFORE ME, OR JOIN YOUR FAMILY IN SLAUGHTER.
I WILL NOT KNEEL, D'LOR. I WILL NEVER KNEEL TO HOUSE MO'KAI, OR ANY OTHER.
RELEASE MY SISTER AND LEAVE.
"RELEASE..."?
DO YOU HEAR THAT, J'ULA? YOUR LITTLE BROTHER THINKS YOU'RE MY PRISONER!
VERY WELL, T'KUVMA. IF YOU WILL NOT KNEEL--

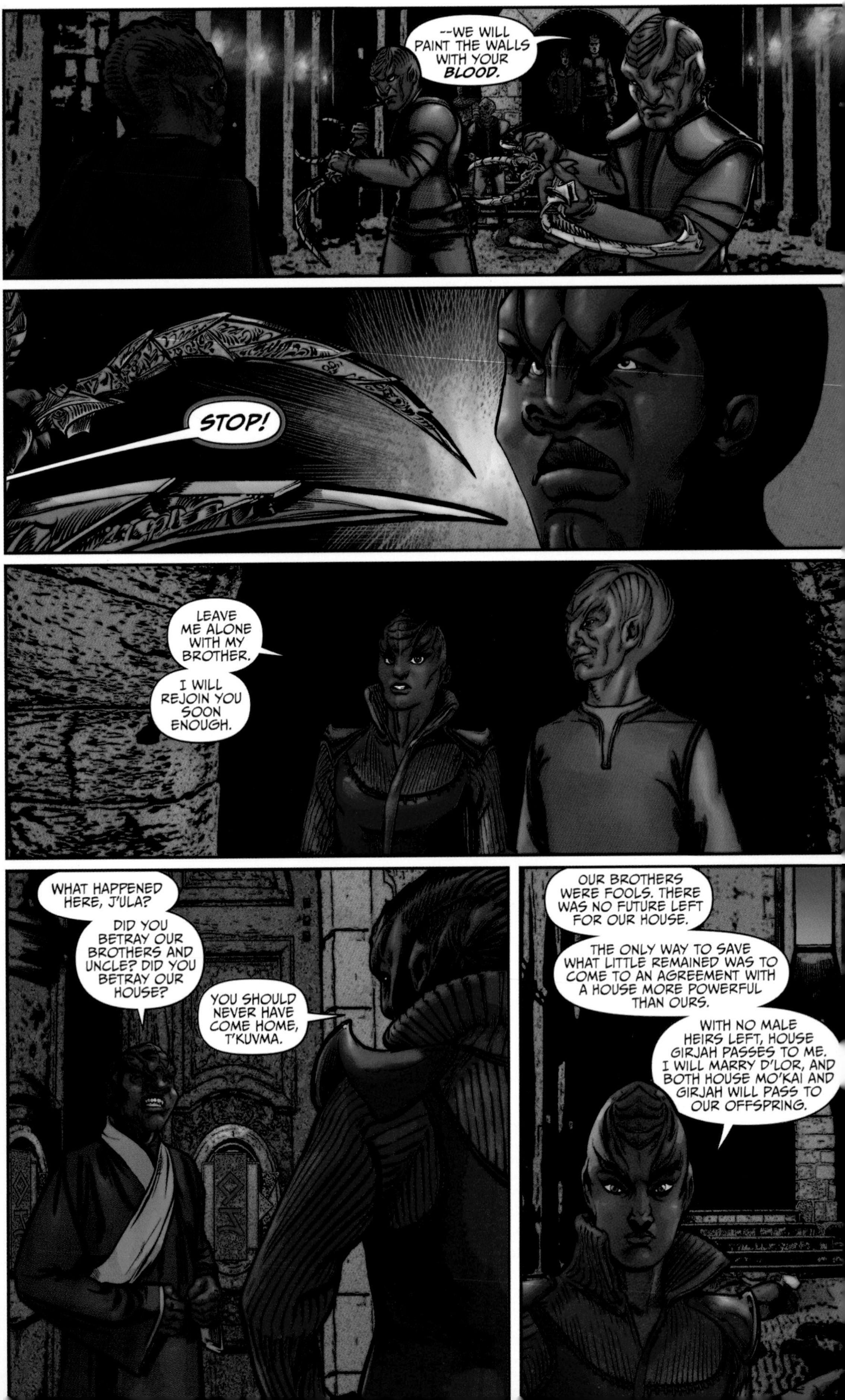
--WE WILL PAINT THE WALLS WITH YOUR BLOOD.
STOP!
LEAVE ME ALONE WITH MY BROTHER.
I WILL REJOIN YOU SOON ENOUGH.
WHAT HAPPENED HERE, J'ULA?
DID YOU BETRAY OUR BROTHERS AND UNCLE? DID YOU BETRAY OUR HOUSE?
YOU SHOULD NEVER HAVE COME HOME, T'KUVMA.
OUR BROTHERS WERE FOOLS. THERE WAS NO FUTURE LEFT FOR OUR HOUSE.
THE ONLY WAY TO SAVE WHAT LITTLE REMAINED WAS TO COME TO AN AGREEMENT WITH A HOUSE MORE POWERFUL THAN OURS.
WITH NO MALE HEIRS LEFT, HOUSE GIRJAH PASSES TO ME. I WILL MARRY D'LOR, AND BOTH HOUSE MO'KAI AND GIRJAH WILL PASS TO OUR OFFSPRING.

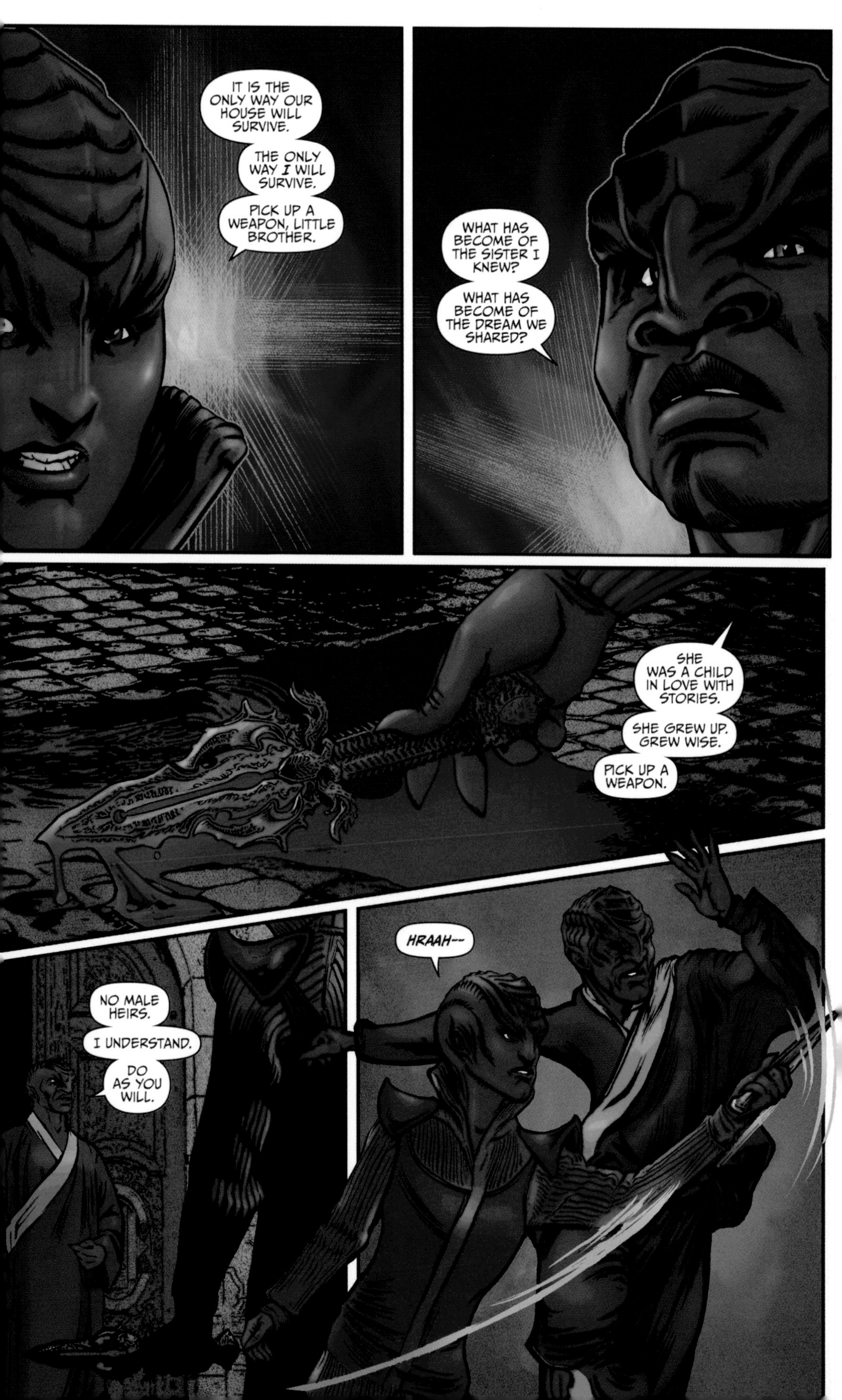
IT IS THE ONLY WAY OUR HOUSE WILL SURVIVE.
THE ONLY WAY *I* WILL SURVIVE.
PICK UP A WEAPON, LITTLE BROTHER.
WHAT HAS BECOME OF THE SISTER I KNEW?
WHAT HAS BECOME OF THE DREAM WE SHARED?
SHE WAS A CHILD IN LOVE WITH STORIES.
SHE GREW UP. GREW WISE.
PICK UP A WEAPON.
NO MALE HEIRS.
I UNDERSTAND.
DO AS YOU WILL.
HRAAH--

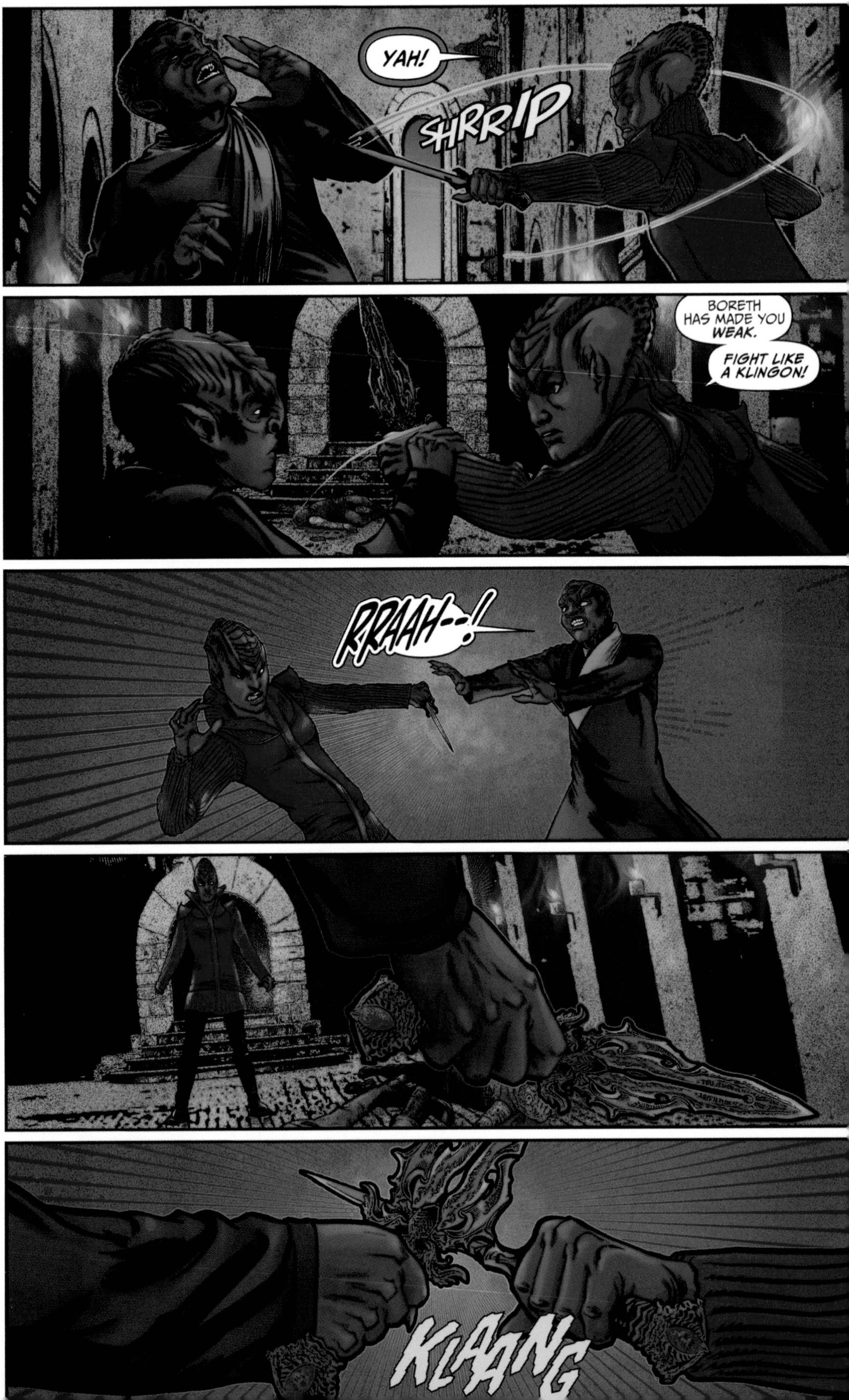

YAH!
SHRRIP
BORETH HAS MADE YOU WEAK.
FIGHT LIKE A KLINGON!
RRAAH--!
KLAANG

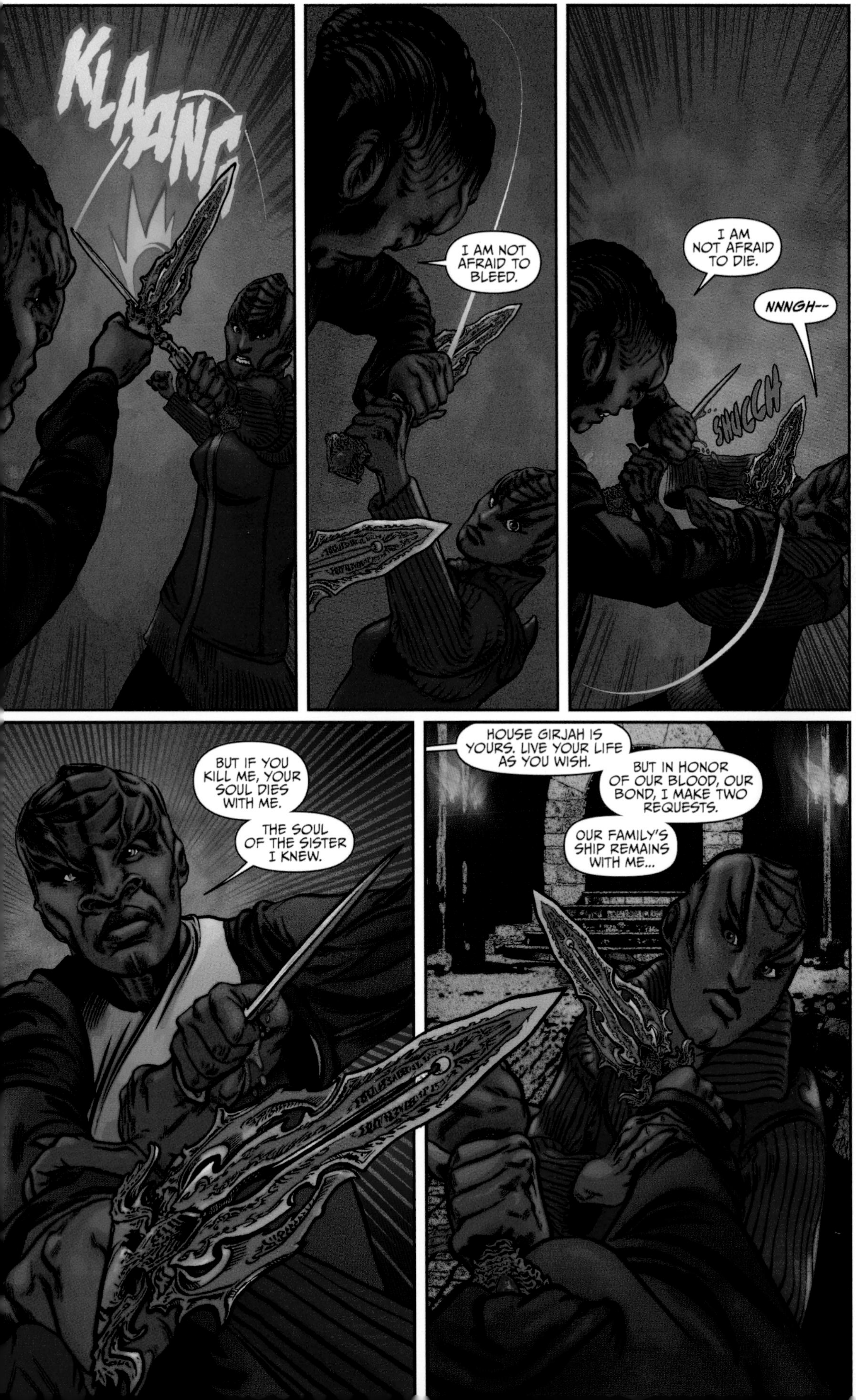
KLAANG
I AM NOT AFRAID TO BLEED.
I AM NOT AFRAID TO DIE.
NNNGH--
SHUCCH
BUT IF YOU KILL ME, YOUR SOUL DIES WITH ME.
THE SOUL OF THE SISTER I KNEW.
HOUSE GIRJAH IS YOURS. LIVE YOUR LIFE AS YOU WISH.
BUT IN HONOR OF OUR BLOOD, OUR BOND, I MAKE TWO REQUESTS.
OUR FAMILY'S SHIP REMAINS WITH ME...

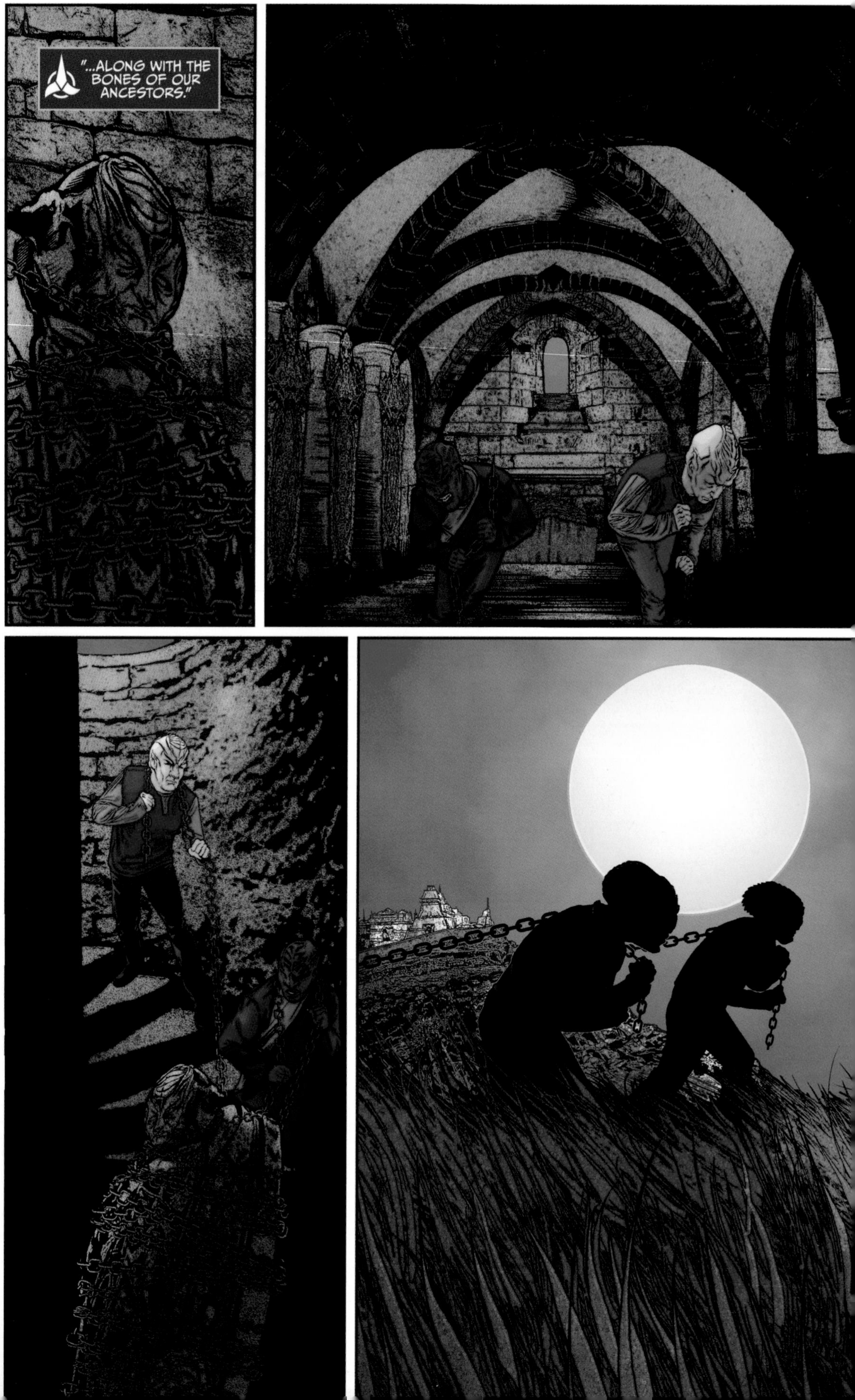
"...ALONG WITH THE BONES OF OUR ANCESTORS."

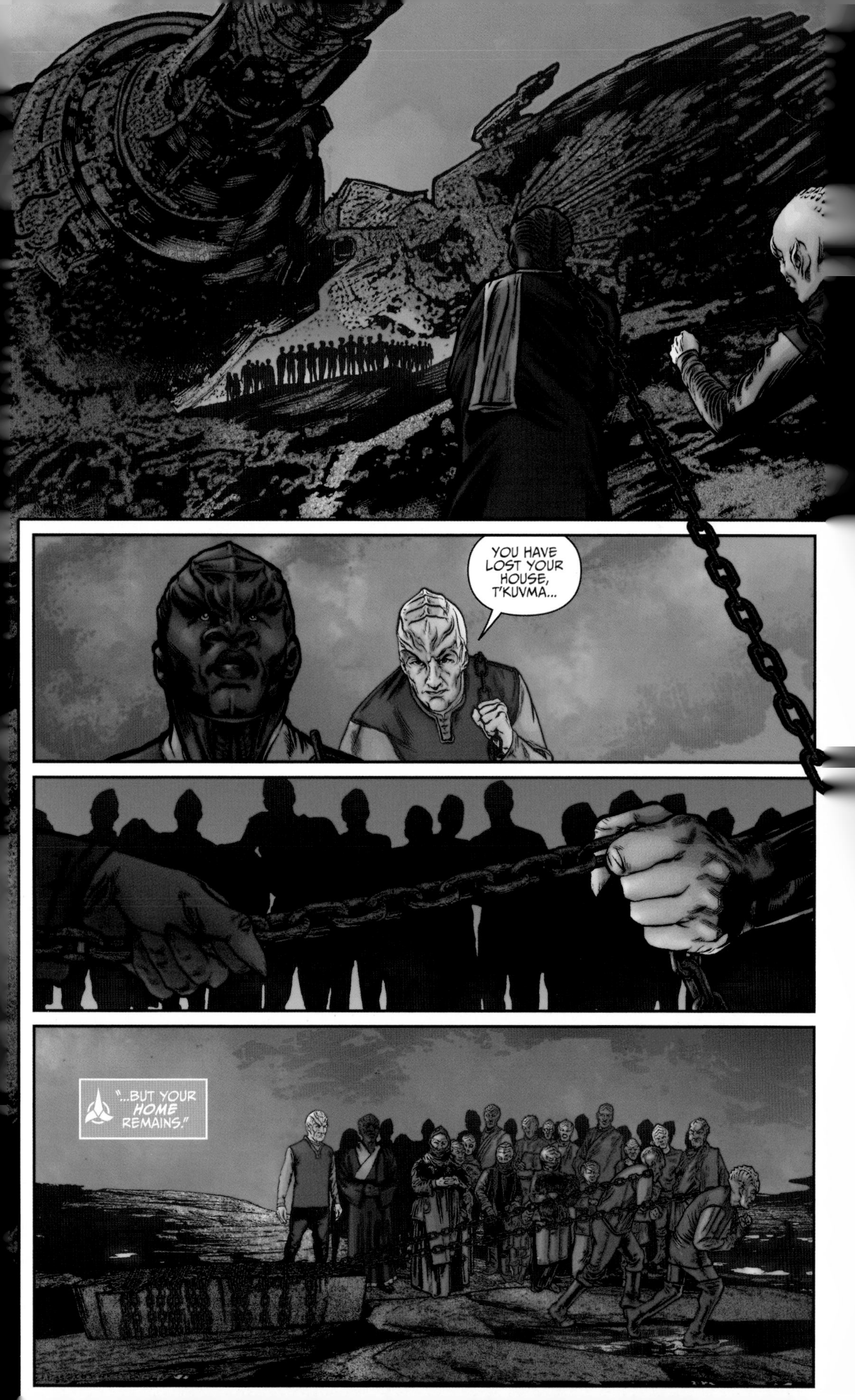
YOU HAVE LOST YOUR HOUSE, T'KUVMA...
"...BUT YOUR *HOME* REMAINS."

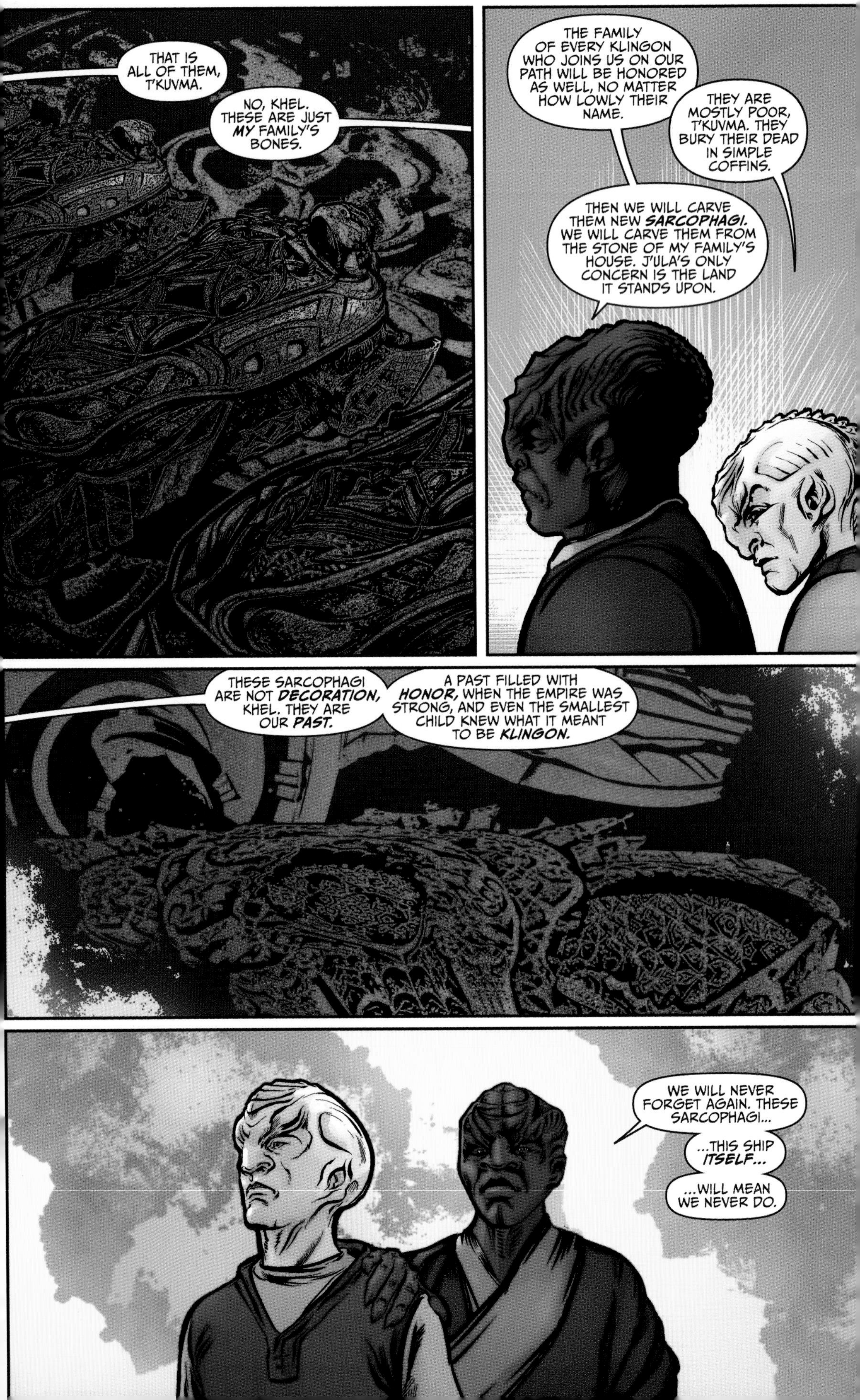
THAT IS ALL OF THEM, T'KUVMA.
NO, KHEL. THESE ARE JUST *MY* FAMILY'S BONES.
THE FAMILY OF EVERY KLINGON WHO JOINS US ON OUR PATH WILL BE HONORED AS WELL, NO MATTER HOW LOWLY THEIR NAME.
THEY ARE MOSTLY POOR, T'KUVMA. THEY BURY THEIR DEAD IN SIMPLE COFFINS.
THEN WE WILL CARVE THEM NEW *SARCOPHAGI.* WE WILL CARVE THEM FROM THE STONE OF MY FAMILY'S HOUSE. J'ULA'S ONLY CONCERN IS THE LAND IT STANDS UPON.
THESE SARCOPHAGI ARE NOT *DECORATION,* KHEL. THEY ARE OUR *PAST.*
A PAST FILLED WITH *HONOR,* WHEN THE EMPIRE WAS STRONG, AND EVEN THE SMALLEST CHILD KNEW WHAT IT MEANT TO BE *KLINGON.*
WE WILL NEVER FORGET AGAIN. THESE SARCOPHAGI...
...THIS SHIP *ITSELF...*
...WILL MEAN WE NEVER DO.

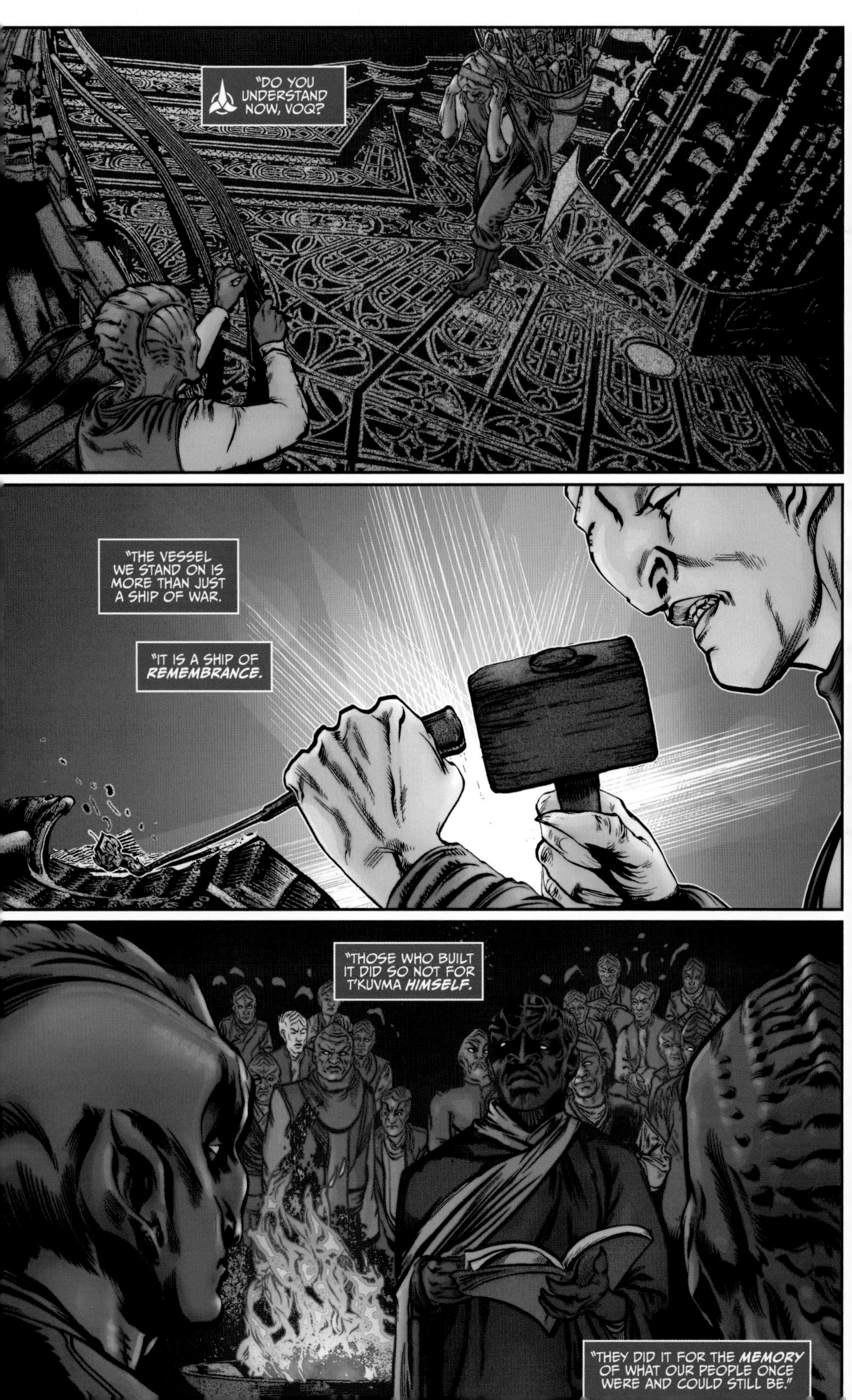
"DO YOU UNDERSTAND NOW, VOQ?
"THE VESSEL WE STAND ON IS MORE THAN JUST A SHIP OF WAR.
"IT IS A SHIP OF *REMEMBRANCE.*
"THOSE WHO BUILT IT DID SO NOT FOR T'KUVMA *HIMSELF.*
"THEY DID IT FOR THE *MEMORY* OF WHAT OUR PEOPLE ONCE WERE AND COULD STILL BE."

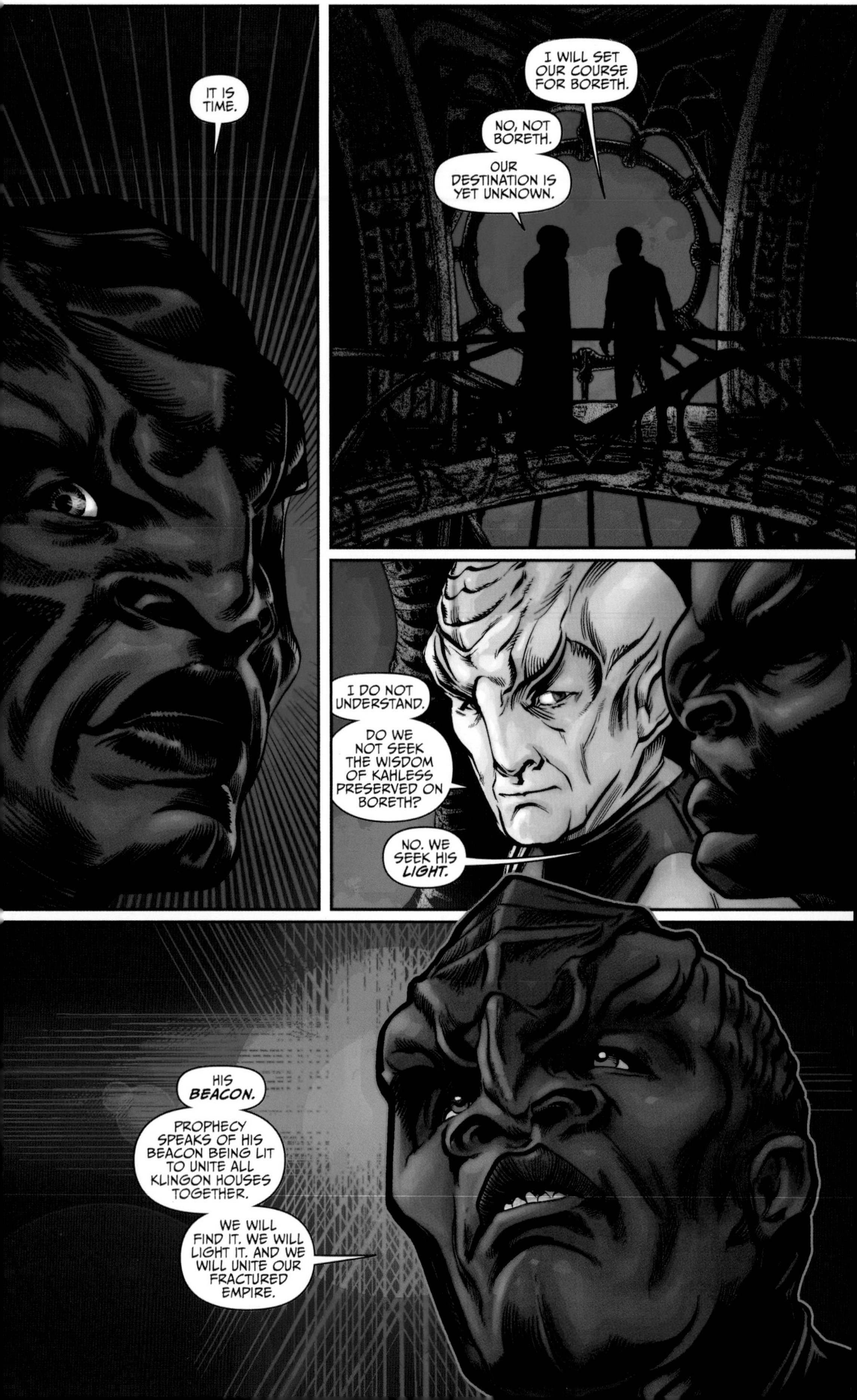
IT IS TIME.
I WILL SET OUR COURSE FOR BORETH.
NO, NOT BORETH.
OUR DESTINATION IS YET UNKNOWN.
I DO NOT UNDERSTAND.
DO WE NOT SEEK THE WISDOM OF KAHLESS PRESERVED ON BORETH?
NO. WE SEEK HIS LIGHT.
HIS BEACON.
PROPHECY SPEAKS OF HIS BEACON BEING LIT TO UNITE ALL KLINGON HOUSES TOGETHER.
WE WILL FIND IT. WE WILL LIGHT IT. AND WE WILL UNITE OUR FRACTURED EMPIRE.

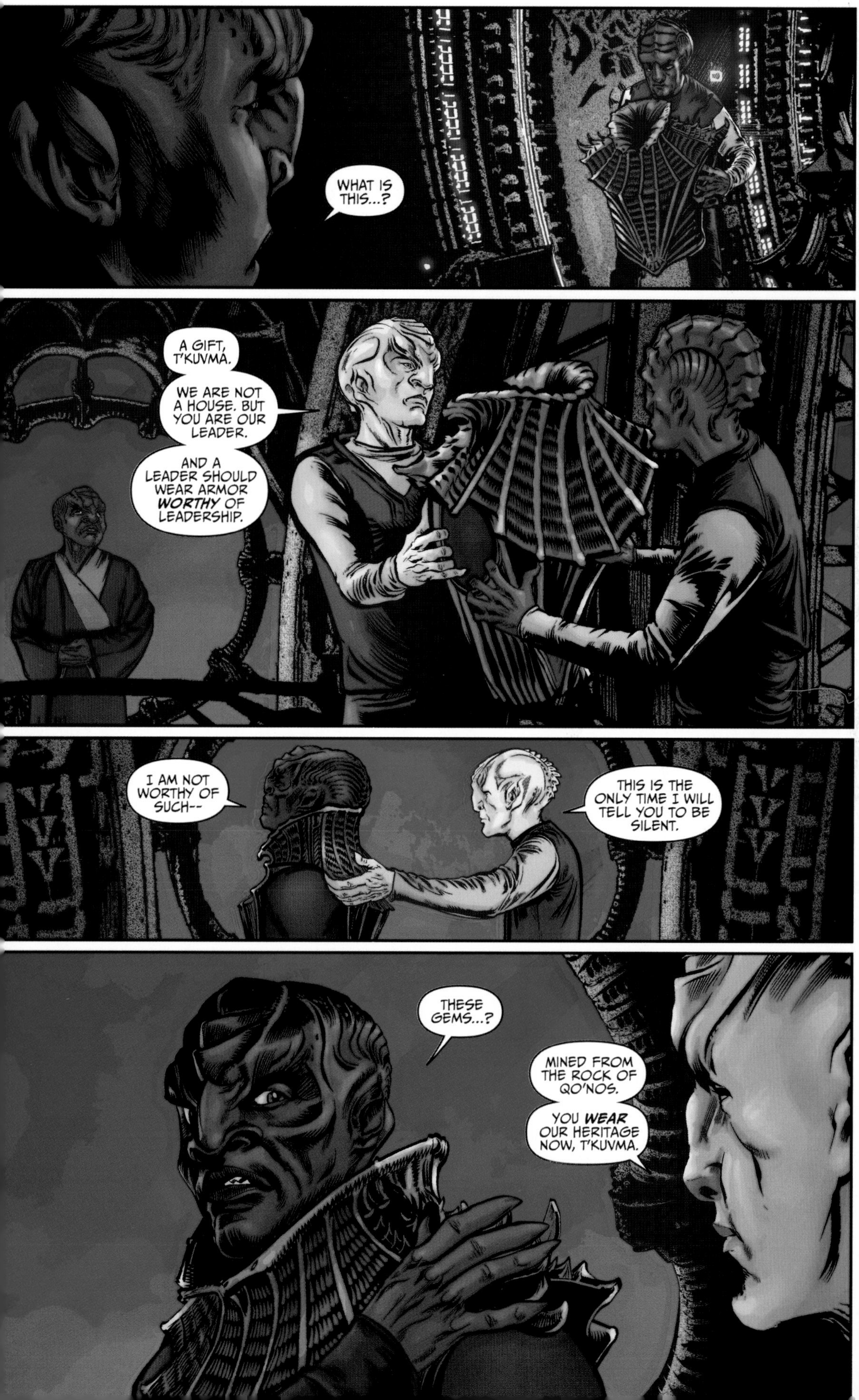
WHAT IS THIS...?
A GIFT, T'KUVMA.
WE ARE NOT A HOUSE. BUT YOU ARE OUR LEADER.
AND A LEADER SHOULD WEAR ARMOR *WORTHY* OF LEADERSHIP.
I AM NOT WORTHY OF SUCH--
THIS IS THE ONLY TIME I WILL TELL YOU TO BE SILENT.
THESE GEMS...?
MINED FROM THE ROCK OF QO'NOS.
YOU *WEAR* OUR HERITAGE NOW, T'KUVMA.

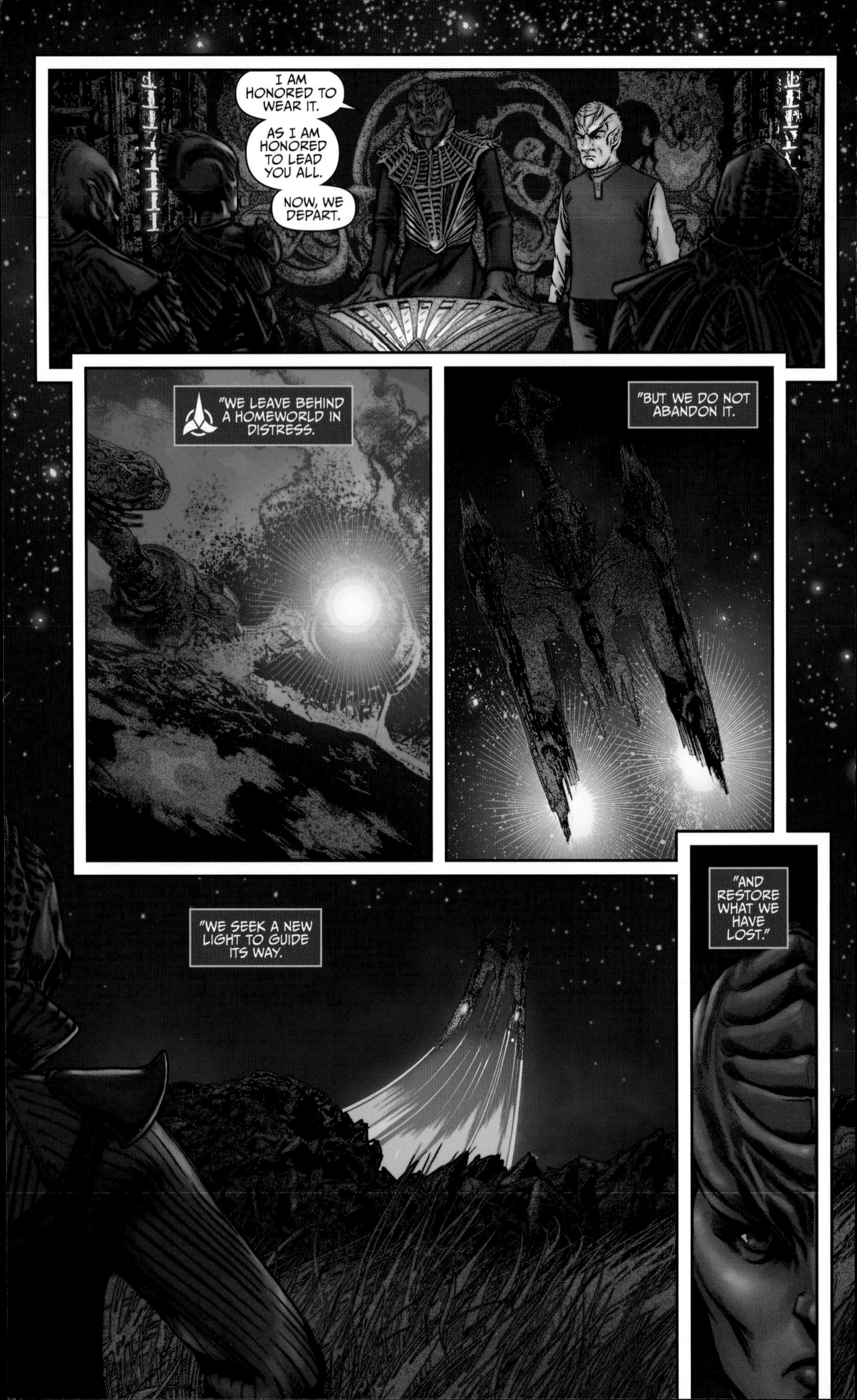
I AM HONORED TO WEAR IT.
AS I AM HONORED TO LEAD YOU ALL.
NOW, WE DEPART.
"WE LEAVE BEHIND A HOMEWORLD IN DISTRESS.
"BUT WE DO NOT ABANDON IT.
"WE SEEK A NEW LIGHT TO GUIDE ITS WAY.
"AND RESTORE WHAT WE HAVE LOST."

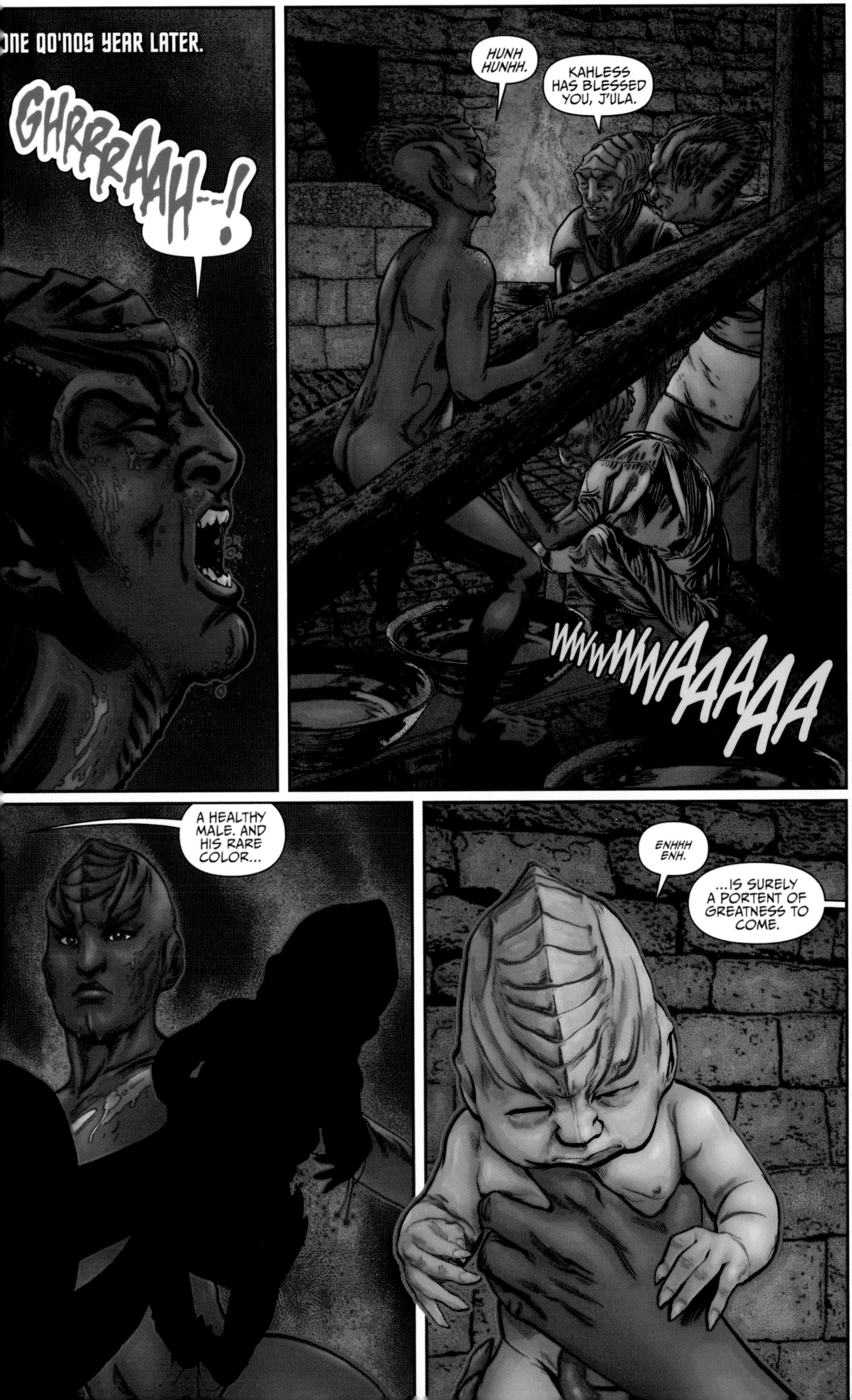
ONE QO'NOS YEAR LATER.
GHRRRAAH--!
HUNH HUNHH.
KAHLESS HAS BLESSED YOU, J'ULA.
WWWWWAAAAAA
A HEALTHY MALE. AND HIS RARE COLOR...
ENHHH ENH.
...IS SURELY A PORTENT OF GREATNESS TO COME.

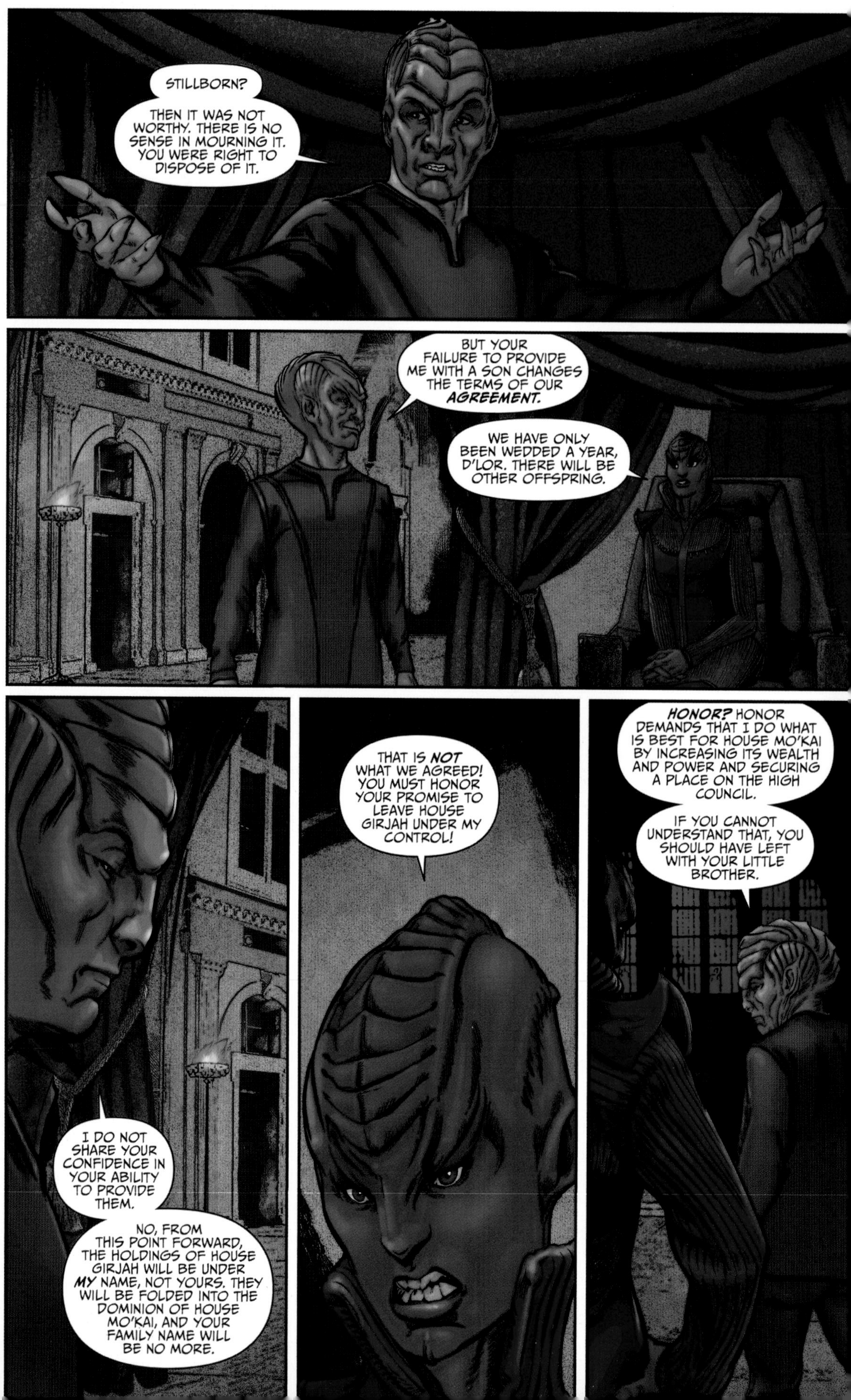
STILLBORN?
THEN IT WAS NOT WORTHY. THERE IS NO SENSE IN MOURNING IT. YOU WERE RIGHT TO DISPOSE OF IT.
BUT YOUR FAILURE TO PROVIDE ME WITH A SON CHANGES THE TERMS OF OUR AGREEMENT.
WE HAVE ONLY BEEN WEDDED A YEAR, D'LOR. THERE WILL BE OTHER OFFSPRING.
I DO NOT SHARE YOUR CONFIDENCE IN YOUR ABILITY TO PROVIDE THEM.
NO, FROM THIS POINT FORWARD, THE HOLDINGS OF HOUSE GIRJAH WILL BE UNDER MY NAME, NOT YOURS. THEY WILL BE FOLDED INTO THE DOMINION OF HOUSE MO'KAI, AND YOUR FAMILY NAME WILL BE NO MORE.
THAT IS NOT WHAT WE AGREED! YOU MUST HONOR YOUR PROMISE TO LEAVE HOUSE GIRJAH UNDER MY CONTROL!
HONOR? HONOR DEMANDS THAT I DO WHAT IS BEST FOR HOUSE MO'KAI BY INCREASING ITS WEALTH AND POWER AND SECURING A PLACE ON THE HIGH COUNCIL.
IF YOU CANNOT UNDERSTAND THAT, YOU SHOULD HAVE LEFT WITH YOUR LITTLE BROTHER.

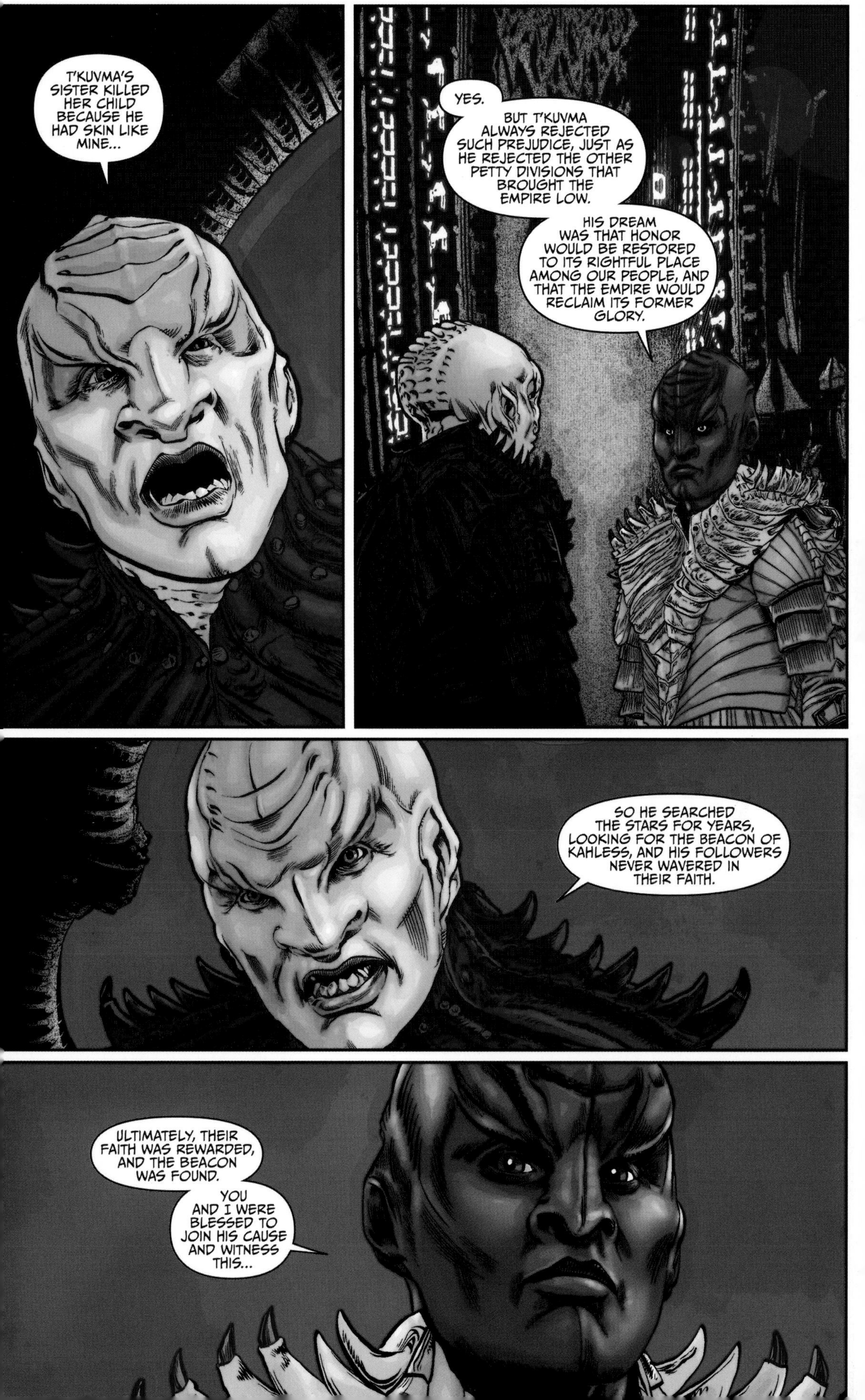
T'KUVMA'S SISTER KILLED HER CHILD BECAUSE HE HAD SKIN LIKE MINE...
YES.
BUT T'KUVMA ALWAYS REJECTED SUCH PREJUDICE, JUST AS HE REJECTED THE OTHER PETTY DIVISIONS THAT BROUGHT THE EMPIRE LOW.
HIS DREAM WAS THAT HONOR WOULD BE RESTORED TO ITS RIGHTFUL PLACE AMONG OUR PEOPLE, AND THAT THE EMPIRE WOULD RECLAIM ITS FORMER GLORY.
SO HE SEARCHED THE STARS FOR YEARS, LOOKING FOR THE BEACON OF KAHLESS, AND HIS FOLLOWERS NEVER WAVERED IN THEIR FAITH.
ULTIMATELY, THEIR FAITH WAS REWARDED, AND THE BEACON WAS FOUND.
YOU AND I WERE BLESSED TO JOIN HIS CAUSE AND WITNESS THIS...

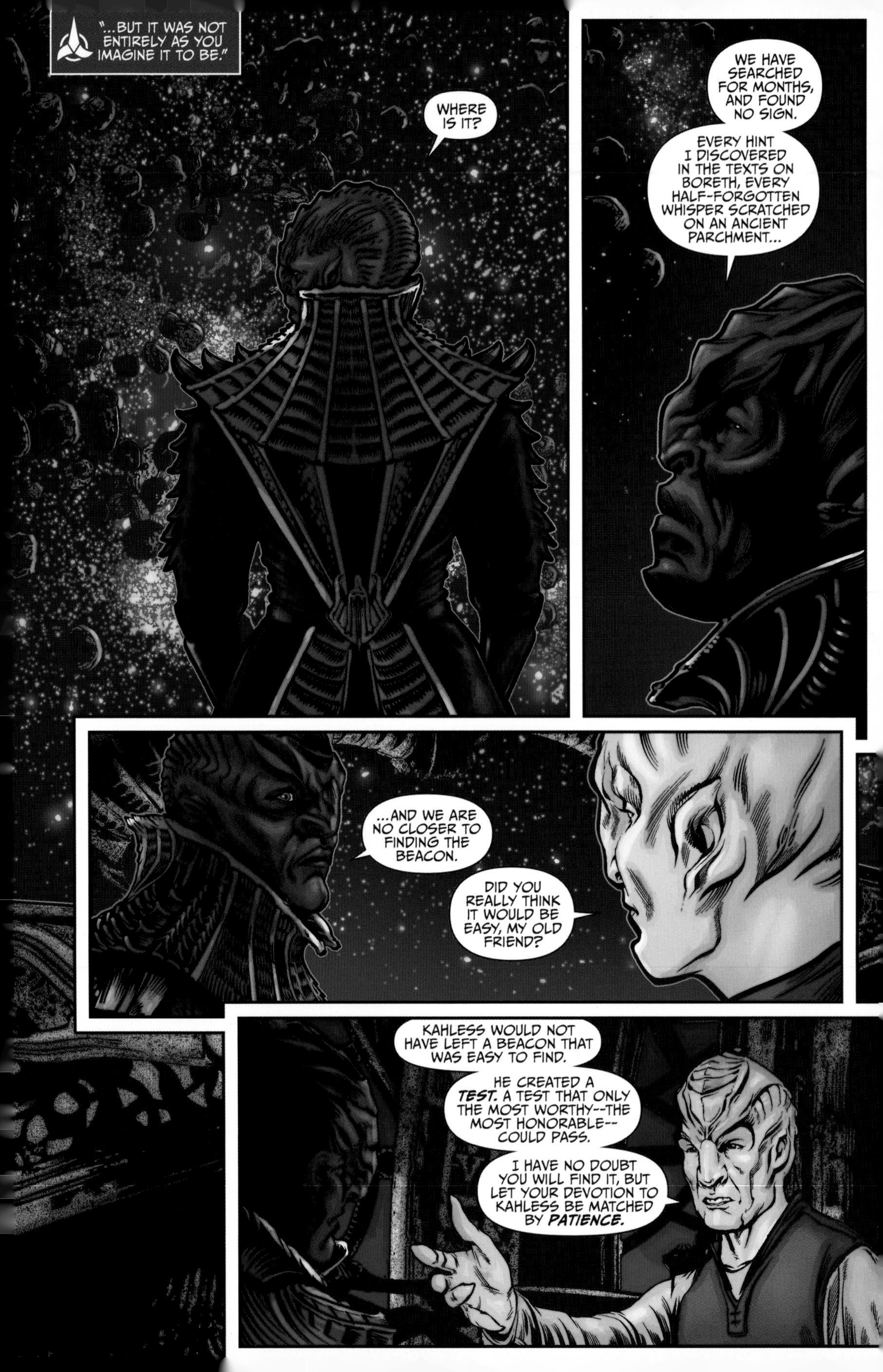
"...BUT IT WAS NOT ENTIRELY AS YOU IMAGINE IT TO BE."
WHERE IS IT?
WE HAVE SEARCHED FOR MONTHS, AND FOUND NO SIGN.
EVERY HINT I DISCOVERED IN THE TEXTS ON BORETH, EVERY HALF-FORGOTTEN WHISPER SCRATCHED ON AN ANCIENT PARCHMENT...
...AND WE ARE NO CLOSER TO FINDING THE BEACON.
DID YOU REALLY THINK IT WOULD BE EASY, MY OLD FRIEND?
KAHLESS WOULD NOT HAVE LEFT A BEACON THAT WAS EASY TO FIND.
HE CREATED A *TEST.* A TEST THAT ONLY THE MOST WORTHY--THE MOST HONORABLE--COULD PASS.
I HAVE NO DOUBT YOU WILL FIND IT, BUT LET YOUR DEVOTION TO KAHLESS BE MATCHED BY *PATIENCE.*

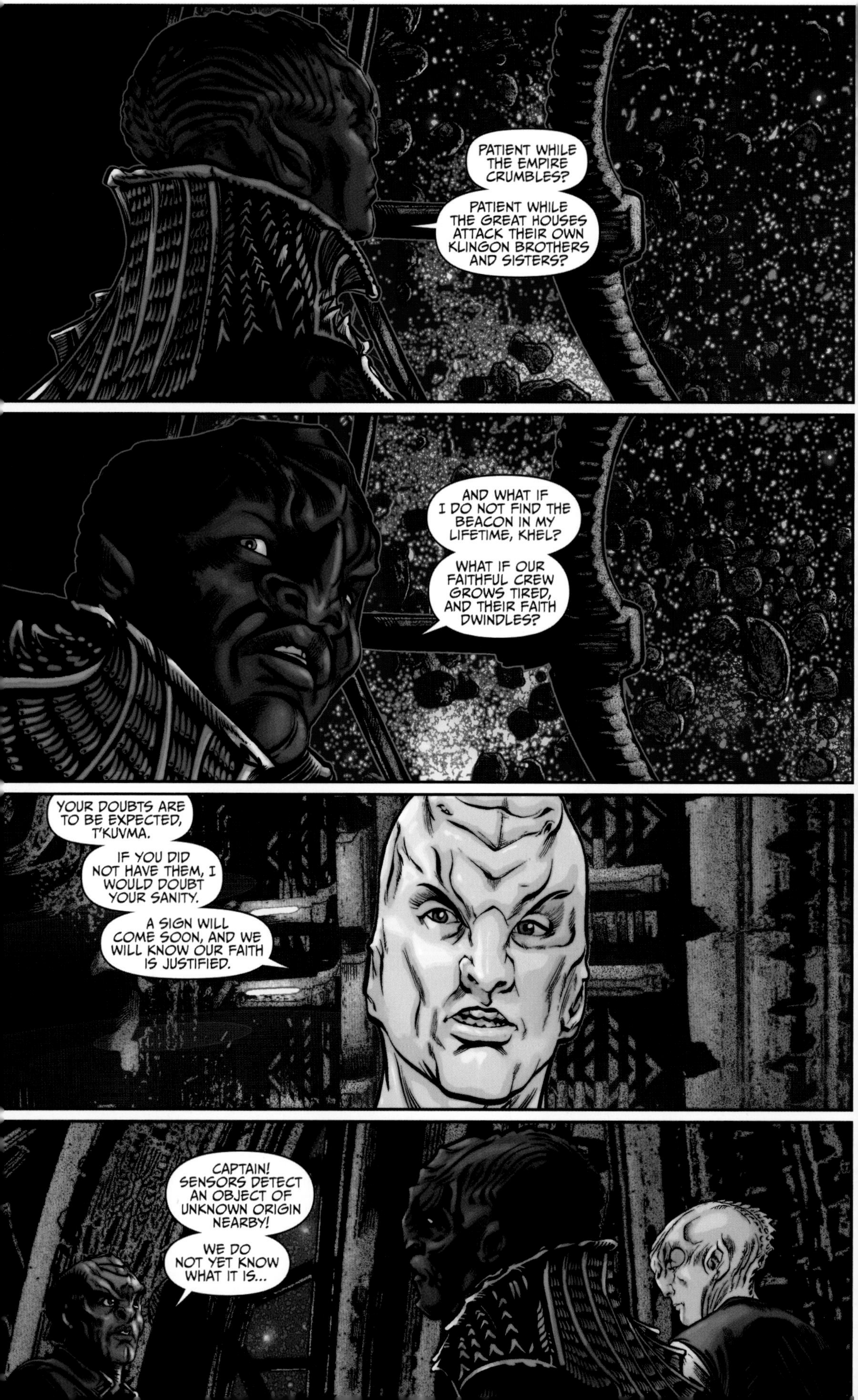
PATIENT WHILE THE EMPIRE CRUMBLES?
PATIENT WHILE THE GREAT HOUSES ATTACK THEIR OWN KLINGON BROTHERS AND SISTERS?
AND WHAT IF I DO NOT FIND THE BEACON IN MY LIFETIME, KHEL?
WHAT IF OUR FAITHFUL CREW GROWS TIRED, AND THEIR FAITH DWINDLES?
YOUR DOUBTS ARE TO BE EXPECTED, T'KUVMA.
IF YOU DID NOT HAVE THEM, I WOULD DOUBT YOUR SANITY.
A SIGN WILL COME SOON, AND WE WILL KNOW OUR FAITH IS JUSTIFIED.
CAPTAIN! SENSORS DETECT AN OBJECT OF UNKNOWN ORIGIN NEARBY!
WE DO NOT YET KNOW WHAT IT IS...

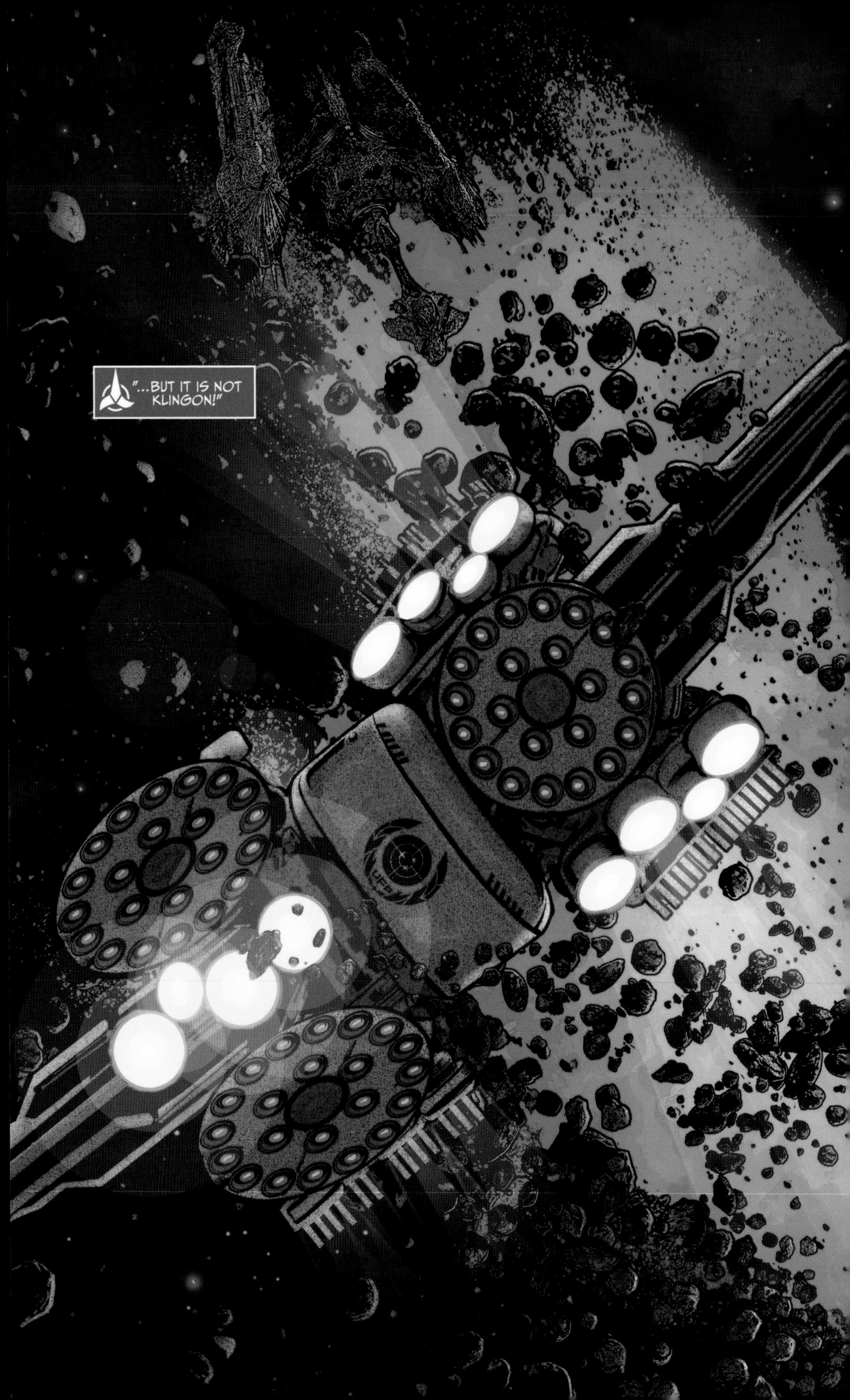
"...BUT IT IS NOT KLINGON!"

ART BY **GEORGE CALTSOUDAS**

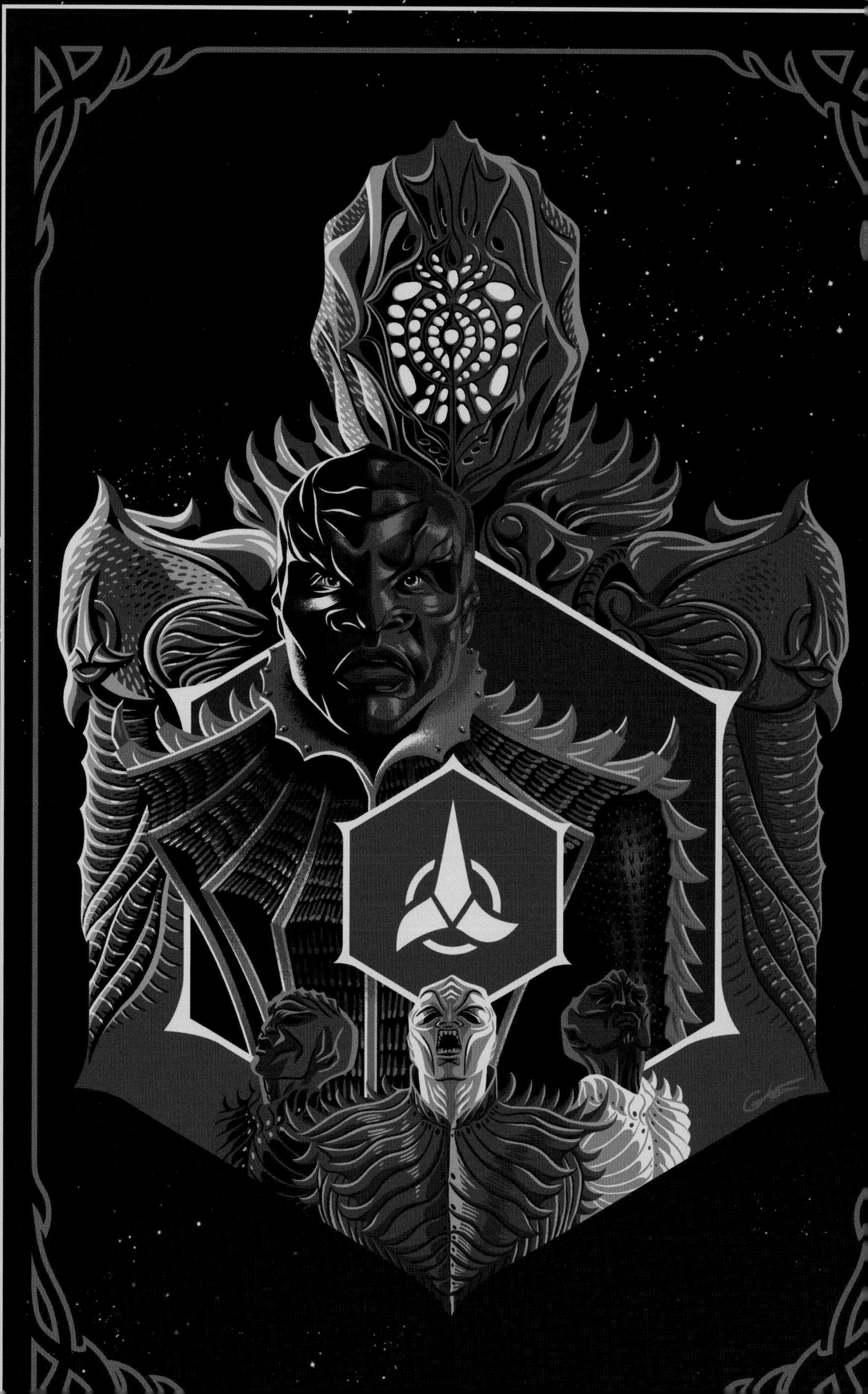

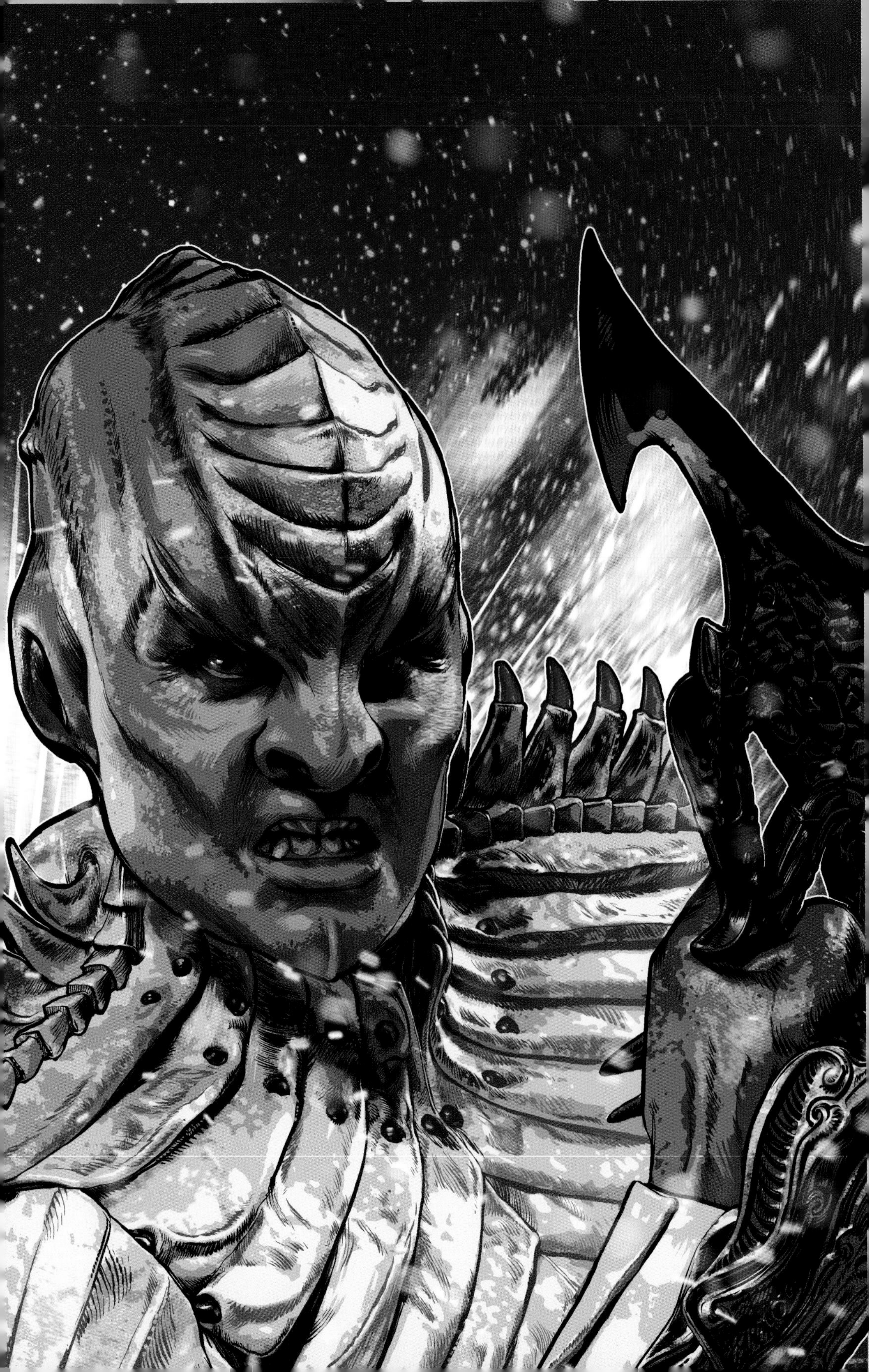

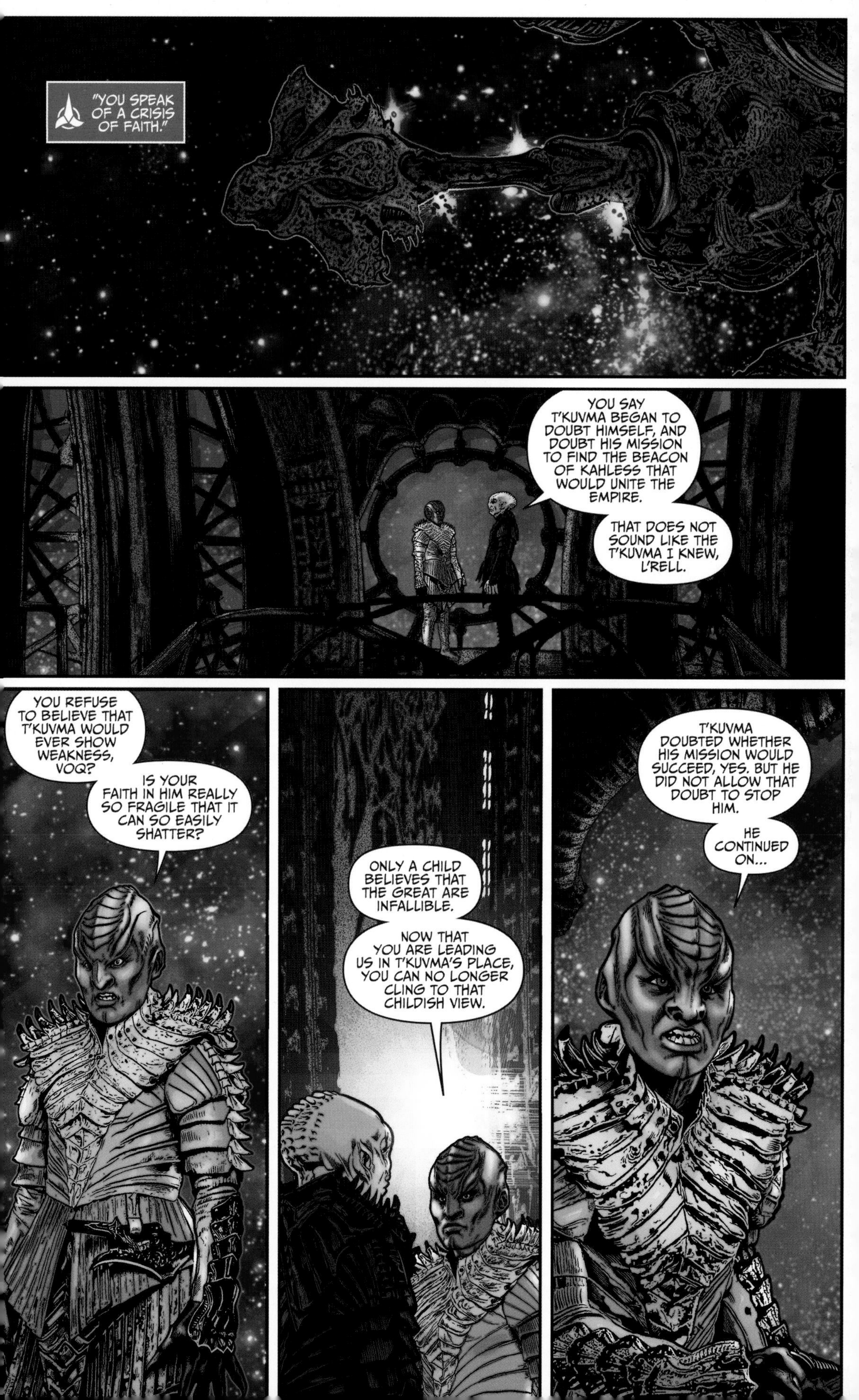
"YOU SPEAK OF A CRISIS OF FAITH."
YOU SAY T'KUVMA BEGAN TO DOUBT HIMSELF, AND DOUBT HIS MISSION TO FIND THE BEACON OF KAHLESS THAT WOULD UNITE THE EMPIRE.
THAT DOES NOT SOUND LIKE THE T'KUVMA I KNEW, L'RELL.
YOU REFUSE TO BELIEVE THAT T'KUVMA WOULD EVER SHOW WEAKNESS, VOQ?
IS YOUR FAITH IN HIM REALLY SO FRAGILE THAT IT CAN SO EASILY SHATTER?
ONLY A CHILD BELIEVES THAT THE GREAT ARE INFALLIBLE.
NOW THAT YOU ARE LEADING US IN T'KUVMA'S PLACE, YOU CAN NO LONGER CLING TO THAT CHILDISH VIEW.
T'KUVMA DOUBTED WHETHER HIS MISSION WOULD SUCCEED, YES. BUT HE DID NOT ALLOW THAT DOUBT TO STOP HIM.
HE CONTINUED ON...

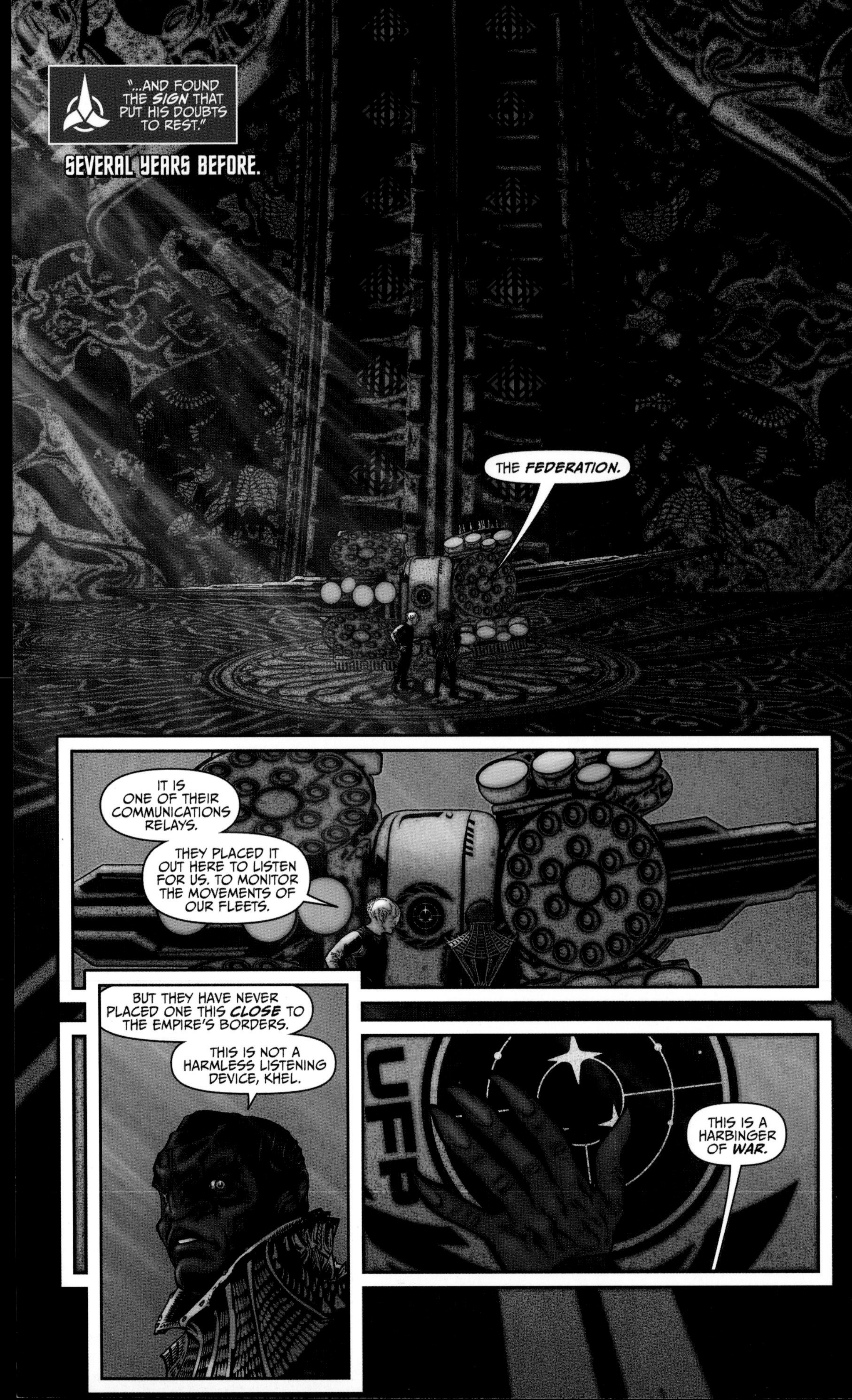
"...AND FOUND THE SIGN THAT PUT HIS DOUBTS TO REST."
SEVERAL YEARS BEFORE.
THE FEDERATION.
IT IS ONE OF THEIR COMMUNICATIONS RELAYS.
THEY PLACED IT OUT HERE TO LISTEN FOR US. TO MONITOR THE MOVEMENTS OF OUR FLEETS.
BUT THEY HAVE NEVER PLACED ONE THIS CLOSE TO THE EMPIRE'S BORDERS.
THIS IS NOT A HARMLESS LISTENING DEVICE, KHEL.
UFP
THIS IS A HARBINGER OF WAR.

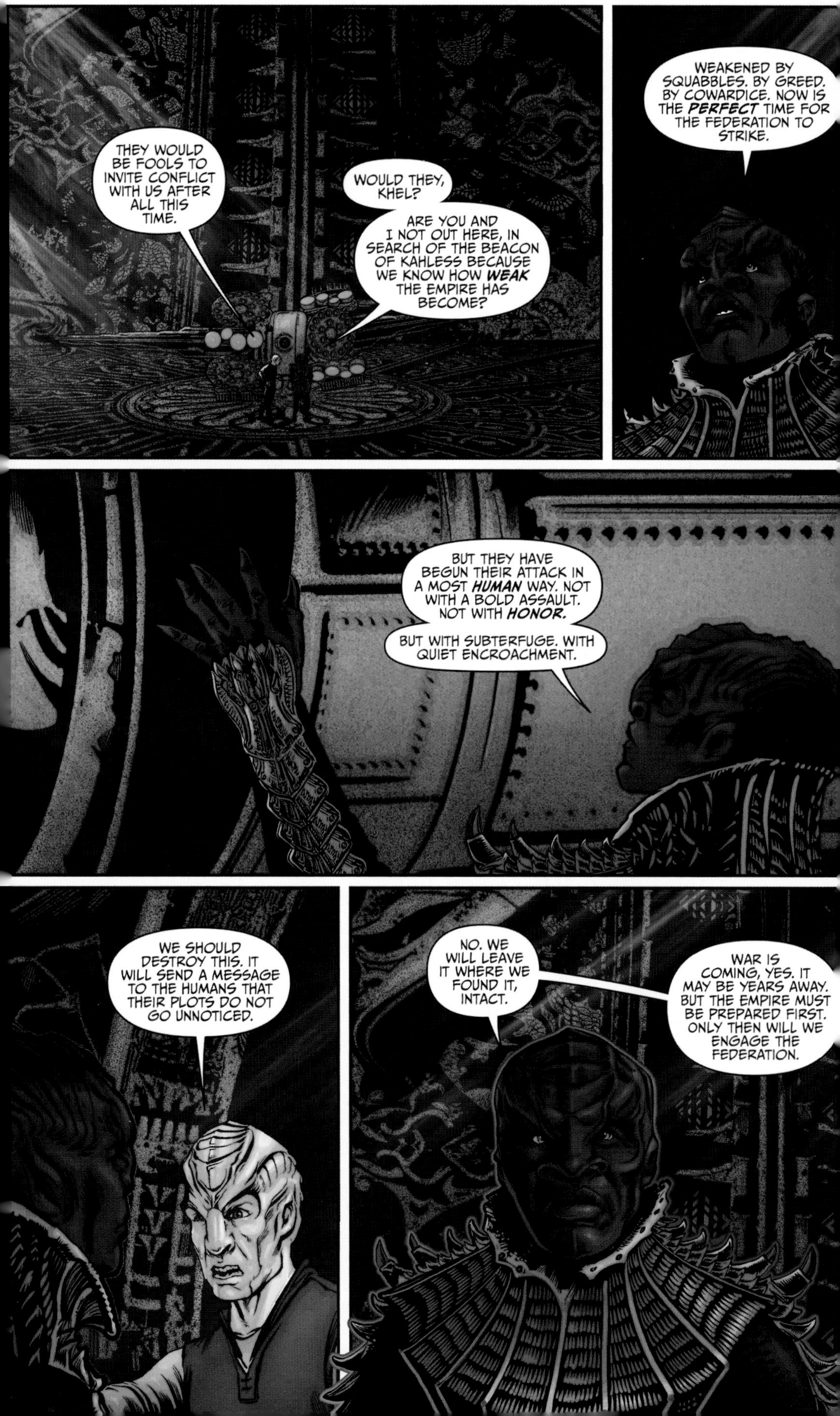
THEY WOULD BE FOOLS TO INVITE CONFLICT WITH US AFTER ALL THIS TIME.
WOULD THEY, KHEL?
ARE YOU AND I NOT OUT HERE, IN SEARCH OF THE BEACON OF KAHLESS BECAUSE WE KNOW HOW *WEAK* THE EMPIRE HAS BECOME?
WEAKENED BY SQUABBLES. BY GREED. BY COWARDICE. NOW IS THE *PERFECT* TIME FOR THE FEDERATION TO STRIKE.
BUT THEY HAVE BEGUN THEIR ATTACK IN A MOST *HUMAN* WAY. NOT WITH A BOLD ASSAULT. NOT WITH *HONOR.*
BUT WITH SUBTERFUGE. WITH QUIET ENCROACHMENT.
WE SHOULD DESTROY THIS. IT WILL SEND A MESSAGE TO THE HUMANS THAT THEIR PLOTS DO NOT GO UNNOTICED.
NO. WE WILL LEAVE IT WHERE WE FOUND IT, INTACT.
WAR IS COMING, YES. IT MAY BE YEARS AWAY. BUT THE EMPIRE MUST BE PREPARED FIRST. ONLY THEN WILL WE ENGAGE THE FEDERATION.

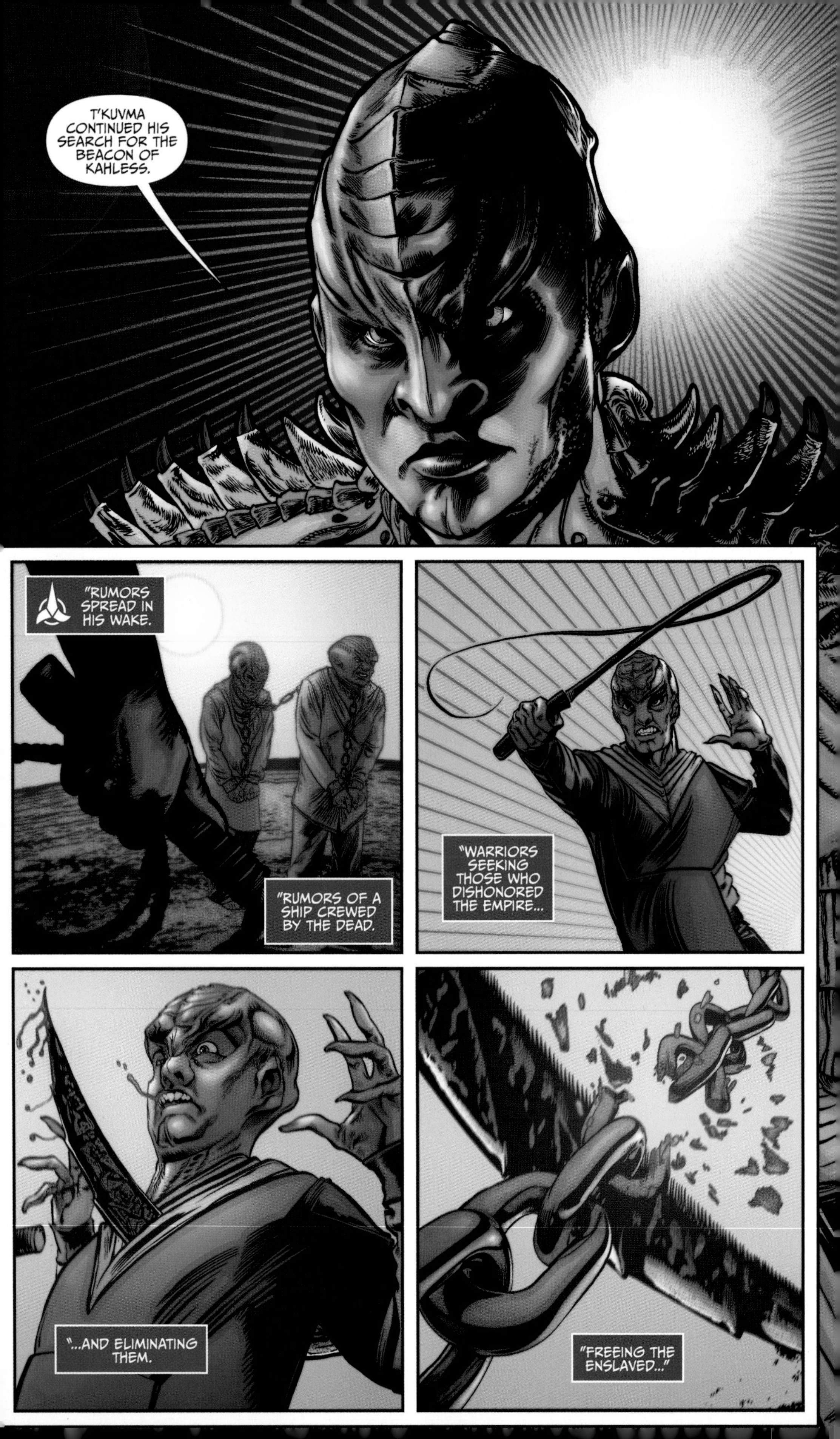
T'KUVMA CONTINUED HIS SEARCH FOR THE BEACON OF KAHLESS.
"RUMORS SPREAD IN HIS WAKE.
"RUMORS OF A SHIP CREWED BY THE DEAD.
"WARRIORS SEEKING THOSE WHO DISHONORED THE EMPIRE...
"...AND ELIMINATING THEM.
"FREEING THE ENSLAVED..."

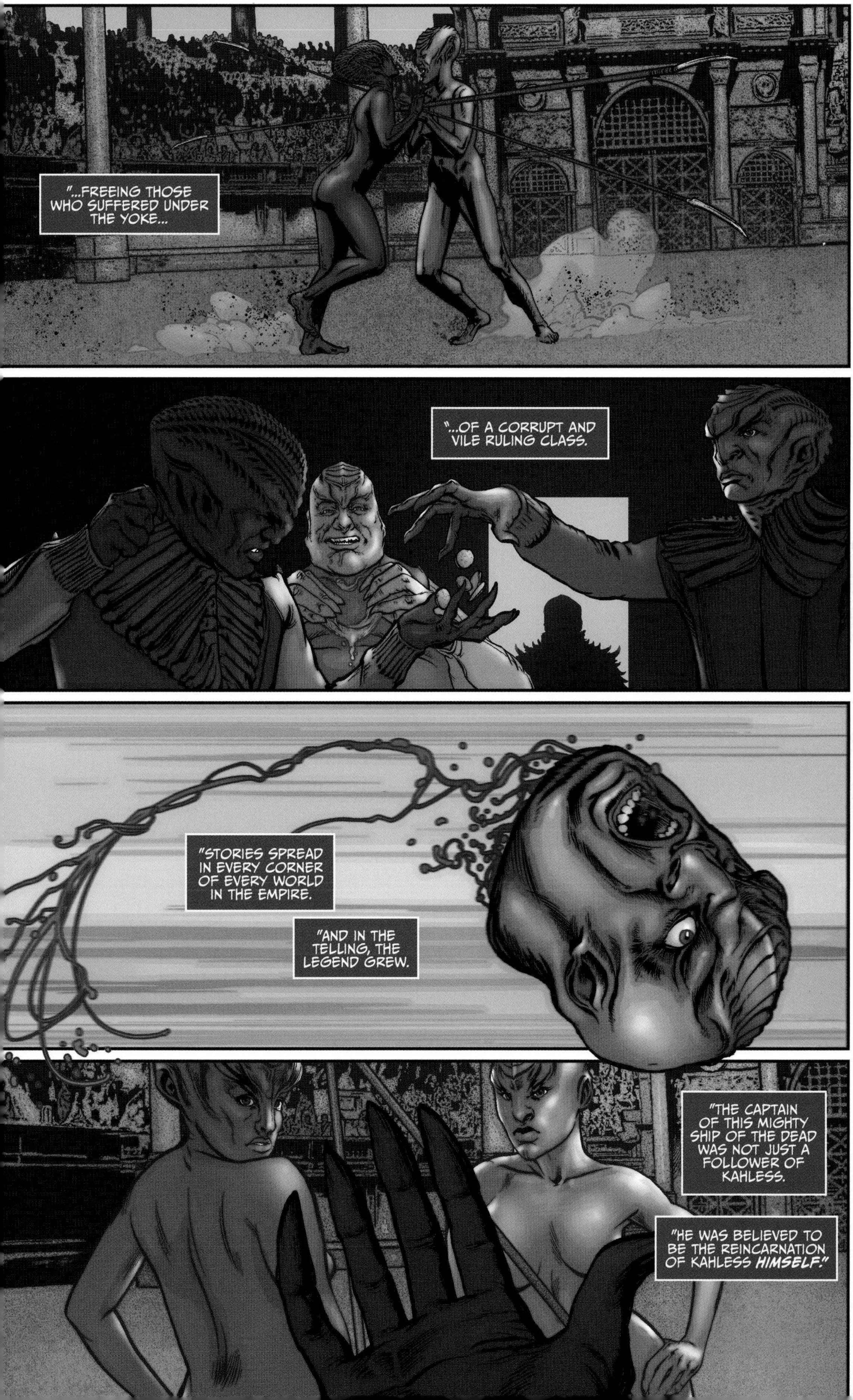
"...FREEING THOSE WHO SUFFERED UNDER THE YOKE...
"...OF A CORRUPT AND VILE RULING CLASS.
"STORIES SPREAD IN EVERY CORNER OF EVERY WORLD IN THE EMPIRE.
"AND IN THE TELLING, THE LEGEND GREW.
"THE CAPTAIN OF THIS MIGHTY SHIP OF THE DEAD WAS NOT JUST A FOLLOWER OF KAHLESS.
"HE WAS BELIEVED TO BE THE REINCARNATION OF KAHLESS *HIMSELF*."

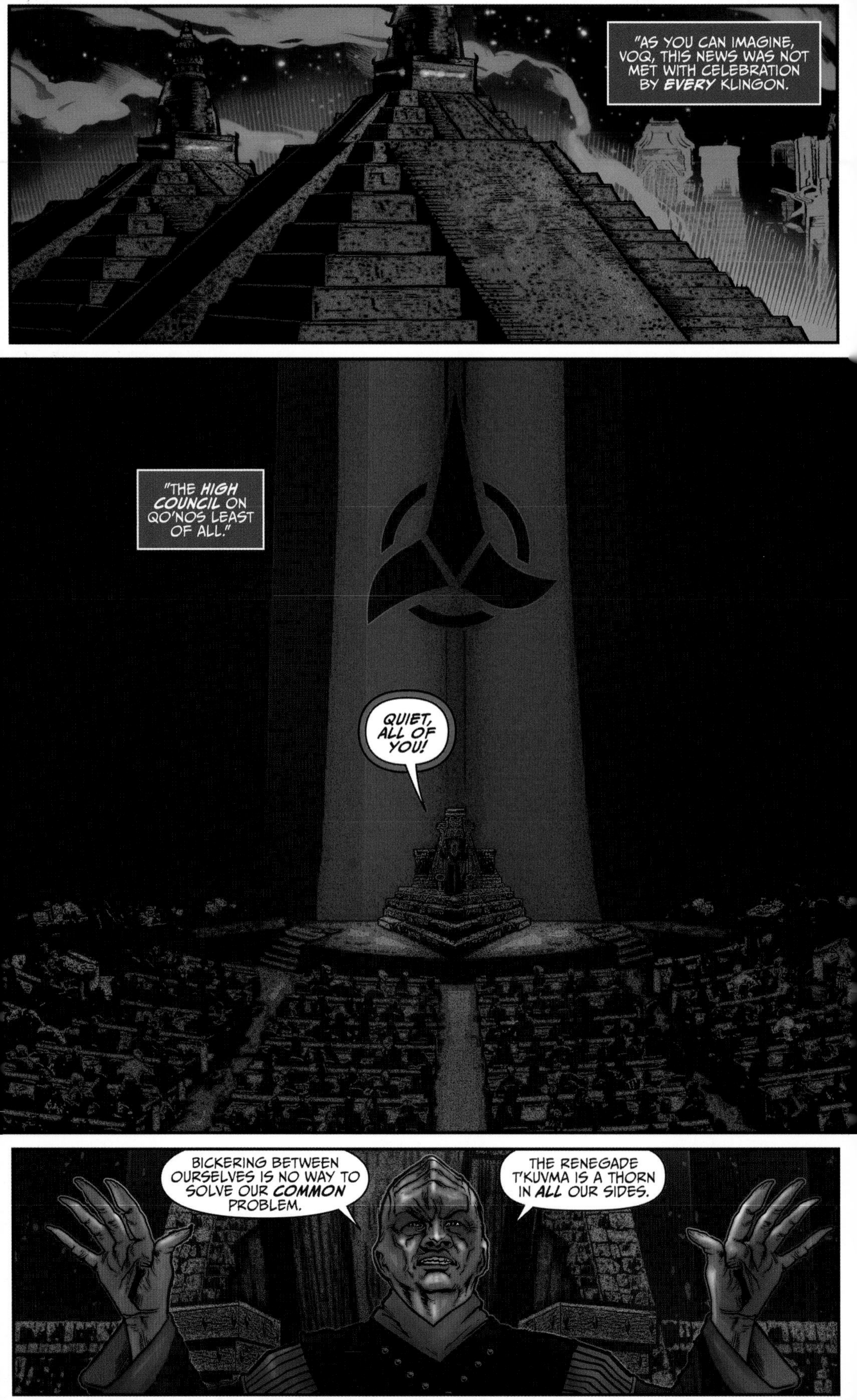
"AS YOU CAN IMAGINE, VOQ, THIS NEWS WAS NOT MET WITH CELEBRATION BY EVERY KLINGON.
"THE HIGH COUNCIL ON QO'NOS LEAST OF ALL."
QUIET, ALL OF YOU!
BICKERING BETWEEN OURSELVES IS NO WAY TO SOLVE OUR COMMON PROBLEM.
THE RENEGADE T'KUVMA IS A THORN IN ALL OUR SIDES.

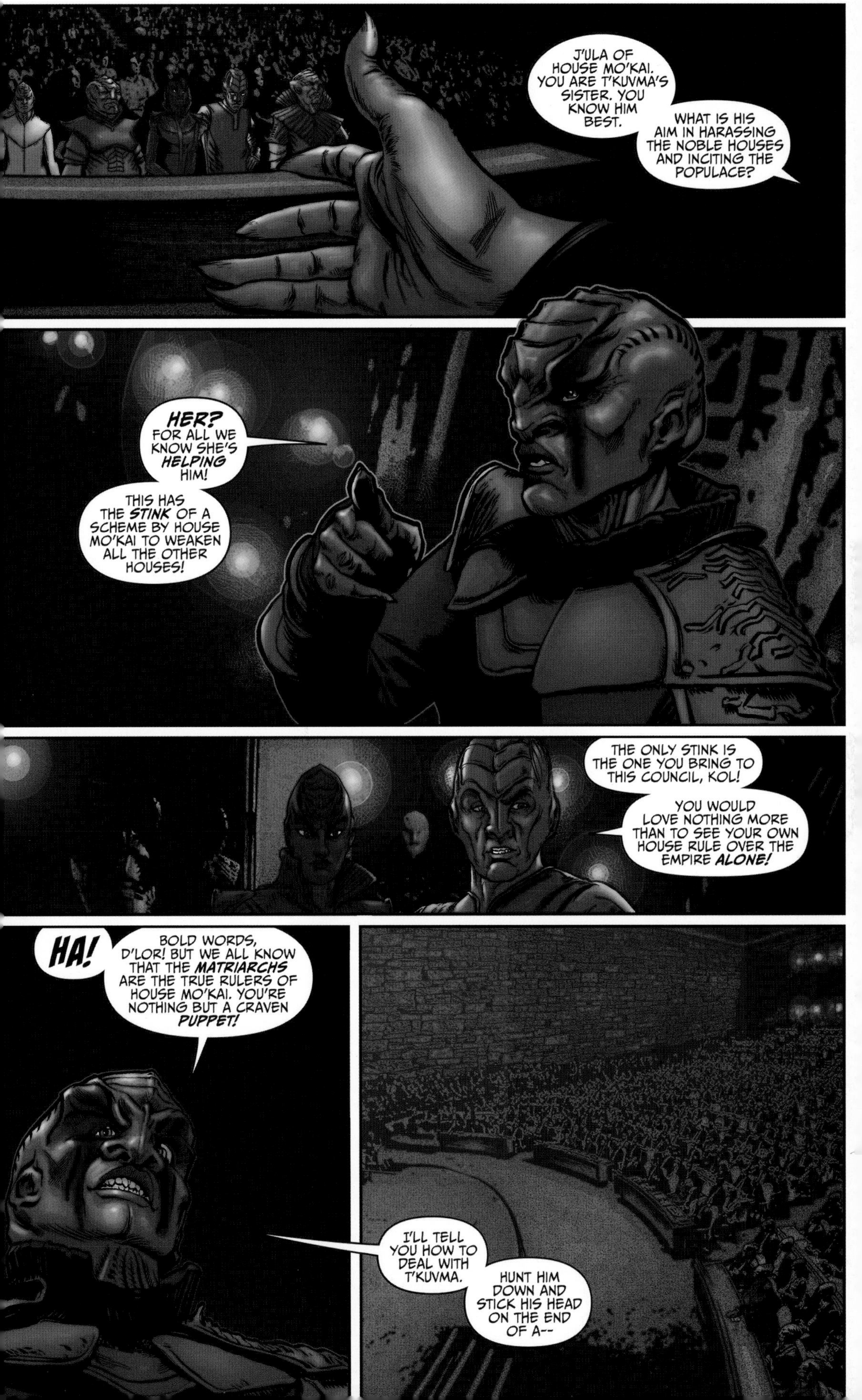
J'ULA OF HOUSE MO'KAI. YOU ARE T'KUVMA'S SISTER. YOU KNOW HIM BEST.
WHAT IS HIS AIM IN HARASSING THE NOBLE HOUSES AND INCITING THE POPULACE?
HER? FOR ALL WE KNOW SHE'S HELPING HIM!
THIS HAS THE STINK OF A SCHEME BY HOUSE MO'KAI TO WEAKEN ALL THE OTHER HOUSES!
THE ONLY STINK IS THE ONE YOU BRING TO THIS COUNCIL, KOL!
YOU WOULD LOVE NOTHING MORE THAN TO SEE YOUR OWN HOUSE RULE OVER THE EMPIRE ALONE!
HA!
BOLD WORDS, D'LOR! BUT WE ALL KNOW THAT THE MATRIARCHS ARE THE TRUE RULERS OF HOUSE MO'KAI. YOU'RE NOTHING BUT A CRAVEN PUPPET!
I'LL TELL YOU HOW TO DEAL WITH T'KUVMA.
HUNT HIM DOWN AND STICK HIS HEAD ON THE END OF A--

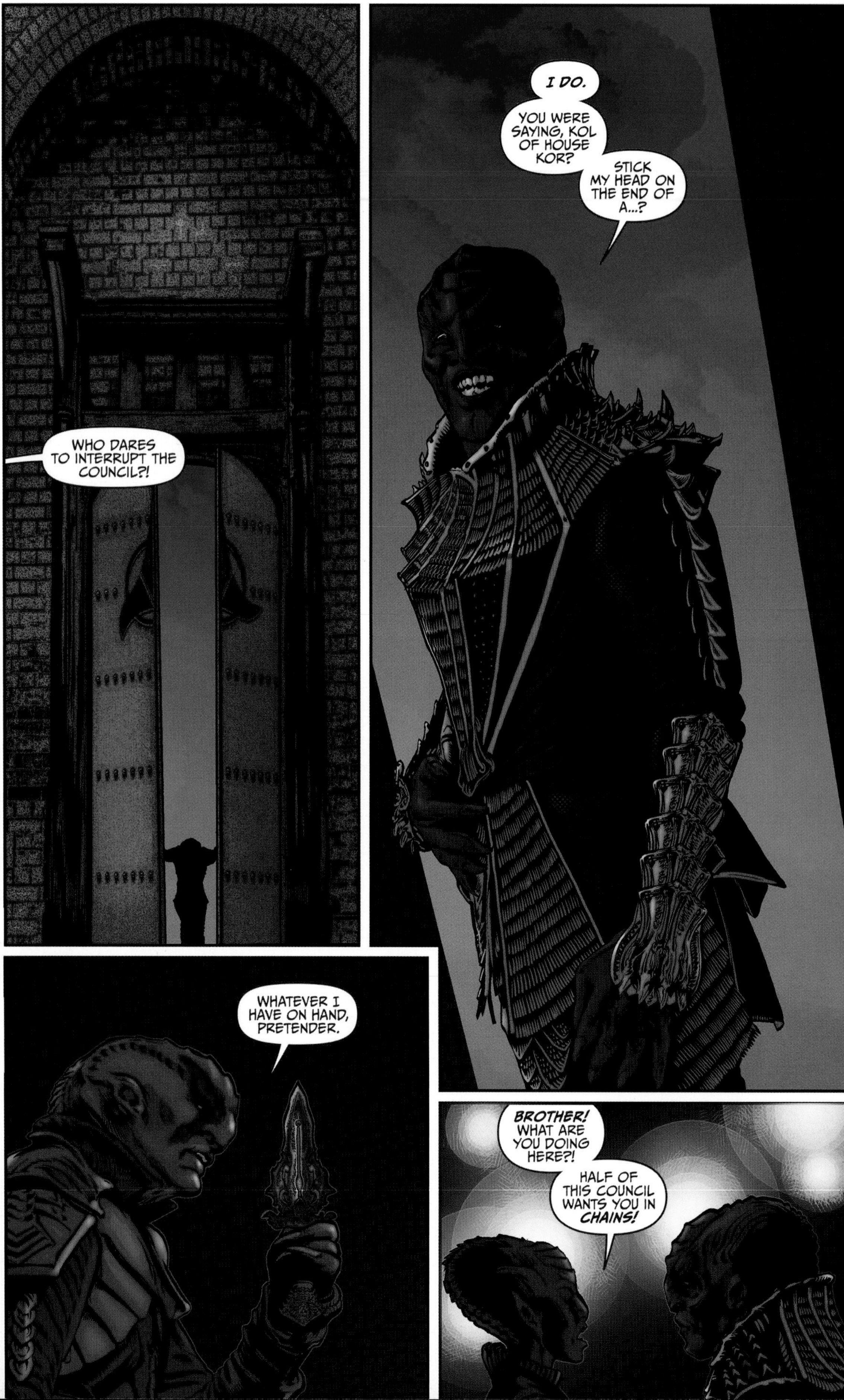
WHO DARES TO INTERRUPT THE COUNCIL?!
I DO.
YOU WERE SAYING, KOL OF HOUSE KOR?
STICK MY HEAD ON THE END OF A...?
WHATEVER I HAVE ON HAND, PRETENDER.
BROTHER! WHAT ARE YOU DOING HERE?!
HALF OF THIS COUNCIL WANTS YOU IN CHAINS!

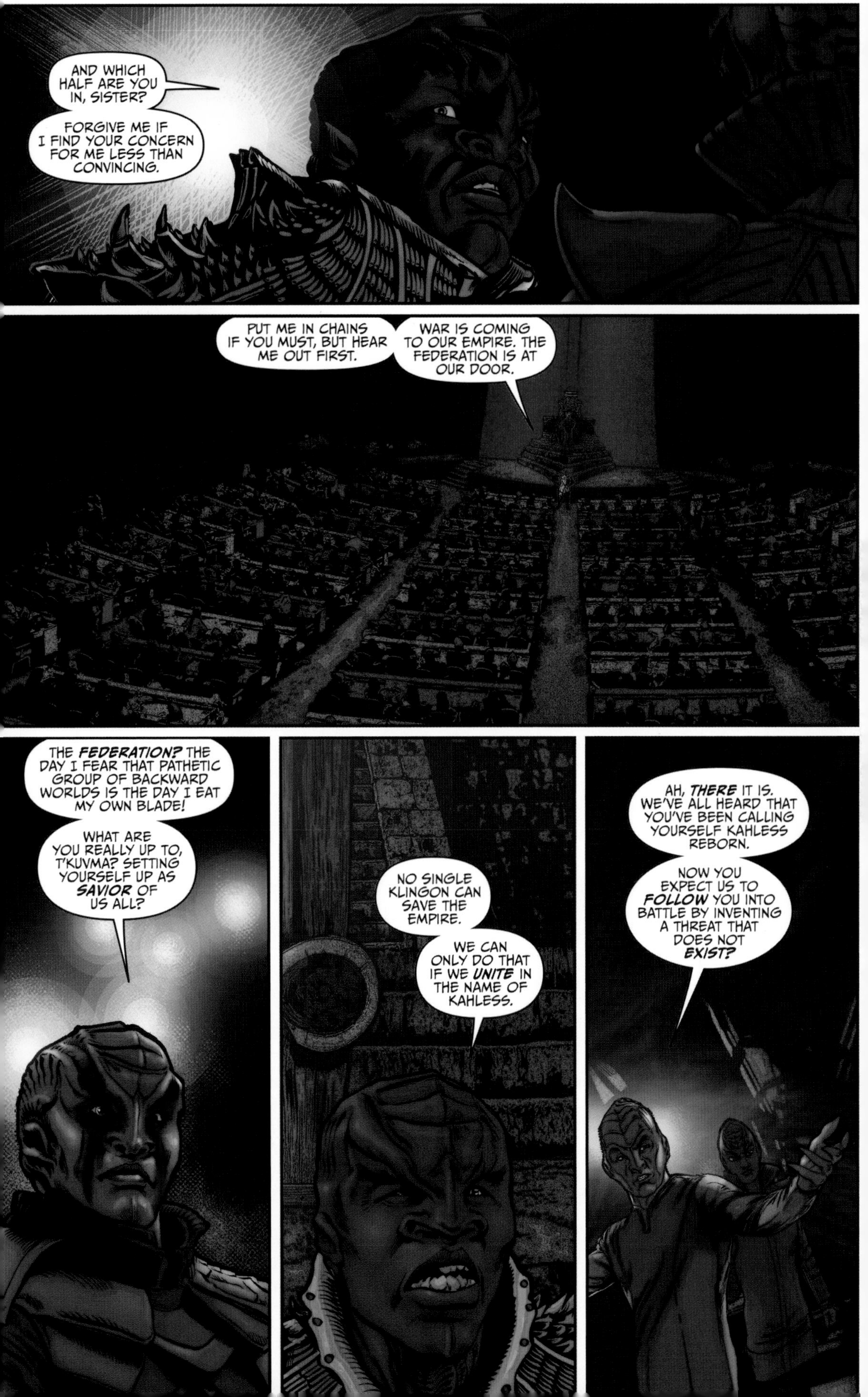
AND WHICH HALF ARE YOU IN, SISTER?
FORGIVE ME IF I FIND YOUR CONCERN FOR ME LESS THAN CONVINCING.
PUT ME IN CHAINS IF YOU MUST, BUT HEAR ME OUT FIRST.
WAR IS COMING TO OUR EMPIRE. THE FEDERATION IS AT OUR DOOR.
THE FEDERATION? THE DAY I FEAR THAT PATHETIC GROUP OF BACKWARD WORLDS IS THE DAY I EAT MY OWN BLADE!
WHAT ARE YOU REALLY UP TO, T'KUVMA? SETTING YOURSELF UP AS SAVIOR OF US ALL?
NO SINGLE KLINGON CAN SAVE THE EMPIRE.
WE CAN ONLY DO THAT IF WE UNITE IN THE NAME OF KAHLESS.
AH, THERE IT IS. WE'VE ALL HEARD THAT YOU'VE BEEN CALLING YOURSELF KAHLESS REBORN.
NOW YOU EXPECT US TO FOLLOW YOU INTO BATTLE BY INVENTING A THREAT THAT DOES NOT EXIST?

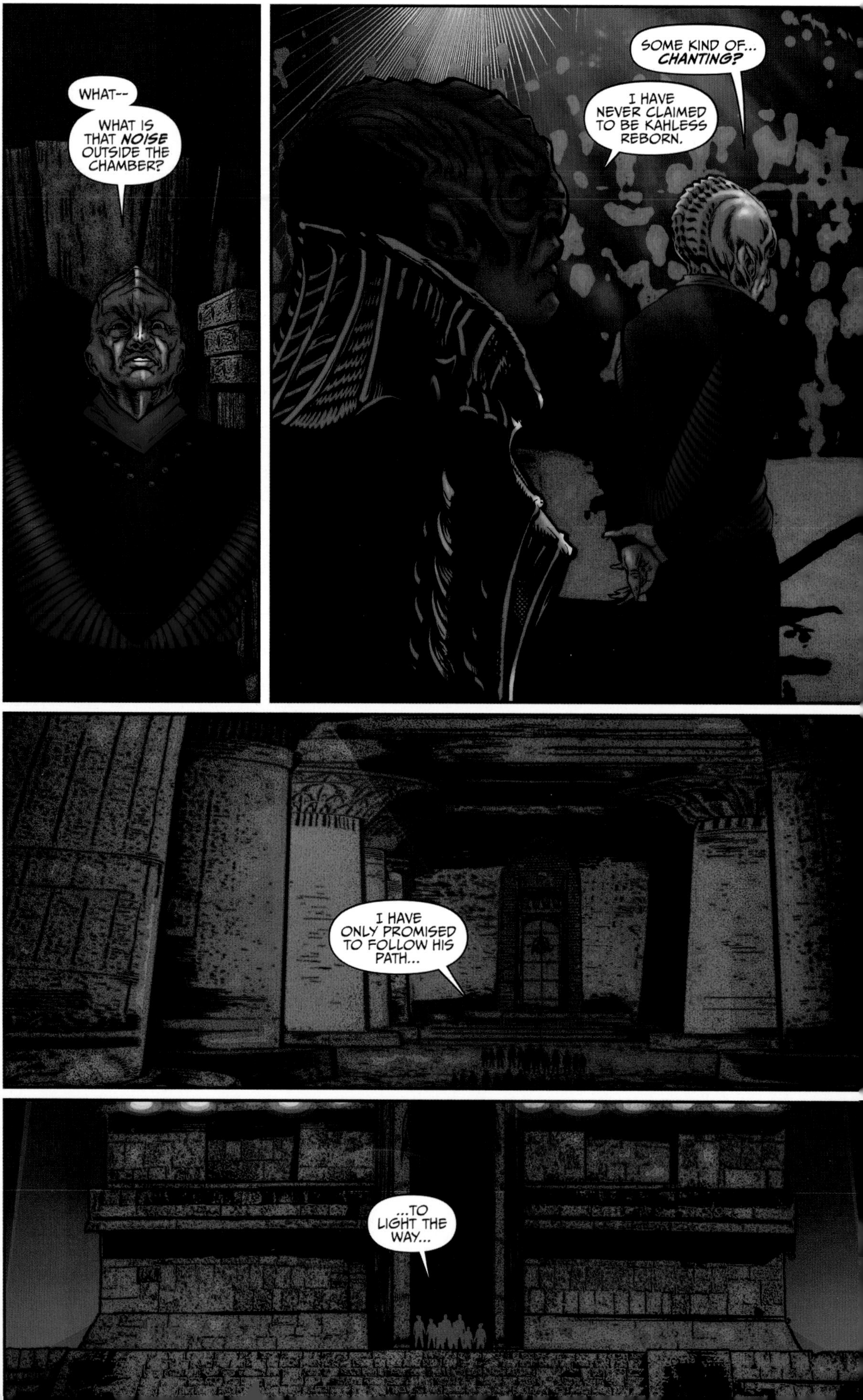
WHAT--
WHAT IS THAT NOISE OUTSIDE THE CHAMBER?
SOME KIND OF... CHANTING?
I HAVE NEVER CLAIMED TO BE KAHLESS REBORN.
I HAVE ONLY PROMISED TO FOLLOW HIS PATH...
...TO LIGHT THE WAY...

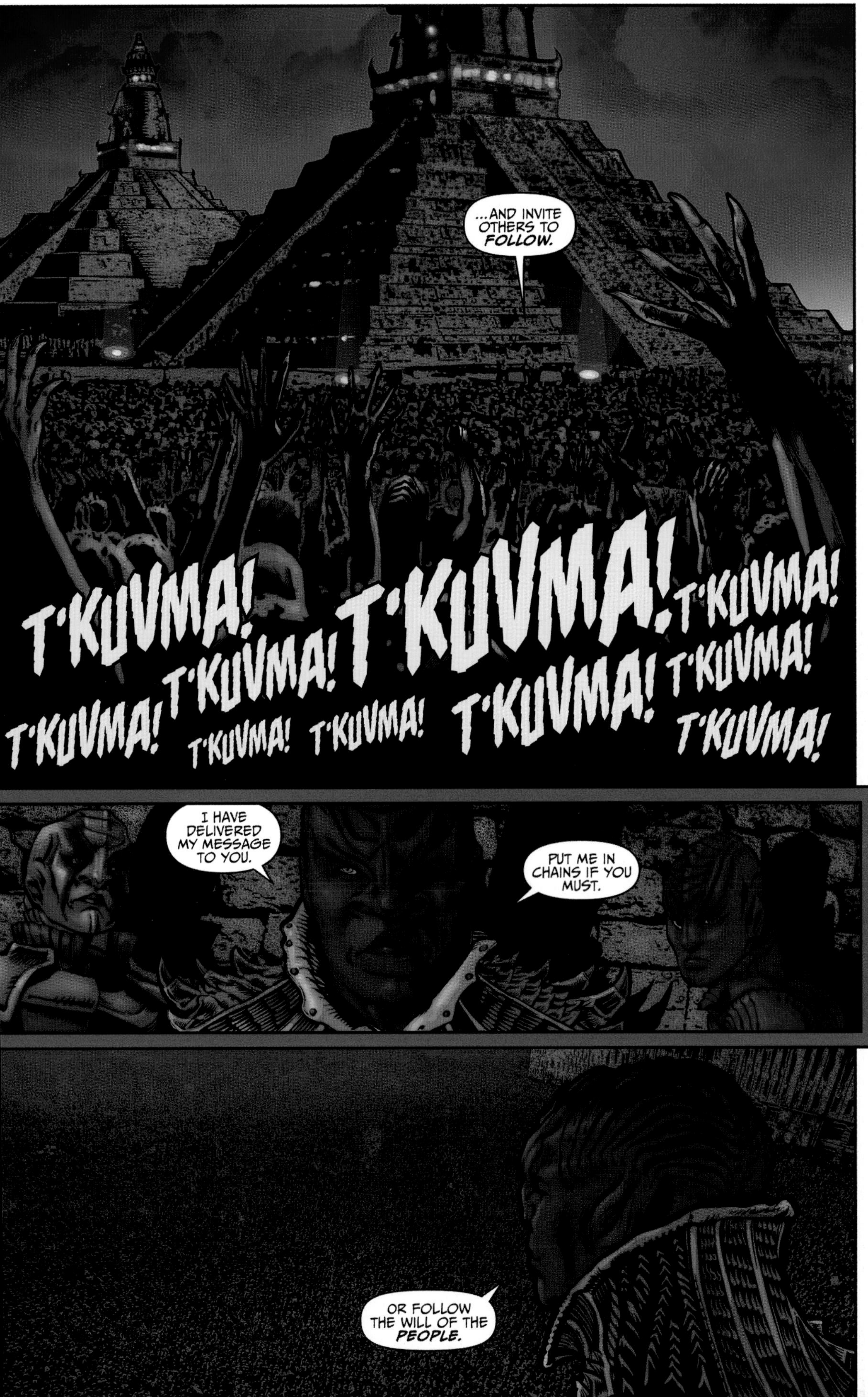
...AND INVITE OTHERS TO FOLLOW.
T'KUVMA! T'KUVMA! T'KUVMA! T'KUVMA! T'KUVMA! T'KUVMA! T'KUVMA! T'KUVMA! T'KUVMA! T'KUVMA!
I HAVE DELIVERED MY MESSAGE TO YOU.
PUT ME IN CHAINS IF YOU MUST.
OR FOLLOW THE WILL OF THE PEOPLE.

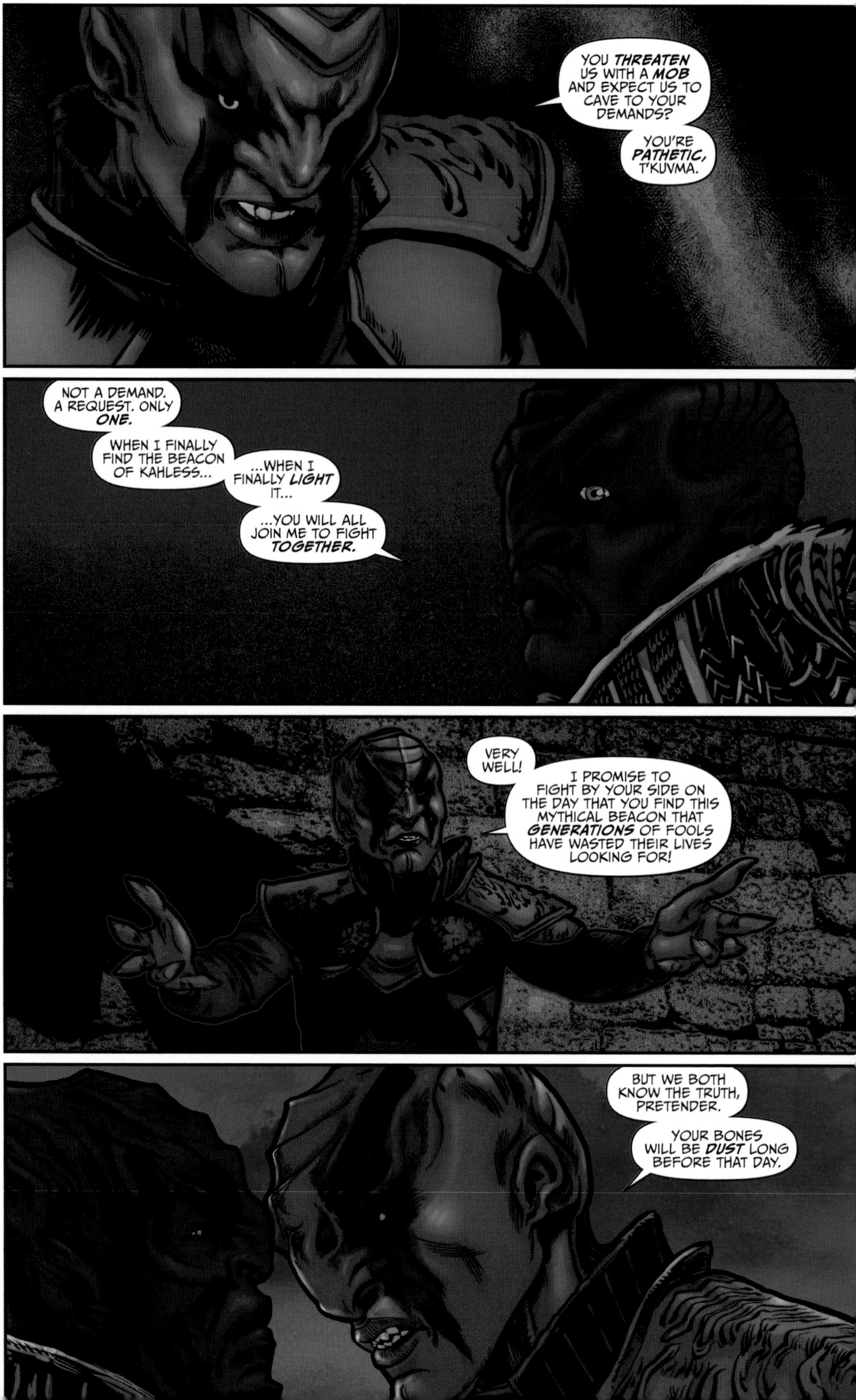
YOU THREATEN US WITH A MOB AND EXPECT US TO CAVE TO YOUR DEMANDS?
YOU'RE PATHETIC, T'KUVMA.
NOT A DEMAND. A REQUEST. ONLY ONE.
WHEN I FINALLY FIND THE BEACON OF KAHLESS...
...WHEN I FINALLY LIGHT IT...
...YOU WILL ALL JOIN ME TO FIGHT TOGETHER.
VERY WELL!
I PROMISE TO FIGHT BY YOUR SIDE ON THE DAY THAT YOU FIND THIS MYTHICAL BEACON THAT GENERATIONS OF FOOLS HAVE WASTED THEIR LIVES LOOKING FOR!
BUT WE BOTH KNOW THE TRUTH, PRETENDER.
YOUR BONES WILL BE DUST LONG BEFORE THAT DAY.

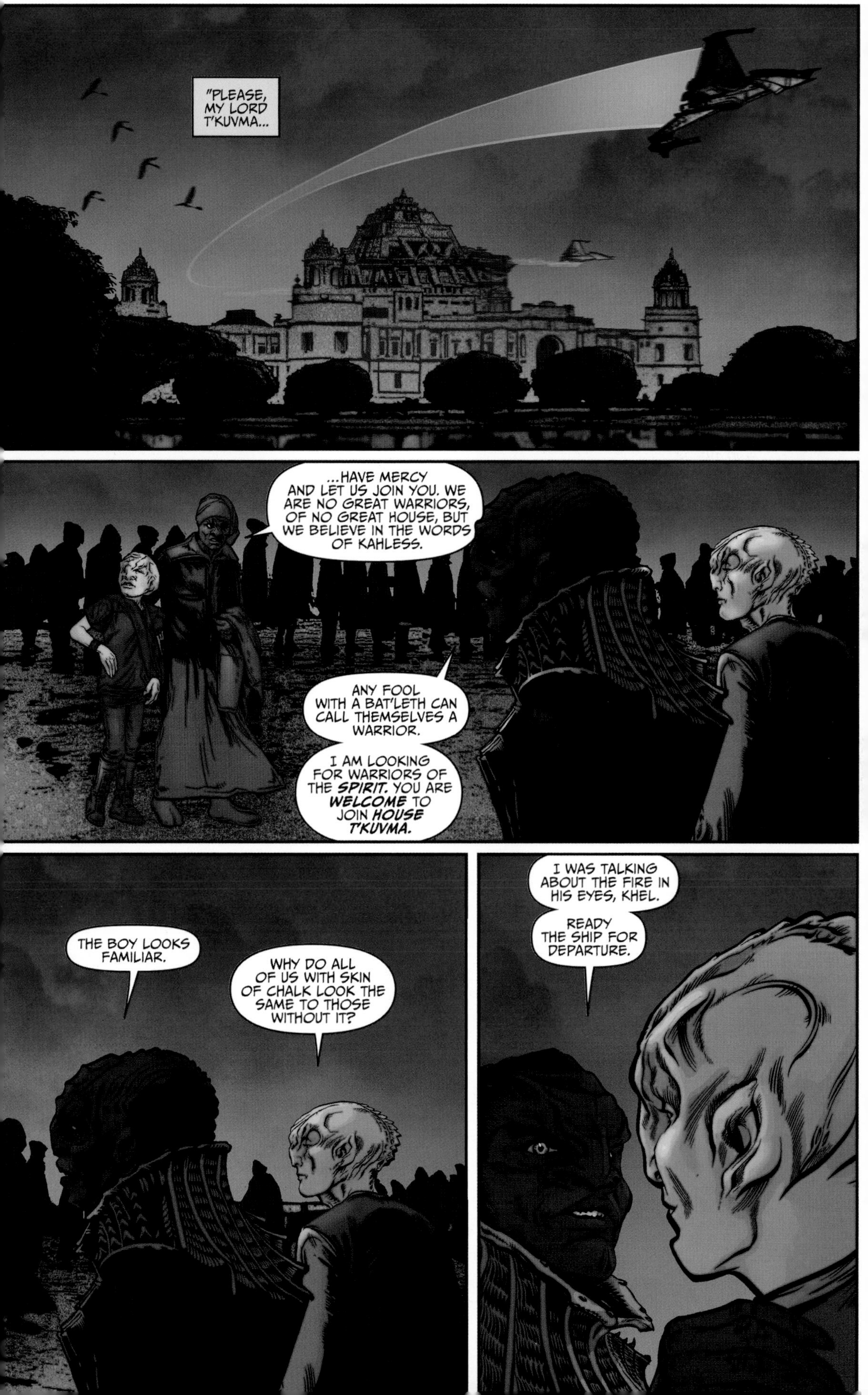

"PLEASE, MY LORD T'KUVMA...
...HAVE MERCY AND LET US JOIN YOU. WE ARE NO GREAT WARRIORS, OF NO GREAT HOUSE, BUT WE BELIEVE IN THE WORDS OF KAHLESS.
ANY FOOL WITH A BAT'LETH CAN CALL THEMSELVES A WARRIOR.
I AM LOOKING FOR WARRIORS OF THE SPIRIT. YOU ARE WELCOME TO JOIN HOUSE T'KUVMA.
THE BOY LOOKS FAMILIAR.
WHY DO ALL OF US WITH SKIN OF CHALK LOOK THE SAME TO THOSE WITHOUT IT?
I WAS TALKING ABOUT THE FIRE IN HIS EYES, KHEL.
READY THE SHIP FOR DEPARTURE.

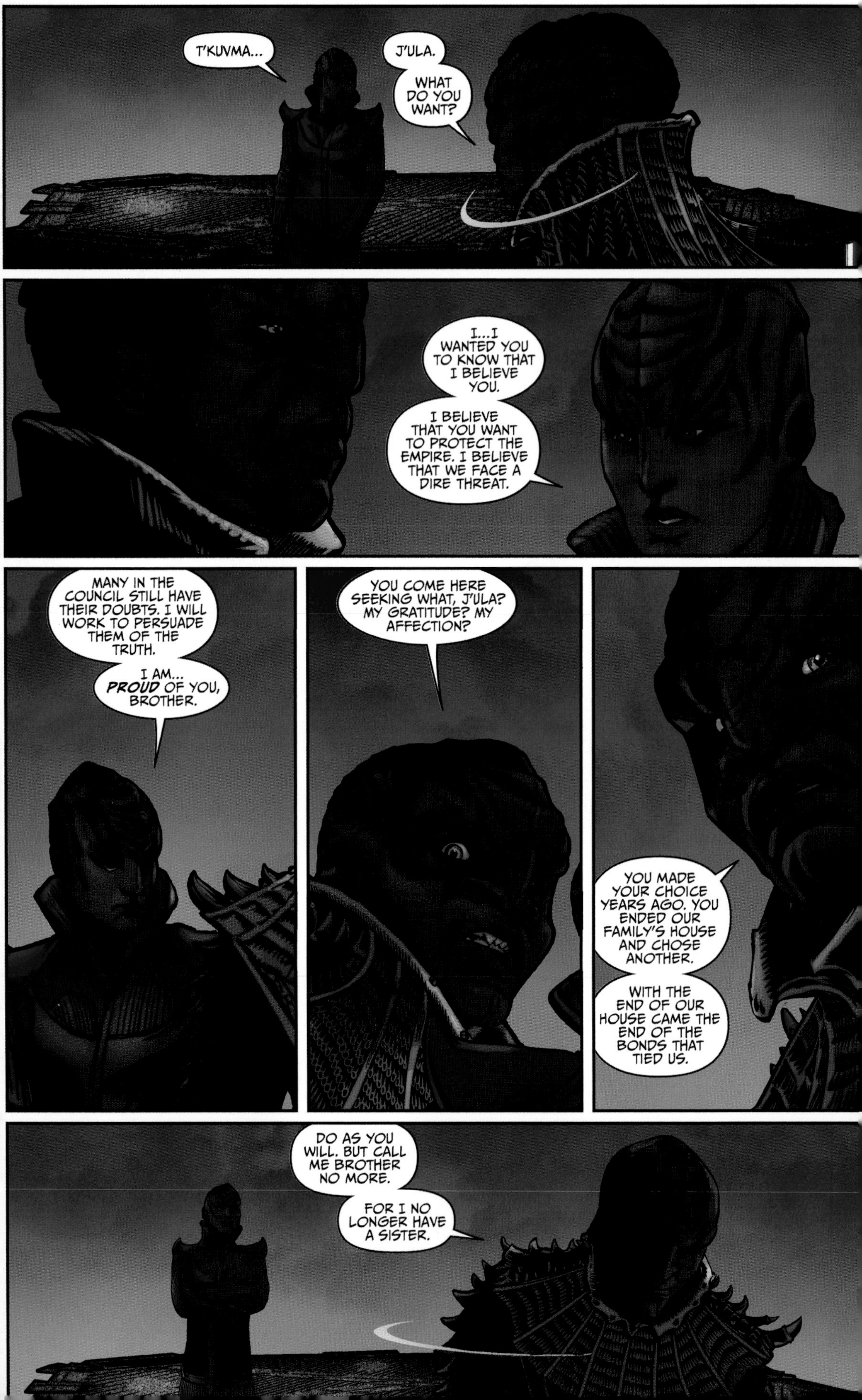
T'KUVMA...
J'ULA.
WHAT DO YOU WANT?
I...I WANTED YOU TO KNOW THAT I BELIEVE YOU.
I BELIEVE THAT YOU WANT TO PROTECT THE EMPIRE. I BELIEVE THAT WE FACE A DIRE THREAT.
MANY IN THE COUNCIL STILL HAVE THEIR DOUBTS. I WILL WORK TO PERSUADE THEM OF THE TRUTH.
I AM... PROUD OF YOU, BROTHER.
YOU COME HERE SEEKING WHAT, J'ULA? MY GRATITUDE? MY AFFECTION?
YOU MADE YOUR CHOICE YEARS AGO. YOU ENDED OUR FAMILY'S HOUSE AND CHOSE ANOTHER.
WITH THE END OF OUR HOUSE CAME THE END OF THE BONDS THAT TIED US.
DO AS YOU WILL. BUT CALL ME BROTHER NO MORE.
FOR I NO LONGER HAVE A SISTER.

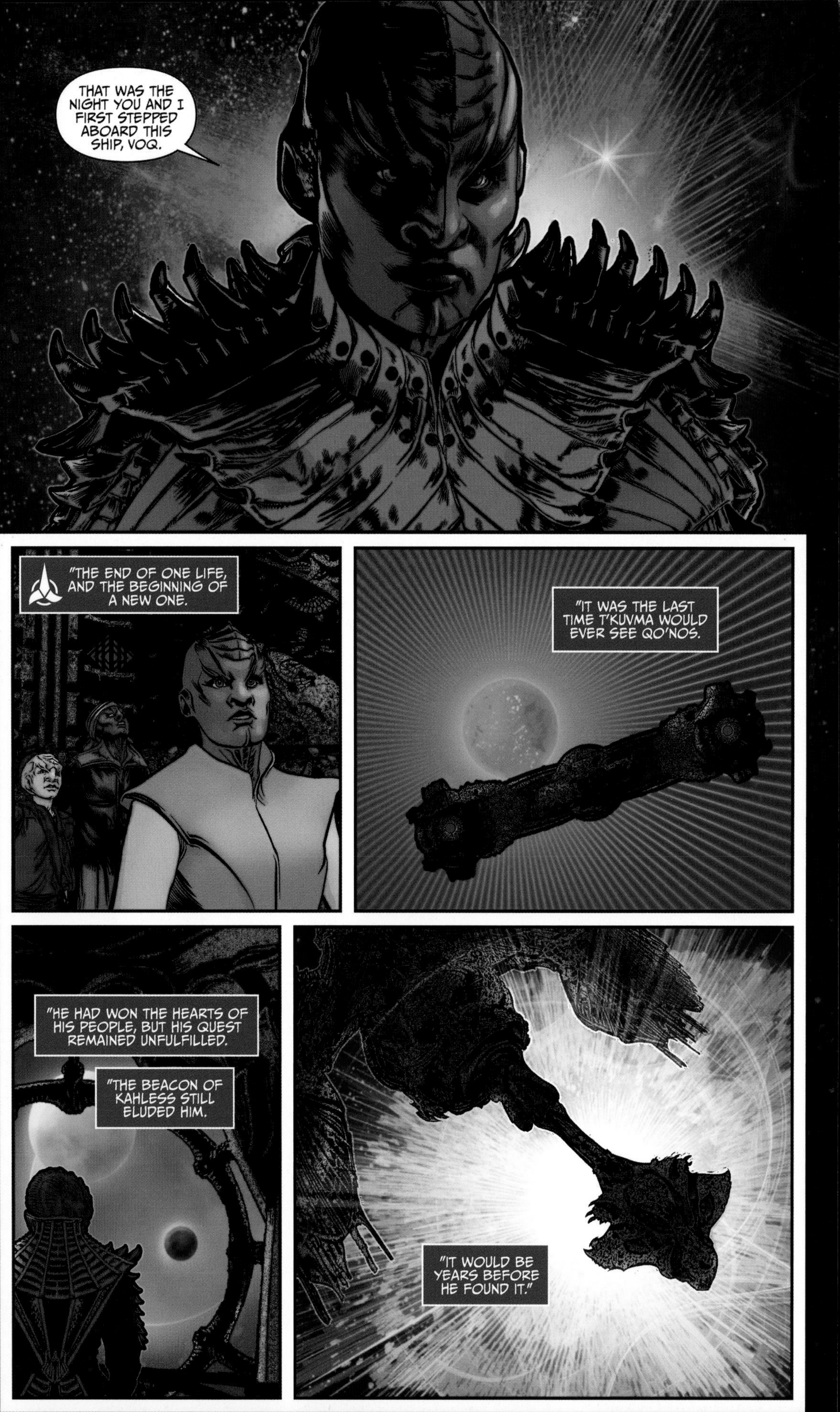
THAT WAS THE NIGHT YOU AND I FIRST STEPPED ABOARD THIS SHIP, VOQ.
"THE END OF ONE LIFE, AND THE BEGINNING OF A NEW ONE.
"IT WAS THE LAST TIME T'KUVMA WOULD EVER SEE QO'NOS.
"HE HAD WON THE HEARTS OF HIS PEOPLE, BUT HIS QUEST REMAINED UNFULFILLED.
"THE BEACON OF KAHLESS STILL ELUDED HIM.
"IT WOULD BE YEARS BEFORE HE FOUND IT."

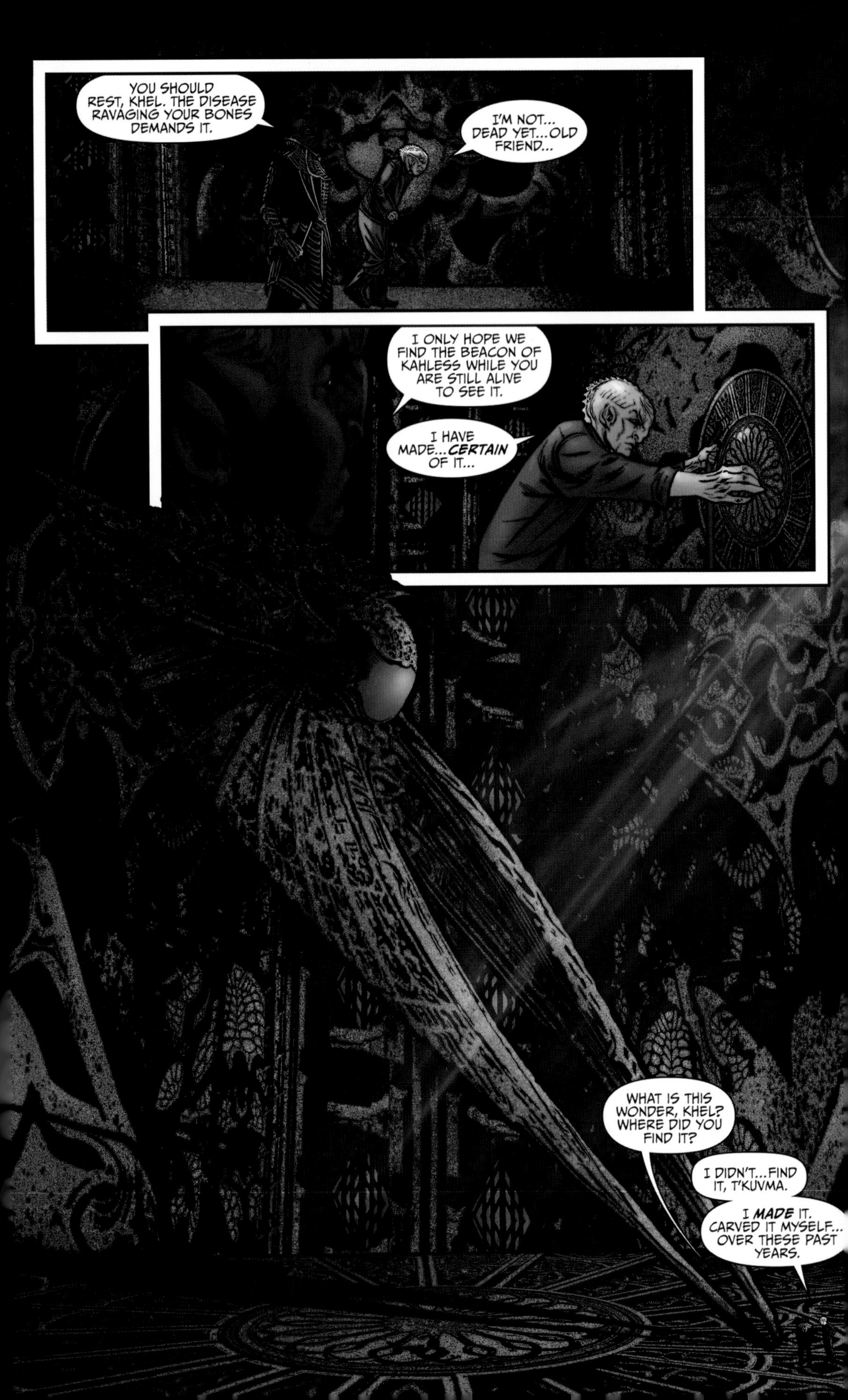
YOU SHOULD REST, KHEL. THE DISEASE RAVAGING YOUR BONES DEMANDS IT.
I'M NOT... DEAD YET...OLD FRIEND...
I ONLY HOPE WE FIND THE BEACON OF KAHLESS WHILE YOU ARE STILL ALIVE TO SEE IT.
I HAVE MADE...***CERTAIN*** OF IT...
WHAT IS THIS WONDER, KHEL? WHERE DID YOU FIND IT?
I DIDN'T...FIND IT, T'KUVMA.
I ***MADE*** IT. CARVED IT MYSELF... OVER THESE PAST YEARS.

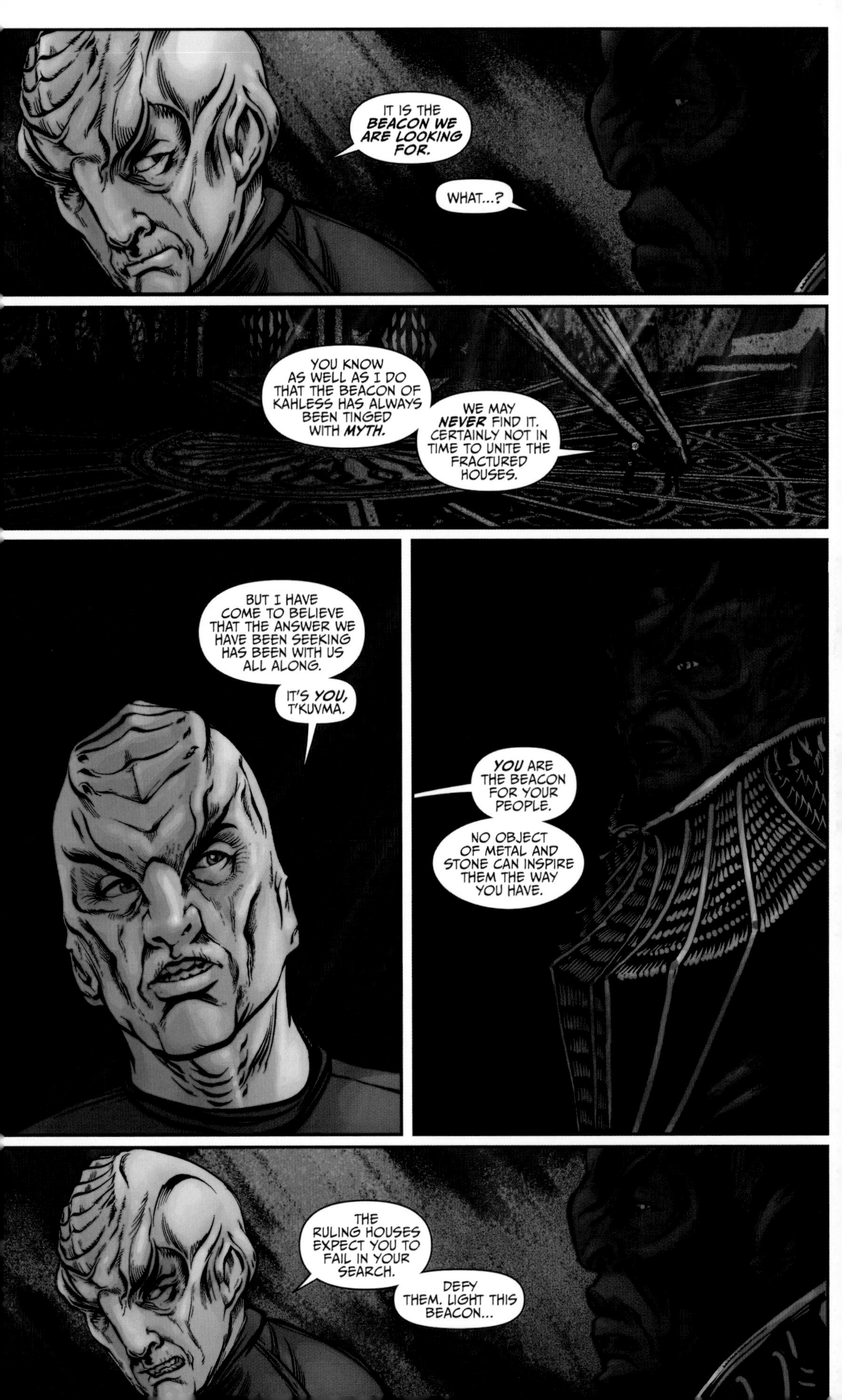
IT IS THE BEACON WE ARE LOOKING FOR.
WHAT...?
YOU KNOW AS WELL AS I DO THAT THE BEACON OF KAHLESS HAS ALWAYS BEEN TINGED WITH MYTH.
WE MAY NEVER FIND IT. CERTAINLY NOT IN TIME TO UNITE THE FRACTURED HOUSES.
BUT I HAVE COME TO BELIEVE THAT THE ANSWER WE HAVE BEEN SEEKING HAS BEEN WITH US ALL ALONG.
IT'S YOU, T'KUVMA.
YOU ARE THE BEACON FOR YOUR PEOPLE.
NO OBJECT OF METAL AND STONE CAN INSPIRE THEM THE WAY YOU HAVE.
THE RULING HOUSES EXPECT YOU TO FAIL IN YOUR SEARCH.
DEFY THEM. LIGHT THIS BEACON...

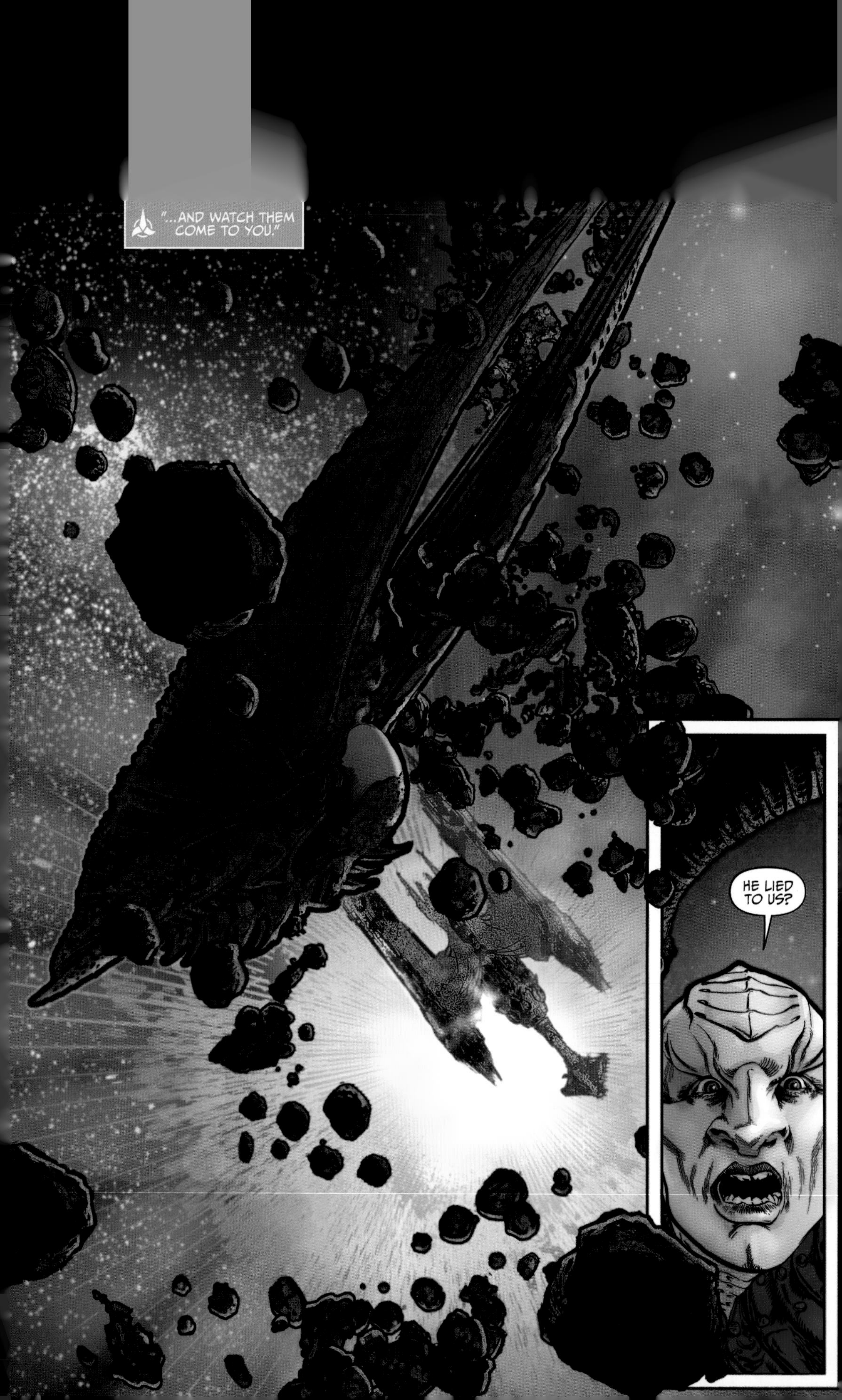
"...AND WATCH THEM COME TO YOU."
HE LIED TO US?

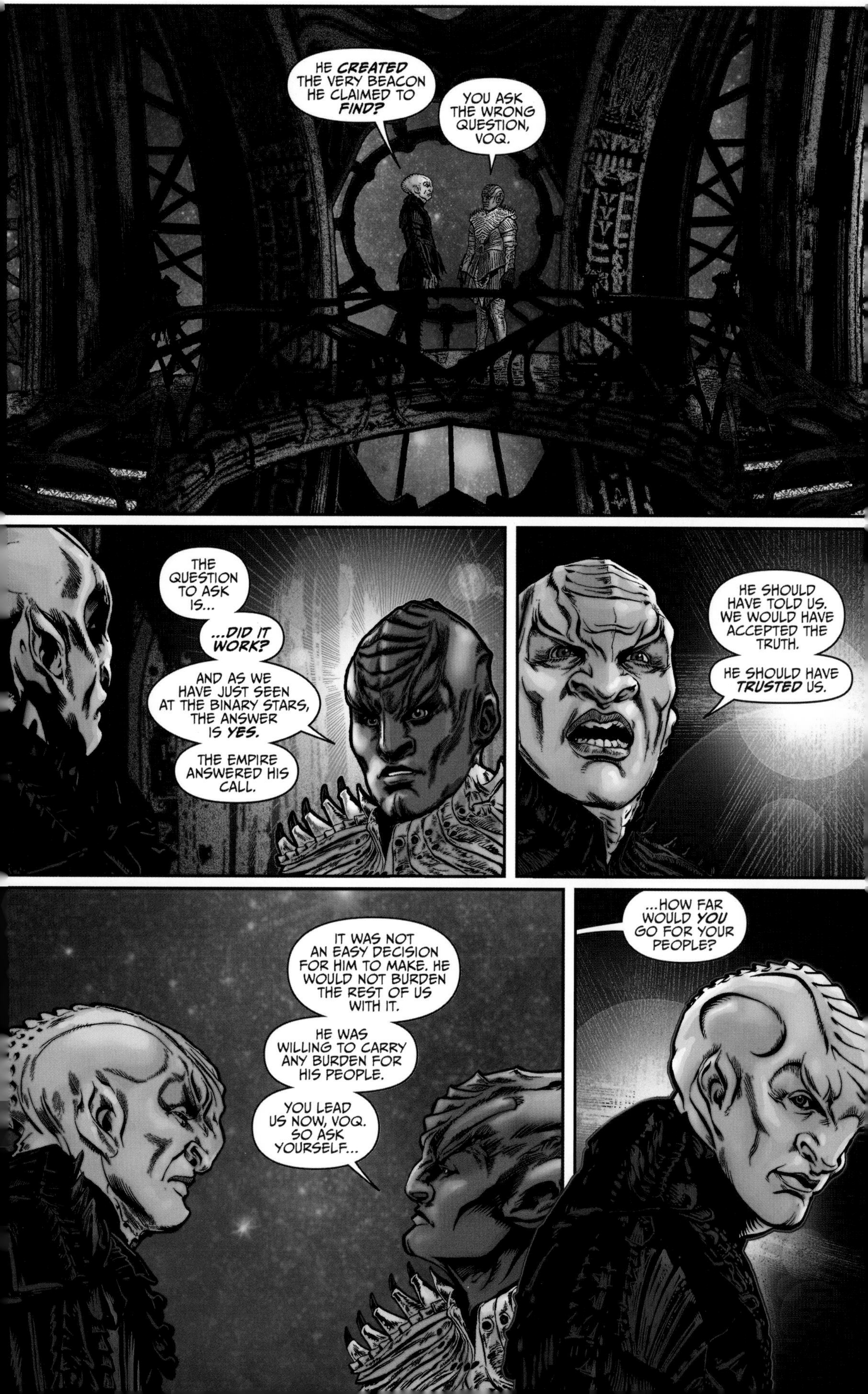
HE *CREATED* THE VERY BEACON HE CLAIMED TO *FIND?*
YOU ASK THE WRONG QUESTION, VOQ.
THE QUESTION TO ASK IS...
...DID IT WORK?
AND AS WE HAVE JUST SEEN AT THE BINARY STARS, THE ANSWER IS *YES.*
THE EMPIRE ANSWERED HIS CALL.
HE SHOULD HAVE TOLD US. WE WOULD HAVE ACCEPTED THE TRUTH.
HE SHOULD HAVE *TRUSTED* US.
IT WAS NOT AN EASY DECISION FOR HIM TO MAKE. HE WOULD NOT BURDEN THE REST OF US WITH IT.
HE WAS WILLING TO CARRY ANY BURDEN FOR HIS PEOPLE.
YOU LEAD US NOW, VOQ. SO ASK YOURSELF...
...HOW FAR WOULD *YOU* GO FOR YOUR PEOPLE?

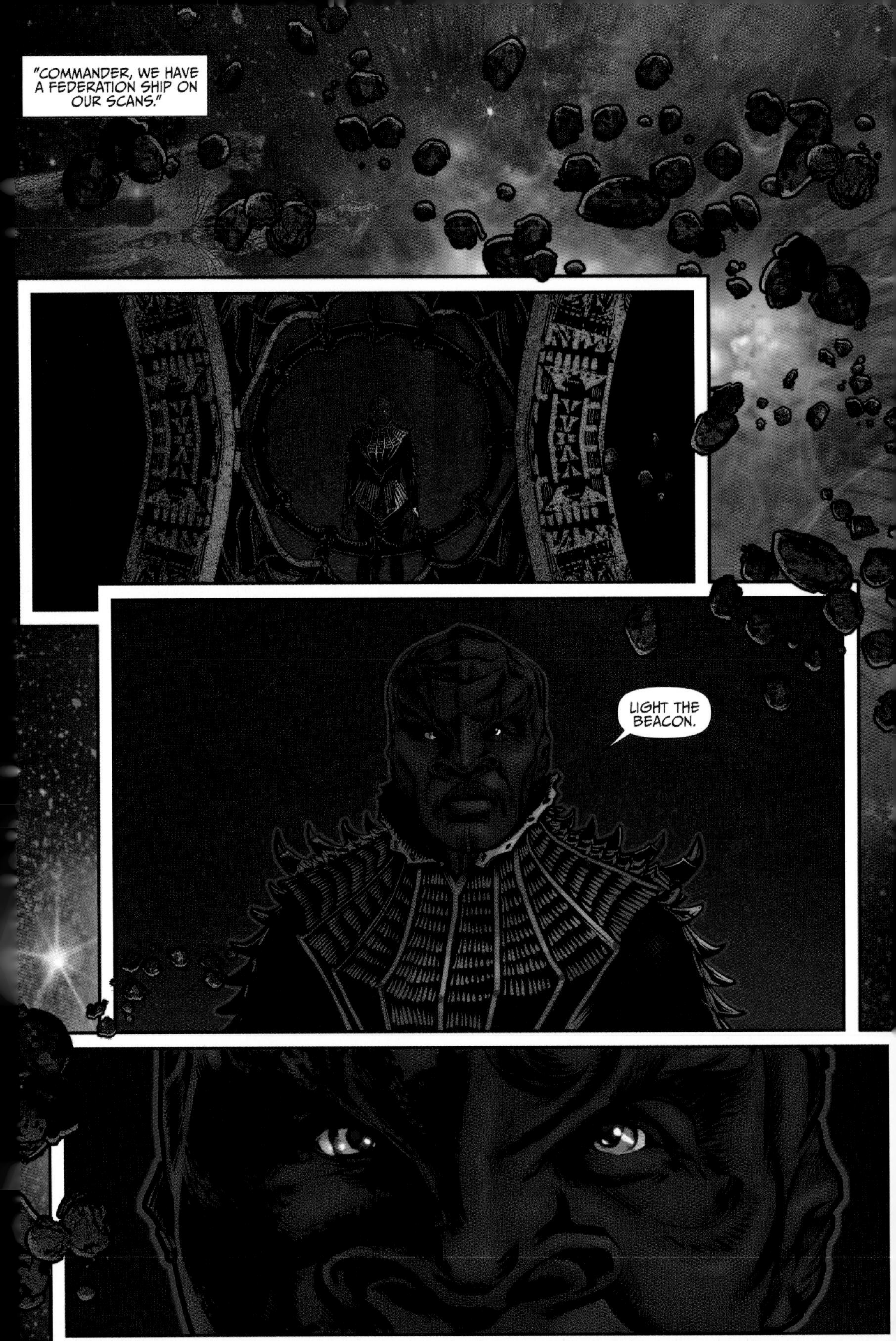
"COMMANDER, WE HAVE A FEDERATION SHIP ON OUR SCANS."
LIGHT THE BEACON.

COLORS BY **ESTHER SANZ**

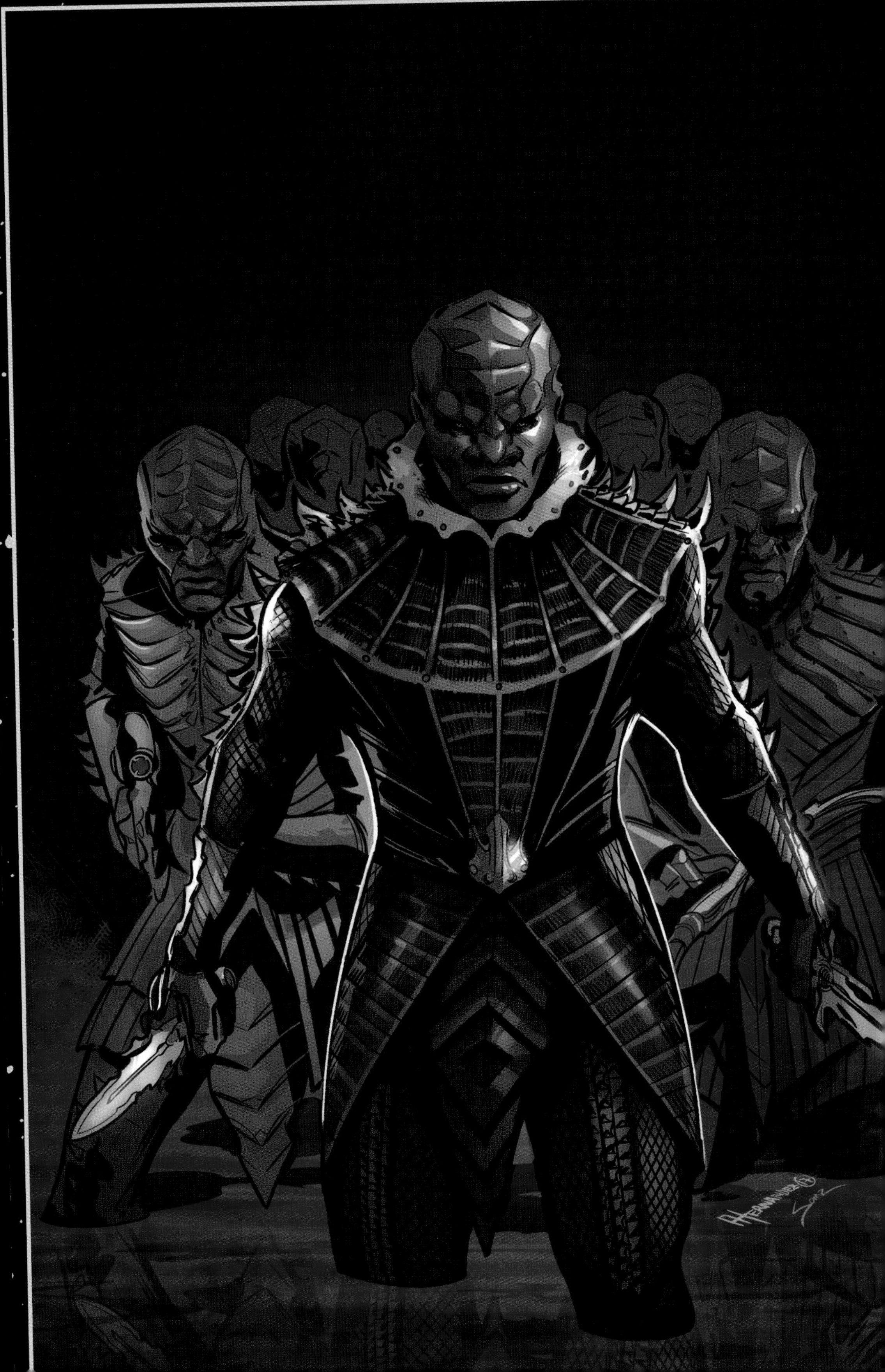

COLORS BY **JORDIE BELLAIRE**

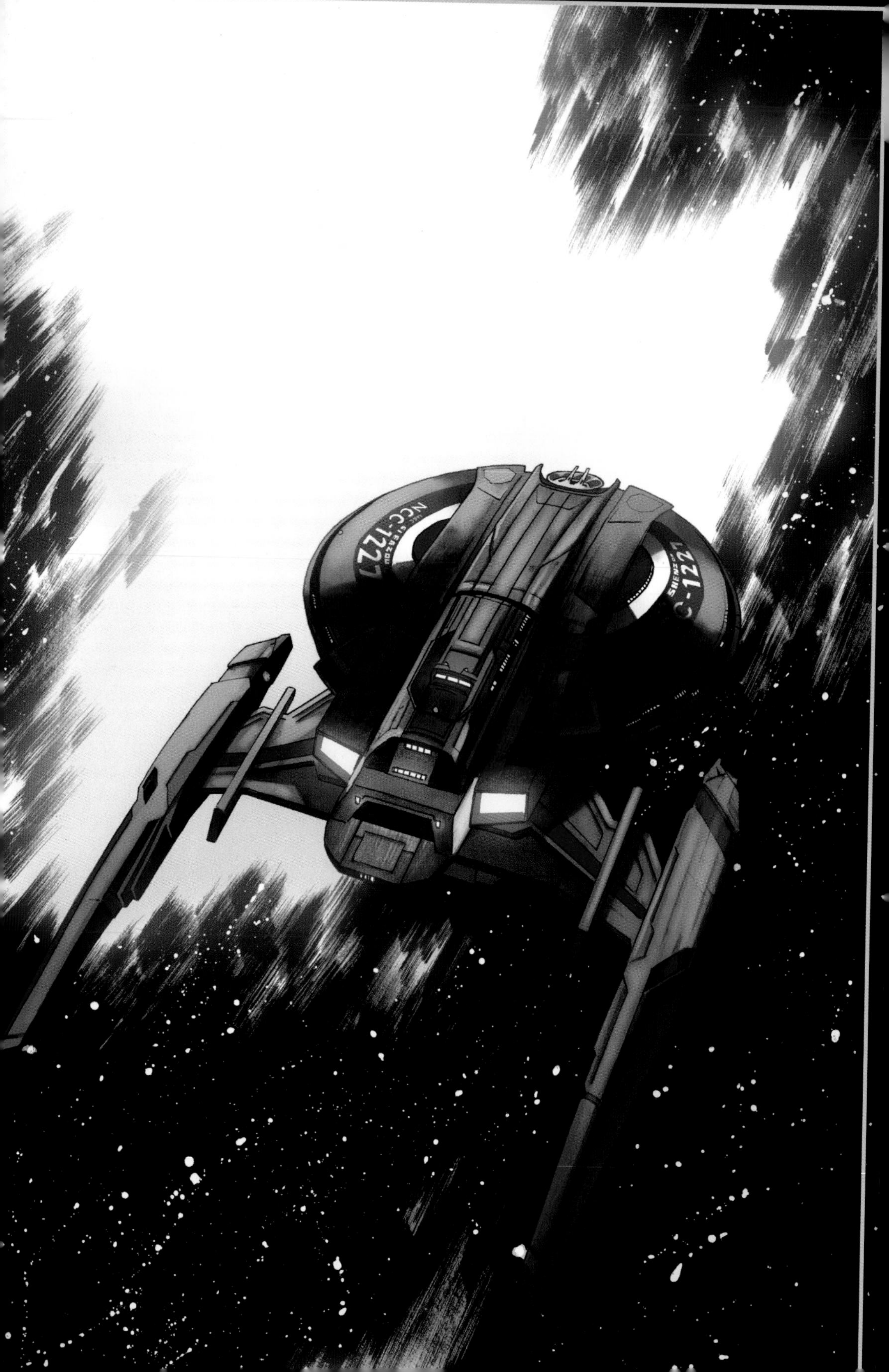
NCC-1227
SHENZHOU
C-1227

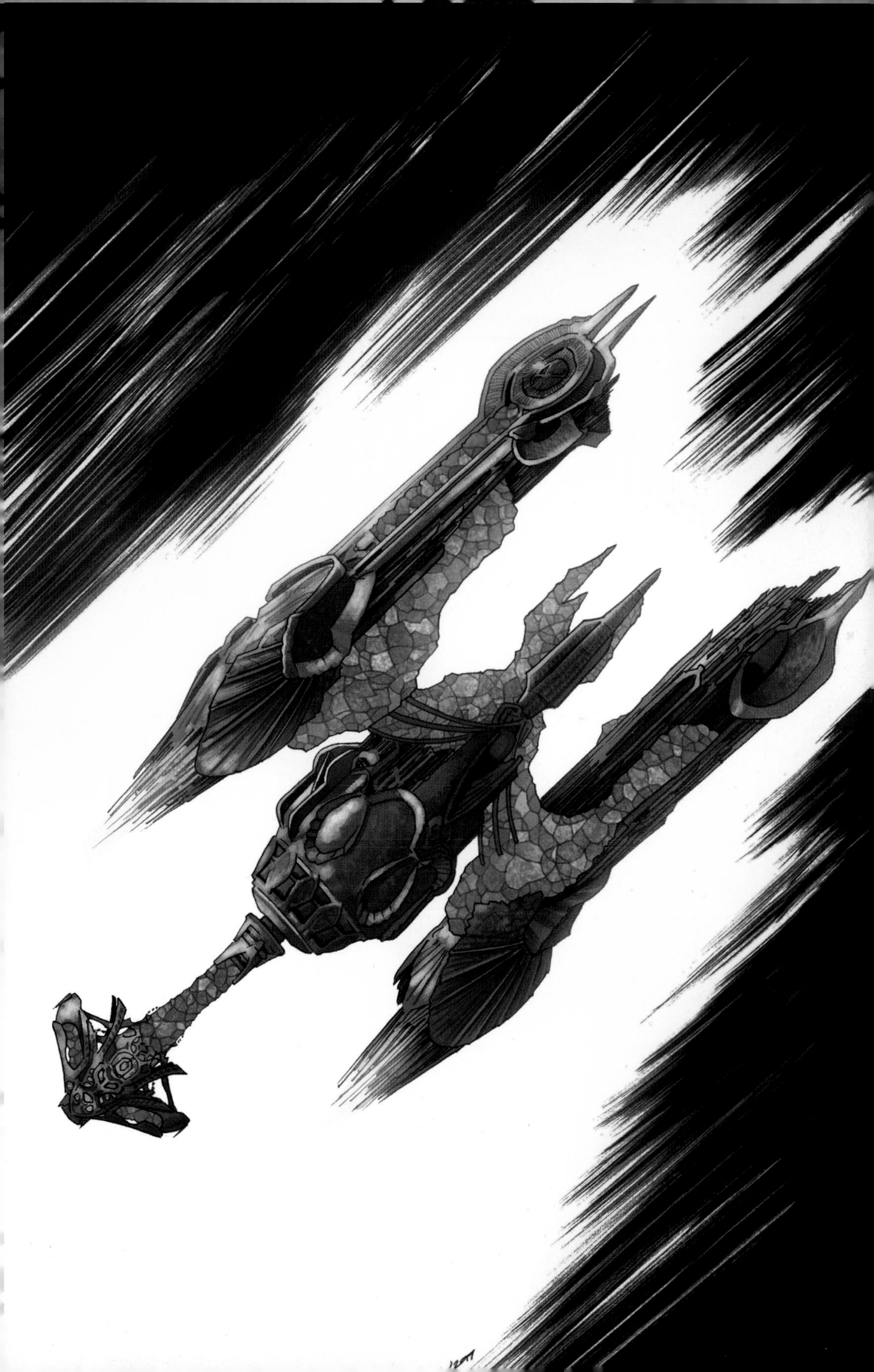

COLORS BY **JORDIE BELLAIRE**

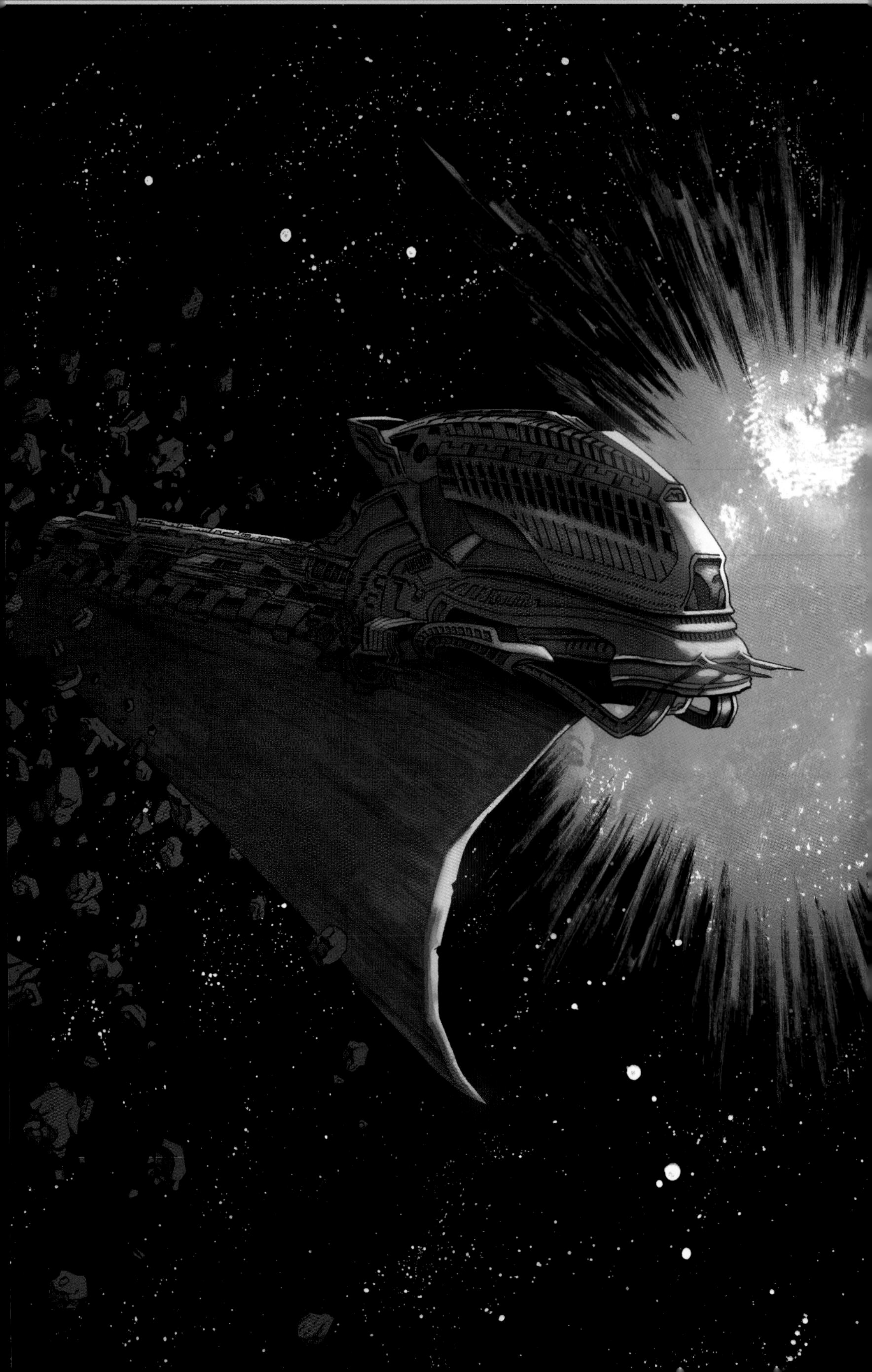

ART BY **DECLAN SHALVEY**
COLORS BY **JORDIE BELLAIRE**

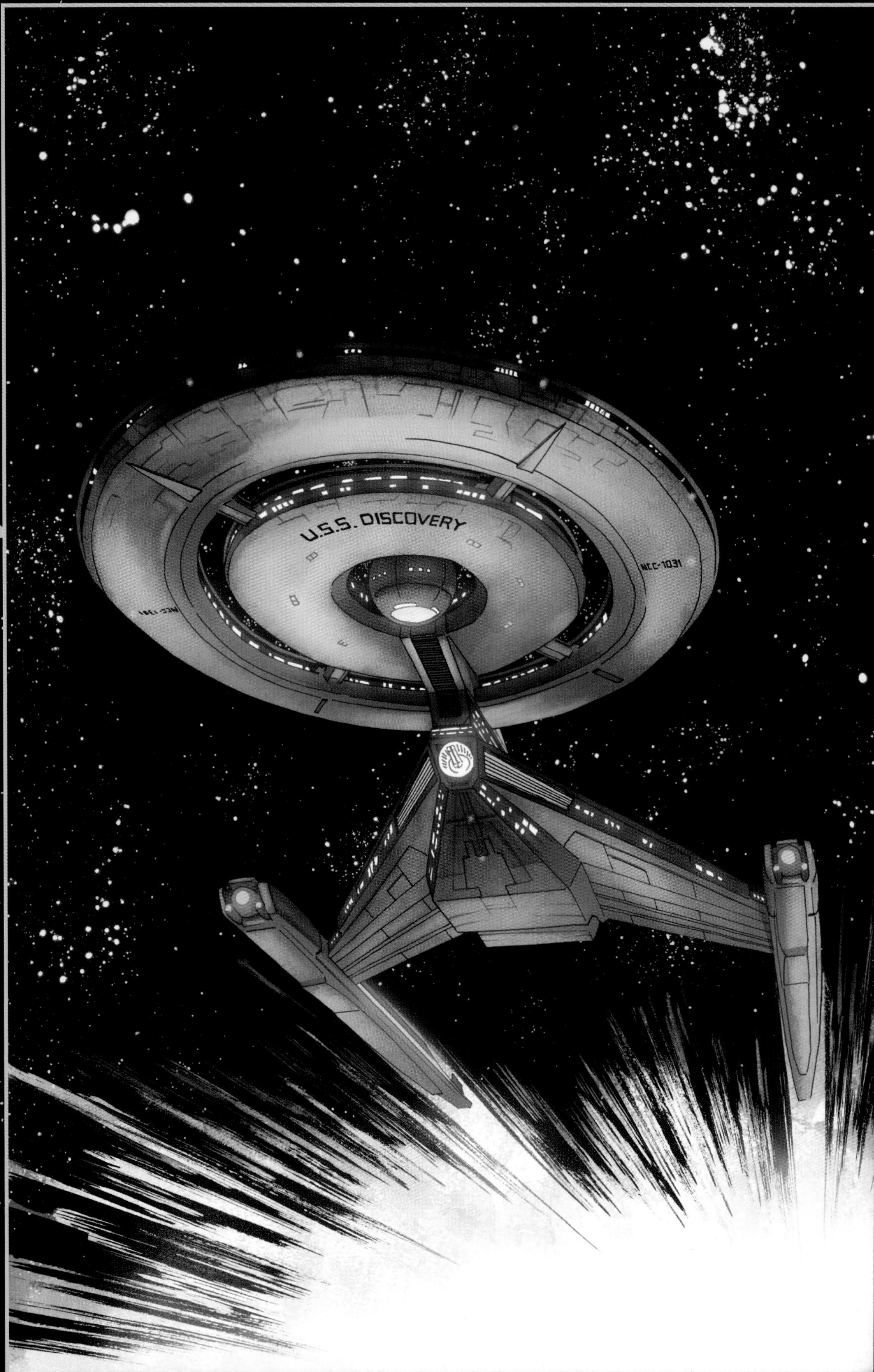
U.S.S. DISCOVERY
NCC-1031